11.18(19)

P9-AOW-752

Yarn Over Murder

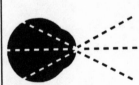

This Large Print Book carries the
Seal of Approval of N.A.V.H.

YARN OVER MURDER

MAGGIE SEFTON

THORNDIKE PRESS
A part of Gale, Cengage Learning

GALE
CENGAGE Learning·

Farmington Hills, Mich • San Francisco • New York • Waterville, Maine
Meriden, Conn • Mason, Ohio • Chicago

GALE
CENGAGE Learning

LIBRARY OF CONGRESS CATALOGING-IN-PUBLICATION DATA

Sefton, Maggie.
    Yarn over murder / by Maggie Sefton. — Large print edition.
        pages ; cm. — (A knitting mystery) (Thorndike Press large print mystery)
    ISBN 978-1-4104-7173-4 (hardcover) — ISBN 1-4104-7173-X (hardcover)
    1. Flynn, Kelly (Fictitious character)—Fiction. 2. Knitters (Persons)--Fiction.
    3. Murder—Investigation—Fiction. 4. Large type books. I. Title.
    PS3619.E37Y37 2014b
    813'.6—dc23   2014018119

Published in 2014 by arrangement with The Berkley Publishing Group, a member of Penguin Group (USA) LLC, a Penguin Random House Company

Printed in the United States of America
1 2 3 4 5 6 7 18 17 16 15 14

ACKNOWLEDGMENTS

I want to thank my Lambspun friend Mary Biggers for her kind cooperation in answering all my questions about her experiences during the High Park wildfire in June 2012. Mary lives in Cache La Poudre Canyon, and she was evacuated in the middle of the night when the wildfire came over the ridge and blazed down into the canyon. Along with the rest of her neighbors who lived closer to the tiny community of Poudre Park, Mary had to leave with just the clothes on her back. She was fortunate to have family in Fort Collins to stay with during the evacuation period. The other Cache La Poudre Canyon residents, along with the evacuees from Rist Canyon (Bellevue Canyon in the mysteries), Glacier View Meadows, and others relied on the Salvation Army and the American Red Cross shelters to provide lodging and hot meals. I made several donations to both these wonderful organizations that came to the aid of our northern Colorado neighbors.

I also want to thank the reporters and staff of the Fort Collins *Coloradoan* for their daily, detailed news reports during the High Park wildfire and the follow-up stories as well. I saved every newspaper from that period so that I could make a detailed day-by-day account of everything that happened. I knew that the newspapers would be essential for including accurate and telling detail in the next Knitting Mystery, *Yarn Over Murder.*

And to everyone else who answered one of my myriad questions, I say again, "thank you." I hope you all enjoy the story.

AUTHOR'S NOTE

Yarn Over Murder takes place as Kelly and friends try to help Jayleen save her ranch in Bellevue Canyon. As I mentioned in the author's note following the previous Knitting Mystery, *Close Knit Killer,* I don't usually set my stories so close together in time. I was finishing that novel in early June 2012, almost ready to submit it to my editor, when the High Park wildfire broke out in Rist Canyon, just northwest of Fort Collins, Colorado, where I live (I call that canyon Bellevue Canyon in the mysteries).

Life as normal changed in Fort Collins and the entire area of northern Colorado at that moment. Even though Fort Collins was never in any danger of the wildfire spreading (a large, long reservoir lies between the city and the western edge of the mountains), we were all riveted by the fast-moving, capricious wildfire.

I realized then that I had to include that

fire in the mysteries. So I totally revised *Close Knit Killer* to include Kelly and friends hearing about the wildfire breakout while at the Estes Park Wool Market — on Saturday, June 9, 2012, the actual day the wildfire was reported.

Yarn Over Murder begins exactly where the previous novel, *Close Knit Killer,* left off, and the High Park wildfire plays a central role. I do not pretend that I have written a newscaster's account of how the High Park wildfire affected all of our city and surrounding counties. But I did try to include real-life details of those life-changing, dramatic events of June 2012 as seen by Kelly and her friends and all of the folks at Lambspun. Jayleen Swinson has her alpaca ranch in Bellevue Canyon, so everything she's spent the last fourteen or more years building is at risk. Kelly and all of the characters — the new ones, too — come to Jayleen's aid. And, as always, a dead body appears, so there's a murder to solve. ☺

CAST OF CHARACTERS

Kelly Flynn — financial accountant and part-time sleuth, refugee from East Coast corporate CPA firm

Steve Townsend — architect and builder in Fort Connor, Colorado, and Kelly's boyfriend

Kelly's Friends:

Jennifer Stroud — real estate agent, part-time waitress

Lisa Gerrard — physical therapist

Megan Smith — IT consultant, another corporate refugee

Marty Harrington — lawyer, Megan's husband

Greg Carruthers — university instructor, Lisa's boyfriend

Pete Wainwright — owner of Pete's Porch Café in the back of Kelly's favorite knitting shop, House of Lambspun

Lambspun Family and Regulars:

Mimi Shafer — Lambspun shop owner and knitting expert, known to Kelly and her friends as "Mother Mimi"

Burt Parker — retired Fort Connor police detective, Lambspun spinner-in-residence

Hilda and Lizzie von Steuben — spinster sisters, retired schoolteachers, and exquisite knitters

Curt Stackhouse — Colorado rancher, Kelly's mentor and advisor

Jayleen Swinson — Alpaca rancher and Colorado Cowgirl

Connie and Rosa — Lambspun shop personnel

ONE

Saturday, June 9, 2012

Kelly Flynn steered her boyfriend Steve Townsend's truck down the main road running from Rocky Mountain National Park into Loveland, Colorado, just south of Fort Connor. Her friends Megan and Marty Harrington said they would meet her with a horse trailer in a shopping center along this street. Scanning a big box parking lot ahead, Kelly thought she spotted Megan and Marty waving at her from the parking lot. Alongside them, there was a large two-horse-sized trailer waiting to be hitched behind Steve's big red truck.

Kelly had never hitched a trailer before, so she was glad Marty was there to help. Like Steve, Marty came from a ranching family and was familiar with hauling animals around. Kelly's sporty car didn't haul anything larger than groceries and potting soil. But today, Steve's truck was needed, as

Kelly and her friends hurried to help their friend Jayleen Swinson rescue her alpaca herd from the wildfire that blazed in Bellevue Canyon, northwest of Fort Connor. Hopefully some of Jayleen's possessions could be tossed into the truck bed as well. But that depended on how fast the wildfire spread.

First discovered earlier that June Saturday morning, the wildfire was raging, according to the scant news reports Kelly had caught on the truck radio while she drove from the annual Wool Market in Estes Park. She and Steve were by Jayleen's alpaca stalls in the livestock exhibition area when the news spread about the wildfire in Bellevue Canyon. Steve volunteered to drive Jayleen's truck and trailer so he could help Curt and Jayleen rush to her ranch in the canyon and rescue her herd.

Meanwhile, Kelly phoned Megan and Marty as well as Lisa and Greg, alerting them to the emergency situation. They could borrow trucks and horse trailers and drive to Bellevue Canyon. Jayleen would need lots of help to move her herd of alpacas down the canyon to safety. Kelly hadn't heard a word from Steve since. Driving in Colorado's beautiful canyons often meant no cell phone signal.

She turned into the shopping center lot and pulled up beside the horse trailer. Marty and Megan already had a trailer hitched behind an old faded blue pickup. "Thank you so much for meeting me, guys," Kelly said, stepping down from the truck. "Did you get that truck and the trailers from Steve's dad?"

"Naw, my mom and dad brought them over. They're driving up to Jayleen's now. So are my aunt and uncle. Jayleen's gonna need a lot of help," tall, skinny Marty said as he reached out. "Gimme the keys and I'll hook this baby up for you. We gotta move fast. I finally reached Steve, and he and Curt and Jayleen just barely got through on Stove Prairie Road, going up the back of Bellevue Canyon. The fire started near there, so the cops are gonna shut down that road soon." Marty climbed inside Steve's truck.

"Oh, no, I was hoping we could drive that way to Jayleen's. It's much faster than going into the canyon from the northwest entrance in Bellevue."

"Don't worry. Marty has some shortcuts," Megan said, handing Kelly a fast-food takeout bag. "I got you a burger and an iced coffee. We're all having lunch on the run today."

13

"Hey, thanks," Kelly said, accepting the bag with the familiar logo. She opened the wrapper containing the juicy burger as she watched Marty expertly back Steve's truck into position right in front of the horse trailer hitch.

"Have you heard from Greg and Lisa yet?" Kelly asked before taking a big bite of burger.

"Yeah, they took Greg's truck over to Steve's parents place and hitched up a trailer. They're already on the way to Jayleen's ranch, too. That road is gonna be crowded for sure." She peered toward the foothills beside them. "We spotted white smoke when we drove over."

White smoke. That was the first sign of fire. Then the smoke would quickly darken as it started to burn trees, especially pine trees with sap in them. Kelly anxiously peered over the uneven rocky ridge called Devil's Backbone that blocked a good view of the foothills. She couldn't see smoke yet.

"Burt is watching over Jayleen's alpacas at the Wool Market, along with Cassie and Eric," Kelly said. "Mimi and Burt will take care of everything up there. Thank goodness Jayleen's got a third of her herd there."

"Okay, it's all hitched. We'd better get going," Marty said, striding toward the faded

14

blue pickup. "There's gonna be a ton of people on the road. We're taking Taft Hill up to Overland Trail then Centennial Road beside the lake. Then cut through the side roads to the mouth of the canyon. Stay right behind me, Kelly, so we don't get separated. Firefighters will be coming in from other counties, so we'll have to fight our way through traffic."

"You got it." Kelly shoved the rest of the burger back into the bag and headed toward Steve's truck. Meanwhile, she sent a fervent plea above that she didn't crash into anything as she maneuvered the truck and trailer around narrow canyon roads.

Revving the engine, Kelly proceeded to follow Marty and Megan out of Loveland and north into Fort Connor. Once they turned onto Overland Trail, which hugged the foothills that ran along the western edge of the city, that's when Kelly saw it. The smoke. White smoke billowing up behind the ridges in the distance. Puffy white clouds climbing into the sky. And nearby, other smoke billowed. Dark smoke, charcoal gray, almost black. The sight of it caused Kelly's heart to lurch.

She followed Marty as he turned left onto a county road that went up into the foothills and skirted the long narrow Horsetooth

15

Reservoir that lay between Fort Connor and the western edge of the foothills. Running nearly the length of the city, it was a popular recreational escape. However, Kelly noticed as many people lining the top of the reservoir this hot, ninety-plus degree Saturday afternoon as those boating and swimming in the waters below. People staring west into the foothills and the canyons beyond, watching the smoke billow and rise.

That fearful feeling stayed with Kelly as she drove along, leaving the reservoir behind as the road wound down into the Bingham Hill valley, usually a beautiful green space of pastures. This summer, barely green. Buffalo once filled this picturesque valley, according to accounts of early pioneers who gazed down from Bingham Hill above. But La Niña's dry weather had chased away all of February and March's normal snows and brought scant April rains. May and June were dry to crackling in the record-breaking heat, in the upper nineties day after day.

The road finally joined another that turned west and headed into the mouth of Bellevue Canyon. Marty slowed ahead, and Kelly watched several cars and pickups pass by. Others were doing the exact same thing. Coming to help out their canyon neighbors any way they could. Kelly stayed behind

16

Marty as they wound their way up into Bellevue Canyon. The horse trailer rattled behind Steve's truck, and Kelly wondered what it would feel like once two alpacas were loaded inside.

Although Kelly could no longer see the smoke plumes as they drove up into the canyon, she could smell the smoke in the air. Strong. Acrid. Pretty soon they would be able to see it. All those billowing clouds of white and black smoke would spread everywhere. All of Fort Connor would soon smell like smoke.

As the road climbed higher, getting closer to Jayleen's ranch, traffic slowed as more trucks appeared. And the smoke got heavier. Cresting the hill right above the ranch, Kelly peered down the hillside. She thought she spotted Jayleen's and Curt's trucks and other trucks clustered below near Jayleen's barn and pastures. Marty's turn signal flashed and she followed suit as they slowed to turn into the long gravel driveway leading to the ranch yard. The horse trailer rattled even more on the gravel road. Curt waved at them and pointed to a place on the right side of the ranch yard where they could park.

Kelly waited for Marty to pull in and park, then she did the same. The acrid smoke smell irritated her nostrils as she breathed it in. Smoke hung in the air now. Steve ran up as soon as she exited the truck.

"Hey, good job," Steve said as he pulled her into his arms for a big hug and kiss. "You guys got here just in time. Cops are gonna close the road soon. Fire has spread from Stove Prairie and jumped the canyon road. It's doubled since this morning, they said."

Kelly hugged him back hard. *Jumped the canyon road.* That means it would start spreading even faster into Bellevue Canyon. Only a couple of ridges separated Jayleen's ranch from the downward slope that led to Stove Praire Road. The small hundred-plus-year-old Stove Prairie mountain school with its wooden building would be right in the wildfire's path, if it wasn't burned already. "I'm so glad you guys got through on that road. The canyon road is packed."

"It's gonna get worse. So we'll have to load up and get out. There'll only be time for one trip." Steve looked over his shoulder. "Damn. Ash is falling already."

Kelly looked up and saw tiny grayish flakes floating in the air above them. Her gut squeezed. That was a bad sign. Burning trees. Lots of trees burning. She brushed her hand across Steve's sweaty, dirt-smeared face. Today's upper nineties heat was even higher this close to the fire. "Do we have enough trailers to get the rest of the alpacas out? Jayleen had a whole bunch at the Wool Market. But most of them are still here, I think, including my six alpacas."

"Yeah, I think so. Some more of Jayleen's friends brought their trucks and trailers. Marty's parents and Curt's daughter and husband already got here, loaded up, and are gone. You probably passed them on the road but didn't recognize their trucks." He ran the back of his hand across his forehead, smearing the sooty dirt even more.

"Hey, you made it!" a familiar voice called from behind.

Kelly turned to see friends Lisa and Greg loading boxes into the back of a green truck. A horse trailer with two alpacas was hitched behind. "Where are we taking the alpacas?" Kelly asked as she raced over to her friends.

"To that woman's ranch in Poudre Canyon," Greg said, jerking his thumb over his shoulder. He dumped the box into the flatbed.

"She's a friend of Jayleen's who lives up the Poudre. Andrea something. She and that guy were here when we drove up." Lisa wiped a bandanna across her face, smearing the dirt. Even Lisa's light blonde hair looked darker, dingy, Kelly noticed.

Kelly looked over at the man and woman who were loading a skittish alpaca onto a trailer. Or rather, trying to. The man, who was wearing a KISS concert tee shirt, appeared unsure of how to handle the alpaca as it danced sideways, clearly frightened by the smoke and smell and confusion. He grabbed for the rope and Kelly noticed a tattoo on his arm. The woman took the rope lead from his hands and started talking to the alpaca, soothing the animal so she could load it safely inside the trailer. When she moved to the side, Kelly spotted a similar tattoo on the woman's arm that looked like a dragon. She figured they must be a couple if they had matching tattoos.

"Kelly, I'm going to grab more of Jayleen's things from the house. We can fill up the back of my truck before we head out." Steve started toward the ranch house.

"I'm gonna grab another load," Greg said. "This will be the only run we can make out of here. Cops are gonna close off the canyon road if they haven't already. You should grab another load, too." He nodded to Lisa.

"Yeah, in a minute." Turning to Kelly, she started to say something, but broke into a cough instead. "Man, the smoke is getting worse. You guys need to load up everything

20

you can and head back. We can meet up once we're out of the canyon. I already talked to Megan and Marty." She coughed again.

"Sounds like a plan," Kelly said as Lisa took off for the ranch house. Kelly's eyes stung already, and she felt the acrid smoke burning her nostrils as she breathed.

The ranch yard was a riot of noise and people. Megan was carrying a box from the ranch house. Marty was loading an alpaca into the trailer behind the faded blue pickup. People she didn't know were on the ranch porch. She spotted Jayleen standing in the corral surrounded by alpacas. Kelly noticed there were a lot fewer animals than usual. *Thank goodness.* Friends rushing to Jayleen's rescue were thinning the herd. She scanned the remaining alpacas and didn't see her six animals. Jayleen must have sent them earlier when Curt's relatives came to help transport them to his ranch.

Curt stood next to the corral fence, clearly giving orders to people. He waved at Kelly, then handed off an alpaca to a bearded man and pointed toward her. The bearded man started walking Kelly's way. He was wearing a faded Springsteen concert tee shirt. She smiled. *What was it with the concert shirts?* She didn't spot any tattoos unless they were hiding under his beard.

"Are you Kelly?" the man called as she approached.

"Yes, I'm here with the guy in the green CSU tee shirt," she said.

The man glanced over his shoulder. "Oh, yeah, Steve. He was already here when I drove up. Said you were coming with the trailer. Which one is it? Curt wants me to load for you."

"The red one," Kelly managed before she coughed several times. She pointed toward Steve's truck.

"Yeah, it's gettin' pretty bad out here. Cops will be starting to chase people away soon."

"You mean evacuate?" Kelly said, as they walked toward Steve's truck.

"Yep. I live up Poudre Canyon, and that's what happened last year with the Crystal Lakes fire. People were all told to get out. We were lucky with that one."

"This is it," Kelly said, and opened the trailer's back doors.

"Hold him for me while I set up the ramp," the man said, handing Kelly the lead to the gray alpaca. It looked like Jayleen's Gray Ghost.

"It's okay, it's okay," Kelly soothed the animal, whose anxious gaze told her how frightening this situation was for gentle creatures who lived simply in the beautiful mountain scenery, grazing on grass surrounded by its fellows. Alpacas were herd animals and did not like being separated.

"Okay, here you go," the man said as he took the gray's lead again and beckoned the hesitating alpaca up the trailer ramp.

Kelly finally realized where she'd seen him before. When he mentioned he lived "up the Poudre" she remembered seeing him a year ago when she and Jennifer were meeting in a real estate client's cabin. This man was the "shaggy guy" Kelly had seen hiding in the bushes outside, spying on them. Burt said he was the neighbor next door.

Since she couldn't remember his name, she decided this was a good time to find out more about this guy. "Thanks so much," Kelly said as the man walked down the ramp. "What's your name? Jayleen has lots of friends." She held out her hand. "I'm Kelly Flynn."

"Dennis. Dennis Holt," he said, giving Kelly's hand a quick shake.

Deep blue eyes, she noticed. And a firm handshake. Rough hands. Outdoor hands. Steve's hands used to be rougher, before he started working down in Denver. "Do you have alpacas, too? On your ranch in the

23

Poudre?"

"Only a few. Used to have more when my wife and I were still married. But she's got most of them now." He glanced over his shoulder toward the brunette woman and man loading a second alpaca into their horse trailer. The woman was stroking the head of a skittish younger caramel brown alpaca.

Kelly didn't know the woman or the man with her. But Dennis Holt's comment aroused her curiosity. "Is her ranch up the Poudre? Is that where Jayleen wants us to take the alpacas?"

"Yep." He nodded his head. "Andrea's got a big pasture. There's plenty of room. I can only add a couple to my little herd since I have less pasture at my place. But I'm right near the water." He gave Kelly a smile.

Nice smile. It softened his bearded features and he no longer looked shaggy and scary. Amazing how a simple smile could accomplish that, Kelly thought. "Boy, are you lucky. I love going up into the canyon and just sitting on a rock beside the Poudre."

Dennis grinned. "You got that right, Kelly. Let me load another alpaca, then you folks can head out of here. Oh, you could check inside the house and see what else needs to be taken out. Some of Jayleen's friends are helping to load up stuff."

"Sure thing." Kelly followed Dennis across the ranch yard, then stopped when Greg and Lisa pulled in front of her in the green truck.

"Hey, let's meet up outside of Landport," Greg said, leaning out the truck window. "One of the fast-foods on North College. Grab something to eat and get gas before we head up the Poudre. Sound okay?"

"Yeah. I'll tell Steve. Drive safely," Kelly said as she waved them off. The horse trailer rattled and shook, moving side to side a bit, she noticed uneasily. *Oh, boy.*

She looked around, searching for Steve, then spotted him dumping a box into the back of Marty's faded blue pickup. He looked up and beckoned.

"Hey, I saw that guy loading alpacas into our trailer, so let's start putting stuff in my truck. We're trying to empty out Jayleen's file cabinet, just in case."

"Thanks, buddy, I think we're gonna head off," Marty said, looking around. "Have you seen Megan?"

"Yeah, she's inside." Steve coughed, long and deep.

"Whoa, you need to get out of here," Kelly said. "Let me grab some boxes inside and

25

start loading. This stuff is getting thick."

"Yeah, it is. We need to grab what we can and head out. Did Greg talk to you, Marty?"

Marty nodded, then waved to Megan. "Yeah, we're meeting at the fast-food plaza on North College," he said, then waved. "Hey, Megan! Let's get going now!"

"See you down below," Kelly called over her shoulder as she and Steve headed for the ranch house.

Just then, Curt started walking their way. "You two better get on that road. Get those animals to Andrea's," he said as he approached. "We moved your alpacas first, Kelly. My daughter and son-in-law both brought trailers, and they took four of yours. I'm carrying the last two with me. We're gonna put them all in that front corral at my ranch along with Jayleen's animals. My sister hauled off two of them, and Jayleen will take the two that are left."

Kelly spotted Curt's truck and peered at the rear ends of two alpacas showing in the back. "Looks like you're carrying my smoke gray and the cinnamon brown."

"Yep. I'm gonna fence off a separate pasture for all of them."

"Let us know when you get to your ranch, Curt," Marty called through the truck window as he and Megan started down the

26

driveway.

Curt waved and nodded in reply as the truck spit gravel.

"We were going to get more of Jayleen's things from the house," Steve said.

Curt's face was smeared with dirt and soot like Steve's. He reached out and clamped his hand on Steve's shoulder. "You've already done more than your share, Steve. Jayleen and I couldn't have gotten those animals loaded as fast as we did without you. Now, you and Kelly get the hell out of here."

Kelly glanced over at Jayleen, who was leading a younger alpaca up the ramp of her truck trailer. "How's she doing, Curt?"

"Okay, once we got to the ranch. It was the not knowing that was killing her." He wiped his sweat-drenched shirtsleeve across his forehead. "Once she saw the animals were still okay, she came back to herself. Saving the animals was all that she cared about. Those are her babies."

Steve stared at the ranch house. "Damn. I'd hate to see this place burn. But I swear if it does, I'm going to rebuild it for her."

Curt gave a crooked smile. "Now, don't you go worrying about that, Steve. Right now, you two have got to get out of here safely. Police will start evacuating people real soon."

"You're sure you've got enough trailers for the animals?" Kelly craned her neck. Jayleen was loading another alpaca.

"Yeah, thanks to Dennis. He brought his trailer and that was nine trailers loaded. We'll worry about the ones up at the Wool Market later. I already talked to Burt and he and Mimi are gonna keep the kids with them at Estes Park overnight at a motel. And they'll be on duty tomorrow until Jayleen and I can get up there. Bless their hearts."

"You're going to have a long drive back to your ranch," Steve said, shaking his head. "With Stove Prairie Road closed by the fire, you'll be going all the way back into Fort Connor then south then west again to get back to the lower Buckhorn Valley."

"Yeah, it'll be a long ride, for sure. My daughter's already there with the rest of the grandkids, finding places for the animals. Bringing in Jayleen's things. It's going to be a busy night, so I sure am glad Burt and Mimi are taking care of things in Estes Park."

The sound of another car pulling up into the ranch yard caught Kelly's attention, and she turned to see Connie Carson from the Lambspun knitting shop jump out of her small black sedan and stride across the ranch yard. She looked like she was headed toward Jayleen's alpaca rancher friend, Andrea, who was opening the door to her navy blue truck, clearly getting ready to drive away. Her male friend stood on the other side of the truck and was staring wide-eyed at Connie.

"YOU! I knew he was with you! You *bitch!"* Connie yelled, face red, arm outstretched as she pointed at Andrea. She reached out and pushed Andrea.

Clearly caught off guard, Andrea stumbled backward a little, but quickly caught herself. She stepped toward Connie, shoving her hand out. "Back off! Get away from me!"

"What the hell? That's Connie!" Steve stared, incredulous.

"Good Lord. That's the last thing we need," Curt said and hurried toward Connie and Andrea, who were both yelling at each other.

"You get away from me!" Andrea warned, pointing her own finger at Connie. "Back off! We're trying to help Jayleen. Go have your nervous breakdown somewhere else."

At that, Connie stiffened and let loose another expletive, then charged toward Andrea again. But this time, Curt grabbed Connie around the waist and pulled her away from Andrea before Connie could get to her. Kelly noticed that Andrea stood her ground and didn't move. The man with her stood beside the trailer and watched wide-eyed.

"That must be Connie's husband," Steve said. "Did you know that they broke up?"

"No, I mean, not officially. Connie's always made it sound like they fought a lot but always made up. So, this is news to me." She shook her head. "Man, this is a bad way to discover your spouse is out with another woman."

Jayleen climbed over the corral fence and raced over to where Curt held a struggling, furious Connie, who was still shouting accusations at Andrea.

"We were getting back together! Then you interfered! You bitch! You have no right!"

"Connie, calm down," Curt said, keeping her trapped in his embrace.

"It's *her* fault! Jim and I were getting together . . ."

"Shut up, Connie!" the man yelled suddenly, his face red. "That's a lie and you know it! We haven't been together for six months!"

Connie looked stunned for a moment, then yelled back. "No! No!"

Jayleen stepped between Connie and Andrea then. "You two better get going," she said over her shoulder to Andrea, then turned to comfort Connie.

Andrea and Jim got into the navy blue truck and revved the engine, then drove slowly down the gravel driveway. Once again Kelly watched a horse trailer sway behind a truck. Slower this time, since two alpacas were aboard.

Connie suddenly burst into tears and buried her face in Jayleen's shirt. Jayleen patted Connie on the back as Curt released her. A personal tragedy or melodrama, in the midst of all this chaos and impending disaster.

"I think we'd better do the same," Steve advised, pointing to his truck. "Cops are going to start clearing folks out, if they haven't already. Roads will be clogged."

Kelly and Steve swiftly walked past Connie and Jayleen. Kelly did reach out and give Jayleen's arm a squeeze. Like one of Mother Mimi's reassuring gestures.

"Call us when you get to your ranch," Steve called to Curt as he and Kelly climbed into the red truck. Curt gave them both a thumbs-up as Steve revved the big engine.

"Traffic will be a nightmare," Kelly predicted as they started down the gravel driveway, slowly.

"Ohh, yeah."

Two

Later Saturday afternoon

Steve turned his truck into the crowded fast-food plaza located in northern Fort Connor. Greg, Lisa, Megan, and Marty were already parked beside one of the familiar fast-food restaurants located in the plaza. Kelly climbed out of the truck the moment it pulled to a stop.

"Whoa! I never thought we'd get off that road," she complained, leaning over toward the ground in a big stretch. "Traffic is really slow going with all the cars and trucks on the canyon road."

"Bumper to bumper for an hour," Megan said as she leaned against the faded blue pickup and sipped from a soda can. "Everyone is evacuating the canyon now."

A steady stream of traffic was turning from the road that led into north Fort Connor from Landport, the small town that sat on Fort Connor's northwestern edge. A main highway ran through the town, branching off for Bellevue Canyon, then continuing farther northwest to the Cache La Poudre Canyon.

"Man, every firefighter in northern Colorado must be here," Steve said as he stretched his arms over his head. "I even saw National Guard guys in Jack's Supply parking lot."

"Yeah, my cousin is in the National Guard unit here, and I betcha they're called in soon. The Armory's over on West LaPorte Avenue," Marty said, a slice of pizza in one hand and a soda in the other.

"The fried chicken is good," Lisa said, motioning to a familiar logo. "Greg's getting a whole bucket, so there'll be plenty."

Kelly's stomach rumbled. "Yum. Fried chicken does sound good. I may snitch some."

"Why don't I just buy us some," Steve suggested. "Who knows how long it will take us to get these animals taken care of at that ranch up Poudre Canyon. Andrea said it was a few miles before Poudre Park, on the right. Yellow ranch house set behind the corrals. What do you want to drink, Kelly?"

"Iced coffee would be great. Fried chicken sounds good. Looks like Greg is enjoying it." She pointed to Greg as he approached, holding a large plastic bucket of fried chicken with one hand while he munched on a chicken leg he held in the other.

Steve grinned. "That's a recommendation. Why don't you catch them up on the soap opera that started before we drove off," he said, then headed for the red-and-white building down fast-food row.

"Ooh, that does look good," Lisa said, taking a crispy brown chicken breast from the bucket. "Thanks, hon." She gave Greg a kiss. He had already polished off the chicken leg and was devouring a large crispy piece.

"What soap opera was that?" Megan asked, lifting a slice of pizza from the carton that lay open on the truck.

"Oh, brother, I can't believe it," Kelly said, brushing hair away from her forehead. There was less smoke down here in town, but the acrid smell was still in the air. "Connie from the shop came driving up Jayleen's driveway, jumped out of her car, then started screaming at Andrea Holt, Jayleen's rancher friend. Calling her names and yelling and even shoving her. Andrea caught herself before she fell over. But Connie was spitting fire. Accused Andrea of stealing her husband. That was the guy with Andrea."

"Whoa!" Marty said, before diving into another pizza slice.

"No way!" Megan looked up, wide-eyed.

"Oh, yeah. Connie's got a temper," Lisa said.

"How do you know?" Greg asked, momentarily distracted from the half-eaten chicken breast in his hand.

"I've heard her on the phone arguing with her husband. Yelling at him sometimes. She's always done it outside, pacing around the parking lot near the golf course. But she gets really riled up. She and he have been in counseling a couple of times over the years. Things will get quieter, and Connie will say how good things are. Then, they explode again." Lisa wagged her head. "I've suggested some individual counseling to her several times, but Connie never wants to go. She always says, 'It'll be all right.' Or, 'We'll get back together.' Something like that. Then, a few months later, it starts all over again." Lisa returned to the crispy chicken.

The steady stream of traffic hadn't let up or slowed down, Kelly noticed. People were evacuating not only themselves and whatever belongings they could carry, but also their pets and livestock. Trucks dragging trailers with horses, alpacas, and all sorts of livestock rolled by. All of them were also loaded with luggage, bags, appliances. Pets

36

poked their heads out of car windows next to children and adults. The evacuation of Bellevue Canyon residents was in full swing.

"Well, it sounds like this time they've split for good," Kelly observed, leaning against Steve's truck.

"What makes you say that?" Megan asked.

"Well, her husband —"

"Jim. Jim Carson," Lisa interjected between bites.

"Husband Jim yelled at Connie to 'shut up' when Connie was shouting that she and he were getting back together and was accusing Andrea of getting in the way and interfering. Anyway, Jim yelled that he and Connie hadn't been together for six months."

"Uh-oh," Greg observed.

"Not good," Marty added.

"Poor Connie," Megan said, looking concerned. "What'd she say after that?"

"She kind of lost it."

"Sounds like she already did."

"Well, she started yelling and getting even redder in the face. And she would have gone after Andrea again if Curt hadn't grabbed her. Then she broke down in tears on Jayleen's chest as Andrea and Jim drove off."

"Oh, brother. She really does need to see someone," Lisa said, tossing the chicken bone into a trash bag.

"Kind of sounds like she's been deluding herself about their relationship," Greg opined sagely, then started on another crispy piece of chicken.

"Very astute. The doctor is in." Kelly teased with a grin.

Greg gave a nonchalant shrug. "I've been sleeping with a psych major. It's rubbed off."

Lisa rolled her eyes and smiled, as Megan giggled. Marty, on the other hand, looked over at Greg with concern.

"Is it contagious? Don't stand too close, Megan."

Kelly joined her friends' laughter as she looked over at the congested flow of traffic. "Man, I sure hope it's easier to get up the Poudre Canyon. This is a mess."

"It should be. I was talking with a guy in the pizza place and he says Larimer County is taking in evacuees' livestock and animals at the county's new exhibition building, the Ranch," Marty said. "So a lot of this traffic will be headed out to the interstate and south of town."

"You hope." Greg glanced over. "I was talking to a couple while I was getting the chicken and they said that the Red Cross has set up a place for Bellevue Canyon evacuees in the Landport middle school gym. And that's right back up this road." He jerked his thumb toward the main road that ran past the fast-food plaza.

"At least we can take the bypass around Landport this time," Lisa suggested.

"Man, the Red Cross is setting up a shelter. The National Guard is probably gathering in the Armory. This is starting to look like a real disaster."

"Don't say it, Marty," Megan said, squeezing her eyes shut. "I don't even want to think it."

Kelly didn't say a word, but it was clear: This was already a disaster. With their forests dry as kindling and pine bark beetle-damaged, and with dead trees mixed in between the green, it was a disaster ready to happen. A strong breeze suddenly blew her hair across her face. *Oh, no. The wind.* That was the worst thing that could happen.

"Uh, oh," Marty said, glancing around. "Wind's picking up. That's bad news."

"Crap!" Greg swore, looking up.

Kelly watched the branches of the tall cottonwoods nearby sway in the strong breeze. "Now that fire's going to spread even faster."

"Oh, Lord," Lisa said, gathering the trash bag and napkins so they didn't blow away.

"Please don't let that fire spread to the Poudre Canyon."

Kelly's gut clenched. *Please, no.* She looked up and saw Steve hurrying their way, a bucket of fried chicken under one arm, drinks in his other hand.

"Hey, guys, we gotta get these animals up the Poudre now. Some guys inside told me they'd just heard on their shortwave radio that the wind has whipped up the wildfire in Bellevue Canyon worse. It's already climbed one ridge and is roaring toward another. Not enough people to stop it, even with all the firefighters from all over northern Colorado. It's out of control." He handed off the drink tray to Kelly.

"We need tanker planes to dump water," Megan said.

"Let's go, hon," Marty said, grabbing the pizza box.

"You ready?" Greg asked Lisa as he pulled out his keys.

"Gotta make a pit stop first," Lisa said. "I'll be quick." She hurried back toward the fast-food restaurant.

"Hey, me, too," Megan said, following.

Not a bad idea, Kelly thought. "Make that a threesome," she said, and took off after her friends. She had a feeling it was going to be a long ride into Poudre Canyon.

■ ■ ■ ■

Kelly glanced out the truck window up at the hazy sky. Smoke from the wildfire in Bellevue Canyon obscured the sun, blowing over from the ridges into Poudre Canyon. There was only one mountain ridge that separated the two canyons. The higher ridge provided one of the walls for the canyon the Cache La Poudre River cut through the mountain millions of years ago. Now, thick gray clouds of smoke and orange haze showed behind the south wall of Poudre Canyon.

"I wish that wind would die down," Kelly said, watching the tops of lodge pole pines sway. "Maybe the firefighters can get a handle on it."

"That's not likely," Steve said, steering the truck around a curve. The Poudre River rushed along beside the road. "With only one air tanker available, and the fire spreading as fast as it is, it's gonna get worse. No doubt about it."

"That's what I'm afraid of. Fire spreading over the ridge into Poudre Canyon. So far, the wind's blowing the fire in the opposite direction. But the wind shifts so fast." She peered up into the sky behind the canyon's tall, steep walls.

"At least they're going to call in the national firefighting units. With luck the Hot Shots could start arriving tomorrow night. Or Monday. We need more manpower. This wildfire has gotten too big already for us to handle.

"And air tankers. *Damn!* How come we only have one on call around here?"

Steve shrugged. "That's all we've ever needed."

He was right, Kelly thought, staring out at the familiar and beloved scenery of Poudre Canyon, high rock walls in one place, gently climbing ridges in another. She peered at a house perched on a rocky hillside.

The Cache La Poudre Canyon was part of the Roosevelt National Forest, and the river itself had been declared a National Wilderness River. Consequently, there weren't as many private homes dotting this canyon compared to other mountain canyons. The few tiny communities of houses and individual homes that appeared infrequently had been built by landowners years ago and were "grandfathered in," as was said in the West.

"We should be seeing Andrea's place pretty soon," she said, scanning the right side of the road.

"Yeah, we should. Yellow ranch house." Steve glanced into the rearview mirror. "Everybody's stayed together. That will help when we unload. Then we can unclog Andrea's driveway in case others are bringing their livestock."

Kelly peered ahead at a structure behind trees. "That looks yellow to me." She pointed out the truck window toward the ranch house farther ahead. "This must be it."

"I think you're right," Steve said, slowing down and flipping on his turn signal. He turned onto the dirt road that led to the ranch house up ahead.

"There's Andrea and Jim. And that looks like Dennis. Curt told me Dennis had brought his trailer to help out." Kelly squinted in the dust that rose as the truck rumbled along. "Looks like they've off-loaded their alpacas. Can't see the animals from here."

"They're in that corral to the left of the ranch house." Steve pointed, then turned the truck to the left as Dennis started directing him to park.

Kelly climbed out of the truck as soon as Steve turned off the ignition. Once again they'd been sitting in backed-up traffic for half an hour until they could get onto the

43

bypass that went around Landport and to the highway that led into Poudre Canyon. Kelly stretched her arms over her head as Steve climbed out of the truck.

"Man, my tailbone is sore from sitting in the truck so long," she complained as Lisa and Greg pulled into a space beside the corral fence. Megan and Marty were right behind.

Now that she was closer and had a better view, Kelly was able to spot a few of Jayleen's alpacas. They clustered together, as alpacas are wont to do, finding solace and protection in their nearness to one another. Their big eyes were even larger than usual, and they were obviously confused about their hasty and rough ride to a strange place. And they were not alone. At the other end of the pasture a larger group of alpacas gathered, watching the newcomers. Andrea's herd, no doubt, Kelly observed.

Andrea Holt strode over to Steve and Kelly. "Hey, guys, you've been great to do this," she said with a wide smile. "You can use that gate over here. That way they'll get right in with their buddies."

"You got it," Steve said, then beckoned Kelly. "You stay with the trailer while I get them into the corral. The less people jostling them, the better. These guys have been

44

through a lot already."

"You've got that right," Andrea said, hands on hips, surveying the corral. "They'll calm down pretty soon, I hope. All that smoke and confusion and fear. Animals can smell fear." Then she turned and strode over to where Dennis was directing Marty where to park.

Greg and Lisa were already out of the truck. Kelly walked around to the back of the trailer where Steve was unlocking the back gate.

"How'd that fried chicken hold out?" she called to Lisa.

"Greg finished it all," Lisa replied.

"Hey, tell the truth. You ate a third of it," Greg protested as he stretched his back. "Man, you're gonna have to give me a back rub when we get home."

"Yeah, then you give me one."

Kelly held the back gate open as Steve brought one alpaca slowly down the trailer ramp. She waved to Marty and Megan farther down the driveway. They, like their friends, were stretching, clearly tired of sitting for long hours, especially bouncing over rough roads while hauling a trailer filled with animals. She looked over her shoulder. Dennis Holt stood near the corral gate, obviously waiting for Steve and the others to bring the alpacas they had hauled.

Glancing around, she spotted Jim Carson standing beside the corral fence closer to the ranch house. He looked kind of lost, Kelly thought, and had the distinct feeling that all this ranching activity was new to him. Clearly he was waiting for directions from Andrea so he'd know what to do. A fish out of water up here in the canyon. Ranching of any kind in the West demanded special skills and a definite hardiness. Only the tough survived in Colorado's ranching community, whether it was cattle, sheep, or alpacas.

Andrea walked over to Greg and Lisa and spoke with them, probably giving them the same instructions she'd given to Steve, Kelly surmised. Greg and Lisa walked around to the back of the trailer, as Andrea walked over to Megan and Marty.

Kelly glanced up at the sky. Still lots of daylight left even though it was nearly six o'clock at night. Another gust of wind blew Kelly's hair across her face, causing that fearful clutch in her gut again. Wind-whipped wildfires were their worst nightmare.

Steve came to retrieve the second alpaca in their trailer, and Kelly watched her friends go through the same routine of off-loading alpacas. The herd in this section of corral was starting to grow.

Kelly watched the animals react each time an alpaca was set loose in the corral; all the others gathered around it, sniffing, looking, nudging each newcomer. It was as if they were checking to make sure the newcomer was still the same member of the herd they remembered. One of the family.

Dennis came out of the barn, dragging a big bag of feed with a rope. Andrea rushed up to him and held the corral gate open so he could drag it into the corral. The alpacas watched with huge eyes, clearly encouraged that dinner was being served.

From the corner of her eye, Kelly noticed Jim Carson approach the periphery of the corral gate. Kelly sensed he wanted to help out but didn't know what to do. Dennis was clearly the more experienced and capable former spouse. She wasn't sure, but Kelly thought she spotted a scowl on Jim's face as he watched the activity.

"Okay, you can close it up and snap the lock," Steve said. "I'll get this one into the corral then see what else Andrea needs."

"I wouldn't make the offer if I were you," Kelly advised, nodding her head toward Andrea, Dennis, and Jim. "It looks like Andrea has already got two guys at her beck and call."

Steve glanced over to the threesome. Dennis was holding open the gate for Marty to bring an alpaca into the corral. "Yeah, Dennis said he and Andrea had divorced about three years ago. Curt told me on the side that Dennis drank too much years ago, that's why he and Andrea split up. But Jayleen got him to join her AA group and he's been sober ever since."

"Wow, this soap opera is starting to sound like one of those on television. There's an ex-husband who clearly wants to get back with his wife —"

"How do you know? Did he say that?"

Kelly smiled at her boyfriend. "I can just tell."

Steve laughed softly. "Well, he's got competition now. And *I* can tell that the other guy, Jim, is getting kind of steamed that Dennis is being super helpful."

"Oh, yeah." Kelly nodded, watching Jim approach Andrea as Greg brought another alpaca into the corral. Then she noticed movement along the driveway to Andrea's ranch. A car was approaching, not a truck. A smaller black car. Kelly thought she recognized it . . . Oh, no. *Connie.*

"Good Lord, that's Connie coming."

Kelly pointed.

"You're kidding!" Steve stared down the road. "Damn, you're right. Let me get this alpaca into the corral in case I have to play Curt's role." He beckoned the caramel-candy-colored alpaca forward toward the corral.

Kelly quickly closed the back gate and snapped the lock, then headed straight for Megan and Lisa. They, too, had noticed someone else arriving. "Hey, guys," Kelly said as she hurried over to them. "That's Connie coming." She pointed.

"Oh, no!" Megan looked shocked. "That's definitely not good, considering what you told us."

"Oh, brother," Lisa said, frowning. "She definitely doesn't want to let this go."

"We're gonna have to make sure she doesn't start another scene like before," Kelly said, glancing toward Andrea, Dennis, and Jim. Apparently they had recognized the small black car, too.

Connie pulled her car beside Marty's blue pickup, then she lifted a box from the back seat and started walking their way.

"Hey, maybe she's just here to bring some of Jayleen's things and that's all," Megan observed.

"Let's hope," Lisa said, walking toward

the approaching Connie.

Kelly joined her and pasted a big smile on her face as they walked up to Connie, who was not smiling. "Hey, thanks for bringing more of Jayleen's things, Connie. I can take them into the house for you," Kelly said, hoping to divert Connie from Andrea.

"That reminds me. We've got a bunch of boxes in our truck," Megan said cheerfully. "Why don't you grab one of those, Kelly, then we all three can take them inside the house."

Great idea, Kelly thought, and was about to add something when Andrea walked up to them. "You can just put them beside the steps. I'll take them inside later. There are a lot of steps to climb."

"Fine!" Connie growled, then stalked over toward the house.

"Go on, you guys," Andrea directed Kelly and her friends. "Bring the boxes from your trucks. The sooner we get everybody out of here, the better." She jerked her head in Connie's direction.

"You got it," Kelly said, then accompanied her friends to their trucks as they all loaded as many boxes as they could carry. As they walked back toward the house, Kelly noticed Jim talking and gesturing to Andrea. Dennis was approaching them on the left.

Kelly deliberately dropped back a few paces behind her friends to watch the intense conversation going on. Then, from the corner of her eye, Kelly spotted Connie approaching the threesome from the right, stalking toward them like she had at Jayleen's earlier that afternoon.

Oh, brother. Sure enough, Connie started cursing at Andrea all over again, gesturing and getting in Andrea's face. Kelly dropped both boxes and started toward the foursome. Dennis had his arm in between Andrea and Connie, trying to calm both women. Jim, on the other hand, was yelling at the top of his voice. Chaos in a ranch yard all over again.

"What are you doing over here?" Connie wailed, tears coming close, face beet red. "You belong at home with me!"

"You're crazy! I can't stand being there with you! Don't you understand!" Jim yelled, gesturing with both hands as he screamed at his wife.

"Hey, hey, that's not helping," Dennis interjected as Connie began to sob.

"*You, shut up!* I've had enough from you!" Jim yelled in Dennis's face, shoving him in the chest.

Dennis jerked back, then grabbed Jim by the shirt and yanked him forward. "Don't you lay hands on me!"

"Stop it! Both of you!" Andrea screamed at them.

Kelly was trying to figure out how to help when Steve and Greg both ran up. Steve shoved his arms between Dennis and Jim as Greg yanked Jim away.

"Okay, okay, that's enough, you guys!" Steve barked, stepping completely between them. "We've got wildfires over the ridge and they may spread this way. Save your energy for fighting the fire, not each other."

Kelly reached over and slipped her arm around Connie, whose sobs had lessened as the violence had ensued. "There, now, Connie. You've got friends here. You'll be okay."

"No, I won't," she whined, wiping the back of her hand across her wet face. "I need Jim. I want Jim back. He's my husband."

Kelly had no answer for that. Lisa rushed up then, and took Connie into her arms.

"Come over here with me, Connie. Let's talk where it's quiet."

Kelly watched both Dennis and Jim quickly regain control of themselves as Steve and Greg hovered on the edges. Megan walked up beside Kelly.

"Boy, you weren't kidding," she said, eyes

wide. "Those two were really getting into it."

"Yeah, it seems to have escalated, not calmed down. Maybe Lisa can work some therapist magic with Connie before we all leave." The wind blew Kelly's hair across her face again.

"Let's hope. I have the feeling we won't be leaving here for a while yet."

Kelly simply nodded as she watched the participants in the mountain soap opera try to pick up the pieces of themselves. Chaos came in many forms.

THREE

Saturday night

"I can't believe you all are just getting back into Fort Connor now." Mimi's voice came over the cell phone. "Those roads must be awful!"

"Yeah, they are," Kelly said, walking away from the splashing fountain in the middle of Fort Connor's Old Town Square. The square was Saturday-night busy, and every café was packed. Even the intense close-to-one-hundred-degree daytime heat earlier didn't keep people from sitting outside. The mountains always cooled down at night, no matter how hot it got during the day. Now, temperatures were pleasant.

"Are you finally at home?"

"No, not yet. We all decided we deserved real food and cold beer for dinner. We've been driving all day. So we're over in Old Town Square at our favorite café, relaxing."

"Well, you folks deserve it. Jayleen

wouldn't have gotten her animals out without your help. All of your help. She told me so on the phone a little while ago."

"I'm sure she'll be staying over at Curt's ranch now to take care of the alpacas, hers and mine. They'll probably gather all her herd there since Curt's got plenty of extra space. He can run a temporary fence off a portion of his pasture for the alpacas."

"Yes, it took them forever to get there, as you can imagine. Thank goodness Curt's family was there to help with the animals."

"How's Jayleen doing?" Kelly asked. "I haven't talked with her since we drove off."

"She's holding up pretty well. And she sounds okay. Worried, of course, poor dear. Her whole livelihood is wrapped up in those animals."

"Well, Andrea has enough space at her place in the Poudre Canyon to keep the alpacas we brought over today."

Unless that fire spreads, a fearful thought intruded.

Kelly pushed that thought away and walked toward a quieter spot in the plaza near the bronze sculpture of a child on a swing.

"I still cannot believe Connie would lose control of herself like that," Mimi said, in the worried tone Kelly recognized. "And to actually try to hurt Andrea . . . that's simply dreadful. I mean, Connie's got a bad temper. Burt and Rosa and I knew that. It was never an issue at the shop or with the customers. But she and her husband have had problems for as long as I can remember."

Kelly leaned back against a stone wall that edged one of the raised gardens situated around the square. "Yeah, Lisa told us that she would see Connie pacing around the parking lot yelling at her husband over the phone. Lisa tried to get Connie into individual counseling several times, she said. But Connie never would."

Mimi's long sigh sounded louder over the phone. "I know, I know. I suggested counseling to Connie years ago. She didn't want to do it. She was convinced the joint marriage counseling would work. But it never did. Oh, things would calm down for a while, but then boom! They'd have another big fight and go into it all over again."

"Yeah, it got pretty ugly up at Jayleen's. Curt had to grab hold of Connie and pull her away before she could push Andrea again."

"*Again?* Oh, no! What'd Connie do? Hit her?"

"No, she pushed Andrea so hard she

stumbled, but regained her footing. And it looked like Connie might try it again, so that's why Curt grabbed her."

"Oh, Lord have mercy!"

"Yeah, she created another scene up at Andrea's when we all were off-loading alpacas. Everybody got hot then. Both Dennis and Jim Carson got into it as well, in addition to Connie and Andrea yelling."

"*Oh, no!* Did they start hitting each other?"

"They wanted to, you could tell. But Steve and Greg pushed in between them, and the guys settled down. Lisa took Connie under her wing and tried to calm her down. Connie was crying. I really felt bad for her. Jim yelled that he couldn't stand being with her. That was pretty harsh."

"Ohh, poor Connie." Mimi made some sympathetic sounds, sort of like a mother hen. Mother Mimi. "Is she back at home? I'll give her a call."

"Well, I certainly hope she is. We took Connie aside before we drove off from Andrea's and talked to her, made sure she was calm enough to drive back down the canyon. She had calmed down and seemed okay. Then we suggested she drive back with our little group. She was right behind Marty, then he said she stopped at one of the turnoffs with outdoor toilets." Kelly looked up at the tree branches swaying in the evening breeze. Wind was still blowing. "So, let's hope she went straight home."

"Please, Lord."

Changing the subject from that afternoon's soap opera, Kelly asked, "How are the kids doing? Cassie and Eric? Did they help with the animals? Burt's not an alpaca guy, so I imagine he was handing out Jayleen's cards to interested buyers."

"Oh, yes. But Eric and Cassie were actually a big help. They stayed in the pen with the alpacas, keeping them calm and showing them to anyone who was interested. Eric is really quite knowledgeable about the animals. And I was amazed how much Cassie remembered from her visit to Jayleen's ranch. That girl is sharp as a tack."

Kelly laughed softly. "That's exactly what Jayleen and Curt say about her. And I'm glad Eric has turned out to be so reliable."

"It's not surprising. Eric's mom is Curt's daughter and has sheep and alpacas of her own. She and her husband operate their own business and then breed both sheep and alpacas as well. So, ranchers' kids become savvy early on."

"The animals are all put up safely for the night?"

"Oh, yes. Burt made sure of that. And Rosa and Sophie closed up our Lambspun booth in the Exhibition Hall a little earlier than usual. That way all of us could go to dinner at the same time. We took everyone to a nice dinner at the Swiss Inn. Cassie and Eric had a ball dipping into the cheese fondue." Mimi's light laughter sounded.

It was good to hear her laugh. Kelly hadn't heard laughter since early that morning when they were all up at the Wool Market enjoying the animals, blissfully unaware of the disaster that was at work in the canyon closer to home.

"If they liked the cheese, I imagine they loved the chocolate fondue."

"Oh, mercy, yes." Mimi laughed again. "They had so much fun dipping marshmallows and fruit. Their faces were smeared with chocolate. We all got a kick out of it."

"I can picture it now. Were you able to get an extra room at the hotel? Wool Market is a busy time."

"Actually, we traded up to a suite. Cassie and I took one bedroom, and Burt and Eric took another. Rosa and Sophie stayed in a separate room. So everyone was taken care of. In fact, Burt's inside with the kids now watching television. I'm outside here on the balcony. Looking out on these beautiful, dark, quiet mountains."

There was a wistful sound to Mimi's voice that couldn't be missed. "Well, I have to admit, our mountains here don't look quiet anymore. Black clouds of smoke are billowing up from even more places than before. More fires haves broken out. That blasted wind has whipped the wildfire, and it's spread like crazy. You can see red flames at the ridge tops. We heard on the radio driving back that it's gone from about two hundred acres this morning to eight thousand this evening. And they think it'll be even more by tomorrow morning. If the wind doesn't stop, the fire can't lay down and get quiet at night. And the firefighters can't get on top of it."

"If only that awful wind hadn't picked up. Awful, awful. And Burt says we're seriously shorthanded with firefighters, even though they've come in from all over northern Colorado."

"Apparently the fire authority has called for national help, so we're hoping some Hot Shot teams will arrive maybe by tomorrow night. We seriously need them."

"I think Burt said he heard that. One of the breeders at the livestock barns was keeping in touch with the police scanners all afternoon and spreading the word."

"That's good. I didn't want you guys to be totally shocked when you finally drive back into town tomorrow. It's bad, Mimi. All of us saw the red and orange flames burning as we drove back into Fort Connor from the Poudre Canyon. It's scary, really. It's spreading fast . . . and everything is so dry."

"It's the drought. Or, that *damn drought,* as Burt says."

Steve walked up to her then and pointed toward the street edging Old Town Square. Then he walked in that direction. Curious, Kelly started to follow him. She noticed several people standing on top of some planters, staring and pointing westward toward the mountains.

"Well, I'd better get back to the others. Give Burt a hug for me, and the kids, too. We'll all see you guys tomorrow afternoon to load up the last of the alpacas."

"Take care of yourselves, Kelly. All of you. You folks have saved the day for Jayleen. See you tomorrow."

Kelly clicked off the phone and caught up with Steve. He was staring westward, too. "What's happened?" she asked, anxious.

"Wildfire's spread. The wind's thrown it all over. See, it's spread up onto that ridge. It wasn't there when we were driving over."

61

Kelly stared westward, but the buildings of Old Town were blocking her view. She saw the billowing smoke of before.

"I can't tell."

Steve climbed up on one of the nearby tall planters and offered Kelly a hand. She scrambled up quickly. "You can see better now," Steve said, pointing. "There . . . see that red orange glow near the top of the ridge?"

Kelly stared toward the mountains, and her heart sank. There was the red orange glow. Flames burning. Burning hot. Burning trees, spreading. Spreading farther.

"Oh, no . . ." she breathed, watching the glow. Dark smoke was billowing from more places now. "It's close to the top of the ridge."

"And the other side of that ridge leads down into Poudre Canyon," Steve said in a quiet voice. Even so, two people who stood nearby turned and stared at him, clearly horrified.

"God, no," the man said while the woman clamped her hand over her mouth.

Kelly felt a cold hand grab hold of her heart this time.

Sunday, June 10
Kelly and Steve wove a path through the

62

crowds of people walking around the Wool Market fairgrounds. Everyone seemed to be eating, Kelly noticed. Either late lunch, early dinner, or snacks. Hot dogs, roasted turkey legs, corn dogs, ice cream. If it was edible, someone was eating it.

"I wish we hadn't gotten separated from the others," Kelly said, glancing toward a livestock corral filled with curly-haired gray Wensleydale sheep. "They haven't been to Jayleen's stall, so it will take them longer to find it."

"Yeah, it seems more crowded today, so parking was a bear," Steve said, creating a path for them between two couples. "But they've been up here before to see Jayleen, so they know where the livestock pavilions are."

"Boy, you forget how large and spread out these stalls are. And we parked toward the back today. Yesterday we came in from the front part of the fairgrounds."

"We're almost there. In fact, I think that's Jayleen's stall up ahead. Isn't that Curt?"

Kelly peered around the moving heads and shoulders in front of her and thought she spotted a familiar Stetson hat. "Yeah, I think it is."

"Okay, let's go," Steve said, shouldering his way between several people. Kelly maneuvered herself right behind him, until they broke free of the crowd and hurried toward Jayleen's stall. There was Jayleen, rubbing a gray alpaca's back. Cassie was brushing another alpaca in the far corner. Eric was raking up some hay. Curt was talking to a man in the next stall.

Jayleen looked up with a big grin as Kelly and Steve approached. "Hey, you two! You made it through the crowds."

"Oh, yeah, it's getting packed out there," Kelly said as she reached out to give Jayleen a big hug. Jayleen hugged back hard. "We heard about the wildfire spreading to the Poudre Canyon. Steve and I wished we could have gone back up there and taken out some of your alpacas to move to Curt's, but the roads are closed now."

Curt clapped Steve on the back as they shook hands. "We can't thank you folks enough for all you did yesterday," Curt said. "We couldn't have gotten all of the herd out if not for you."

"Lord-a-mighty, that's the truth," Jayleen said, reaching over to give Steve a hug. "Thank God for good friends."

"What have you heard from Andrea or Dennis?" Steve asked. "We've all been glued to the radio, waiting for updates. Last we heard was this morning on television, the sheriff said the wildfire had come over the ridge into Poudre Canyon last night. Police have evacuated everyone in the Lower Poudre Canyon around Poudre Park."

"Not a word from either of them so far," Curt said, shaking his head.

Kelly recognized his worried expression. She didn't see it often. Her mentor-advisor was an experienced rancher and had seen just about anything that happened in these northern Colorado mountains; the foothills, as the locals called them.

"Their phones are probably out of signal range. You know how that happens when you get into that canyon."

"I sure hope so," Jayleen said, her face revealing her concern. "Someone told us they heard from the police scanners that the fire came down right around Poudre Park. And there were only five volunteer firefighters on duty. Everyone else had gone into Bellevue Canyon where they were needed."

Kelly and Steve looked at each other. "Does anyone know how far it spread?"

"Not yet. They have another briefing tonight. Good thing Andrea's place isn't right in Poudre Park. It's a few miles away, so she should be okay. But we'll all feel better when we can hear something."

"Amen," Jayleen said.

"Hey!" Cassie called out, as she scrambled over the stall fence. Dropping to the ground, she ran over and threw herself into Kelly's embrace. "So glad you're all right! Jennifer and Pete said you were okay."

Eric climbed over the fence and dropped easily to the ground. He walked up beside his grandfather and smiled. Steve reached out and gave Eric's hand a firm shake, man to man.

"I hear you and Cassie held down the fort here for Jayleen. Burt says all he did was hand out cards to customers, but you were able to answer their questions. Good job, Eric."

Curt reached over and touseled his grandson's light brown hair. "Eric's got the makings of a good rancher. Gotta be able to talk about the livestock, right, son?"

"Yeah," Eric said, a slight flush creeping up his neck and ears with the praise. "Cassie helped, too."

"It was kind of fun!" Cassie said. "They asked all sorts of stuff. Eric knew most of it. But I could tell them about the hair and stuff because Jayleen let me brush 'em."

Jayleen smiled and gave Cassie a hug, which Cassie returned. "They were real troupers, from what Burt said."

"Hey, your ears are all red!" Cassie said,

then giggled, pointing toward Eric.

"Yeah, well, you've got dirt on your face!" Eric retorted, pointing.

"Do not!"

Kelly laughed. "Well, I heard that both of you were smeared in chocolate last night. What'd you two do, swim in the fondue pot?"

Both Cassie and Eric broke into high-pitched laughter as they started throwing hay at each other.

"Listen, young'uns, now that Kelly and Steve are here, we'd better start loading up these animals," Curt announced. "It's gonna be another long drive back to the ranch, and I'm sure these good folks would like to get a decent night's sleep before going to work tomorrow morning."

"Yes, sir," Eric said, walking back to the corral. Cassie started to follow.

"Cassie, why don't you get a lead on Shasta. And Eric, you get a lead on Blondie, okay?" Jayleen said. "Kelly and Steve can take them to their trailer and get 'em loaded up.

Cassie nodded then climbed back over the fence into the corral stall.

"Where did you folks park?" Curt asked.

"Way in the back of beyond," Kelly said, jerking her thumb over her shoulder. "Can we take them around the side away from all the crowds? It'll take forever to get through all the people. Plus everyone is going to want to stop and pet them."

"Sure, you can. Did the others park near you?" Jayleen asked.

"We got separated, so they should be here pretty soon." Steve craned his neck and peered over the top of the passing visitors walking by the stalls, exclaiming at the animals.

"I think I spy Marty," Curt said, squinting into the distance. "Yep, there's that redhead."

"Well, that's good. We've got to drive all the way down the Big Thompson Canyon, so it'll take a while," Kelly said, checking her watch. "Do you want us to pick up some food for you and Curt once we get out of the canyon? We'll pass by lots of food places."

"That's sweet of you, Kelly, but Jennifer and Pete brought a whole spread over to Curt's ranch yesterday afternoon. Curt's daughter, Cindy, and her family were there helping with the animals. I swear, it was enough for a whole army." Jayleen smiled. "That was so sweet of them to do that."

"I figure they must have emptied out the café. There's plenty for tonight as well."

Curt waved at the approaching Megan and Marty. "Hey, there. Did you get lost behind the barns?"

"No, we had to stop because Marty and Greg were hungry, of course," Megan said with a smile. "Hey, Jayleen, how're you doing?" She and Jayleen embraced.

"I'm doing better, but worrying about those folks in Poudre Canyon."

"Yeah, we've been listening to news alerts on the radio on the way over," Marty said, corn dog in one hand, soda in the other. "Wind has whipped the wildfire back into Bellevue Canyon and away from the Poudre. And it's moved up toward Whale Rock Road."

"Oh, Lord!" Jayleen closed her eyes.

"That's a four-by-four road," Steve said. "It'll be almost impossible for firefighters to get equipment up there."

"Lord, Lord," Curt said grimly. "Any word about air tankers coming in? We need them to drop retardant on the flames."

"I think Greg heard that some were going to come in tomorrow." Marty beckoned Greg and Lisa out of the crowd. Like Marty, Greg had a corn dog in one hand and a soda in the other. Staff of life.

"Sorry to be late, guys," Lisa said as they joined the rest. "Of course, food slowed us down as usual."

"Sustenance," Greg said, then took another bite of corn dog.

"Didn't you say a water tanker plane is coming tomorrow?" Marty asked him.

Greg swallowed quickly and nodded. "Yeah. And the national fire teams are arriving now, we just heard. First team of Hot Shots arrived. They're setting up in Landport over near the Armory."

"Thank God," Megan said, closing her eyes. "Let's hope they can hit the ground running. This fire overwhelmed our limited resources, for sure."

"Hot Shots will get right on it. They could see how bad it was when they were flying in," Marty added.

"Let's hope," Lisa said. "Have you heard anything from Andrea? We're all worried sick about Poudre Canyon."

Jayleen shook her head. "Not a thing. We figure nobody up there can get a cell phone signal. So we'll all just have to say a prayer and hope."

"They probably don't want to talk to anybody after fighting the fire," Greg observed, after he'd finished off the corn dog. "Man, those folks had more than their share to deal with yesterday. Fighting couples. Then fighting the wildfire. Too much."

"What do you mean?" Curt asked, narrowing his gaze on Greg. "Don't tell me Connie had another outburst?"

"Oh, yeah," Marty said with a nod.

"It got ugly. Steve and I had to separate Dennis and Jim."

"Oh, Lord have mercy," Jayleen said, wagging her head. "Not again."

"Well, it's nothing you and Curt have to worry about," Kelly said, giving Jayleen's arm a squeeze. "It's their problem to work out. You and Curt have enough on your plate. So now that the troops are all assembled, let's get these animals loaded and head down Big Thompson Canyon and back to Curt's ranch. At least your place is not that far from the mouth of this canyon, Curt."

"Yeah, with luck we can come back for a second load before dinner," Steve added.

Curt wagged his head. "You folks are lifesavers, you surely are. That way Jayleen and I can manage the rest in a couple of trips."

"Bless your hearts," Jayleen said, her eyes shining. "I feel like I've got a flock of special angels helping me out. I can't thank you enough."

"Yeah, you can," Greg spoke up. "You can make us all a pot of your chili."

"Angels, huh? I'm gonna put that on a tee shirt," Marty said with a grin.

Megan rolled her eyes while Kelly and everyone else laughed.

"All right, then, let's get this show on the road." Curt clapped his hands. "I think I'll load up two of these animals and join your convoy. Maybe we can finish up faster tonight."

"Sounds like a plan," Kelly said. "There will be a lot of traffic on that road leaving the Wool Market, so we might as well join in."

"Okay, head 'em up, and move 'em out!" Marty called, waving his arm as he headed toward the corral.

FOUR

"Kelly, I've been hoping you'd come in this morning," Mimi exclaimed as Kelly stepped inside the Lambspun knitting shop foyer. Mimi rushed over and gave Kelly a big hug. "Jayleen called us after you folks had dropped off the animals. You all came to the rescue once again."

"Well, we were glad we were able to help," Kelly said. "Curt and Jayleen will have their hands full caring for all those animals at Curt's ranch. They'll have to fence off a portion of the pasture. Meanwhile, we're all keeping our fingers crossed that the animals we took to Poudre Canyon are okay. Thank goodness they weren't near Poudre Park and the wildfire. Andrea's ranch is a few miles away."

She walked toward the main knitting room where the long library table was located. Knitters and fiber workers of all persuasions

73

could be found sitting around the welcoming table any time of day, asking for help with a project and receiving help. There was always someone at Lambspun who could help someone with questions and give how-to demonstrations.

Mimi followed after her. "Have you talked to Jayleen today? Has she heard anything from Andrea? I've tried calling several times but the phone doesn't even take messages anymore. The mailbox is full." Mimi had a worried expression.

Kelly dropped her shoulder bag onto the knitting table. "No, I haven't heard a thing. She's bound to check in sometime. We heard last night on the news that all of the Poudre Park and lower canyon residents were evacuated right when the fire started spreading into Poudre Canyon. Andrea is bound to call her friends sometime. She must know they're worried."

Mimi's brow furrowed. "The problem is, Andrea may still be in the canyon. After all, her ranch isn't right at Poudre Park, so if it wasn't in immediate danger, maybe she wasn't evacuated."

"I don't know, Mimi," Kelly said skeptically. "I'm pretty sure I heard the sheriff say they were evacuating everyone in the lower Poudre Canyon."

"Oh, dear. Now, I'm really worried she hasn't called." Mimi's concerned look deepened.

Kelly recognized it and sought to reassure her, much as Mimi did for so many others. "She's probably so busy juggling everything she hasn't had time. I mean, she had a ranch filled with alpacas up there. Maybe she and Jim and Dennis have been transferring the animals all this time. Maybe they had help. Who knows? We'll simply have to wait until we hear something." Changing the subject slightly, Kelly asked, "By the way, how's Connie doing? I'm hoping she used Sunday to calm down. Maybe talk with someone, a counselor, hopefully."

Mimi leaned closer to Kelly and lowered her voice so the customers in the next room browsing the yarn bins wouldn't hear her. "I hope so, too. But I don't know. She didn't come in today. There was a message left on the shop voice mail from her saying she didn't feel good, and she was staying home." Mimi frowned. "That's not like Connie to leave a message on the Lambspun line like that. Usually in the past, she's called my cell phone and told me personally."

"She's probably simply embarrassed, that's all. Connie no doubt figures that we told you guys what happened, so now she feels embarrassed by all those emotional scenes over the weekend. I wouldn't worry."

"Burt said the same thing this morning," Mimi said with a slight smile as Kelly withdrew her laptop computer from her shoulder bag. "So with two of you in agreement, I guess it's all right."

"Is Burt off on errands? Or is he in the café having a late breakfast?"

"No, he went off early to see how he could help with the Salvation Army over at the Ranch or the Red Cross in Landport, where they've set up a disaster shelter. Meals are being served there now. Burt's going to volunteer to help drive in supplies if they need extra hands."

Kelly smiled. "That sounds like Burt. Believe me, I'd go help, too, but I've got to see what client work is waiting for me in my inbox first."

"You and the gang have done your fair share of helping. And would you believe that Jennifer and Pete had a whole dinner waiting for Burt and Cassie and me when we arrived back home yesterday? Jennifer called and said they were bringing food over so we could all have supper together. Then they took Cassie home with them afterward. Wasn't that sweet of them?"

"I'm sure they wanted to do their part.

Jen told me over the phone yesterday that she and Pete wished they could drive animals but figured they could help in other ways."

"Well, they were right. We were all hungry again after a quick fast-food break when we left Estes Park and the Wool Market. Rosa and Sophie didn't want to stay for dinner, since they were anxious to get to their homes. So, Pete's cooking was really welcome. Burt and I both will have to exercise extra to work off those additional pounds." She laughed lightly.

"I'm so glad you two got to relax. You've been on oversight and supervisory duty all weekend."

"Where did you folks go for dinner? Back to Old Town?"

"Yes, we went to a steakhouse and indulged ourselves. Looks like Greg has completely fallen off the vegetarian wagon. He was gorging on fried chicken Saturday," she said with a grin.

Mimi laughed again as she walked toward the adjoining workroom. "Well, I'd better get back to work. I have to find room for the Wool Market items that were extras. That will take me a while. Cassie promised she'd unpack those Wool Market boxes for me once she finishes helping Jennifer and Pete."

That sounded different so it caught Kelly's attention. "What's she doing? Don't tell me they've got her waitressing?"

"Actually, Cassie is clearing and cleaning tables because Julie couldn't get in today. She was up in Steamboat for the last couple of days and the wildfire closed off Colorado 14 through the Poudre Canyon. She's had to drive back the other way from Steamboat, down on Route 40 to Kremmling, then east to Granby, then drive up to Fort Connor. Poor girl. She's not getting back until this afternoon."

"And she'll be exhausted," Kelly added as Mimi disappeared into the workroom.

Kelly opened her laptop and was about to press the start button when she paused, then leaned back against the wooden chair.

Julie wasn't the only one who was exhausted. Both she and Steve woke up groggy that morning. Lisa called and said she and Greg felt like they'd been hit by a truck. Megan said even Marty wasn't as talkative as usual this morning. Exhaustion had set in. Kelly was amazed at how tired they all were. It wasn't as if they had been moving furniture all weekend. They'd been sitting in trucks, driving, loading and unloading alpacas, driving through bumper-to-bumper traffic going into and out of mountain canyons. Watching the wildfire spread, tossed by the wind, igniting treetops and ridgetops into flames.

And all the while there was the inescapable heat. Upper nineties. That only added to the efforts. Not to mention the constant worry about their friends and their properties. Of course, the soap opera dramatics that interrupted both the Bellevue Canyon and Poudre Canyon alpaca transit didn't help matters.

Kelly pushed back her chair. She was still tired, even after a hot shower, breakfast, and morning coffee at home. Clearly, this exhaustion called for a dose of Eduardo's high-octane brew. The cook at Pete's Porch Café at the rear of the Lambspun knitting shop made coffee exactly the way Kelly liked it: black and thick and super strong. Black Gold, Kelly called it.

Instead of heading straight to the café, however, Kelly took her time and strolled from the main knitting room of her favorite knitting shop to the adjoining central yarn room. Right off the foyer, this room was filled with even more yarns and fibers to touch and enjoy.

Summer colors burst from every corner.

Raspberry reds, blueberry blues, mint greens, lemon yellows. She stroked the bamboo and cotton yarn, always surprised at how soft bamboo could be. It was such a sturdy plant with a tough protective coating, and yet it could be made into a yarn that was softer than some cottons. She moved to the many bins lining the walls and fondled the delicate merino light wools, the silk and cotton combinations, and the sinfully soft coil of pure silk yarn. Luscious.

As always, Mimi and the shop elves had all sorts of knitted and crocheted and woven garments draped over tops of tables, hanging from the ceiling, tacked on the walls, and dangling along the sides of bookcases and shelves. Everything asked to be touched, so Kelly obliged, reveling in the feel of each fiber.

"Hey, Kelly! Have you seen Mimi?" Cassie said as she rounded the corner from the hallway that led to the café. A few weeks shy of her twelfth birthday and tall for her age, Cassie was still skinny, on the edge between childhood and adolescence. "I told her I'd help find places for all the extra yarns and stuff they took to the vendor booth at the Wool Market."

"Yeah, she's in the workroom," Kelly said, giving Cassie a quick hug. "I heard that you were helping out Jennifer and Pete by cleaning and setting up tables in the café. Good job!"

Cassie brushed a lock of dark brown hair away from her forehead, her enormous bright blue eyes alight. "Oh, yeah. Julie was stuck up at Cameron Pass hiking this weekend and couldn't get through on the road back to Fort Connor. So she had to go all the way around Granby to get here." Cassie made a face.

"Well, you stepped up, Cassie. That was good. Pete and Jen really needed your help. Just like Jayleen did. So I salute you with my empty coffee mug." Kelly held it high with a smile.

Cassie giggled. "It was fun, actually. Even though it was scary what was happening. Eric taught me a lot of stuff about the animals, too."

Kelly looked out into the yarn room. "That was one heckuva weekend, wasn't it? That wildfire has scared everybody. We've never had a wildfire in Bellevue Canyon or Poudre Canyon like this one. There have been little fires that were put out faster, but nothing like this."

Cassie's eyes got even bigger. "Pete and Jennifer told me. When we drove in last night, Mimi and Burt and I could see the red orange fire right there on the mountains! It was so scary! I couldn't believe all the smoke."

"Well, some Hot Shot firefighter teams got in last night, so I heard they've already started on the fire. So that'll help. But we need more."

"Oh, I thought I heard your voice, Cassie," Mimi said, coming around the corner from the hallway.

"We were just sharing wildfire info," Kelly said, patting Cassie's shoulder. "I'd better get some coffee so I can stay awake long enough to get client work done. I'm afraid I'll fall asleep. See you guys later."

Kelly walked down the hallway and into the back of Pete's café. She spotted her dear friend Jennifer serving breakfast to a group at a nearby table. Jennifer glanced up and spied Kelly. Then she put her coffeepot aside and walked over to embrace her friend. Kelly gave her a big hug.

"Thank goodness you guys were there to help," Jennifer said. "This is bad. I've never seen it like this."

"I know," Kelly said, drawing back and looking into her friend's concerned face. "This is the one we've always dreaded."

Kelly took another deep drink of Eduardo's

black nectar. *Ahh.* Caffeine. Thanks to the rich, strong coffee, Kelly had been able to actually start working on her client's accounting spreadsheets. She'd switched locations from the knitting table to the café. The added stimulus would help in her efforts to stay awake. Both she and Steve were definitely going to get to sleep early tonight and catch up, if that was possible.

The back door of the café opened and Burt stepped inside. Since Kelly was seated at her favorite small table beside the windows, Burt couldn't miss her.

"Hey, Kelly. Getting back to work in the real world, right?" he said with a big smile.

"Trying to, Burt. But it's not coming easily. Pull up a chair and catch me up on what's happening at the front lines. Mimi said you went over to help the Salvation Army and Red Cross."

Burt pulled out a chair across from Kelly. She noticed even more worry lines on Burt's crinkled face than usual. He was a retired Fort Connor police detective, and a lifetime of dealing with serious crimes and criminals had left signs on Burt's face. But nothing took away his wide smile. Kelly always found that reassuring.

Along with rancher Curt Stackhouse, Burt had become Kelly's second father figure and advisor ever since she'd arrived in Fort Connor four years ago for her aunt Helen's funeral. Curt advised Kelly on all things ranching and land-related, including natural gas deposits that were found on Wyoming land she inherited from another distant relative.

Aunt Helen had left Kelly the beige stucco, red-tile-roofed cottage across the driveway from her aunt's favorite knitting shop, Lambspun. It was a smaller version of the Spanish Colonial–style former farmhouse that now housed the popular knitting shop. Her aunt Helen and uncle Jim had lived there when Kelly was a child. Sheep once grazed on pastures where golfers now chased balls. Located on the edge of Fort Connor's Old Town, the city-owned golf course was bordered on one side by the Cache La Poudre River and trail. The Cache La Poudre flowed out of the canyon of the same name and ran diagonally across Fort Connor before it joined the South Platte, those waters rushing to meet the great Mississippi.

Mimi's husband, Burt, advised Kelly on all detective-related matters. Ever since Kelly had joined the warm family atmosphere at Lambspun, she'd found herself involved in helping to solve various murders of local residents. Several of them were friends of the Lambspun family and staff. Her friends called it "sleuthing." Burt, however, always took Kelly's efforts seriously. He was quick to point out that her track record of discovering the real guilty party in a murder had been "impressive" over the years.

"It's crazy over there in Landport," Burt said, holding out his cup for Jennifer as she approached with the coffeepot. "Kelly, did you know Jennifer and Pete brought a feast over to our house when we arrived home last night?"

Jennifer gave a dismissive wave. "We just packaged up extras from Sunday's brunch and lunch. We figured you folks were tired of eating corn dogs." She winked.

Burt closed his eyes. "If I never see another corn dog again, it'll be too soon."

"Mimi told me you two would have to run extra miles to compensate."

"I don't even want to think about it," Burt said, blowing on his coffee before he took a sip.

"Oh, pooh. You two deserved a good meal. Cassie must have had two slices of pecan pie. After eating dinner, of course," Jennifer added.

"Don't tell Marty. He'll be over here for

lunch to finish off that pie." Kelly laughed.

"That means Cassie's going to have a growth spurt. Kids' appetites always pick up right before they shoot up in height," Burt said. "I remember watching my daughter grow up, and my grandkids. It happened like clockwork."

"Wow, she's pretty tall for her age now."

"When's her twelfth birthday?" Kelly asked.

"July tenth. It's a Saturday, so we'll have a big party late that afternoon. With all this heat in June, it's bound to be broiling by July." Jennifer glanced around at the smaller amount of midmorning customers starting to thin out before the lunch crowd arrived. "I'll check on you two later," she said, turning away toward the other tables.

"I only stopped in for coffee before I pick up some supplies for the Salvation Army folks. All of their staff are on duty out there at the Ranch, serving hot meals from their special food truck. So I volunteered to run stuff from town out to Landport for the Red Cross and to the Salvation Army at the Ranch by the interstate. Trying to be useful."

"How's that fire look from the highway outside town? You can get a better long-range view of the mountains from there.

Last night, Steve and I drove out to the interstate for a long-distance view. Black clouds were glowing red, orange, and yellow. Even the setting sun glowed bloodred. It was frightening."

Burt's expression sobered. "Fire's gotten worse, judging from all the smoke. The national incident commander gave the news update this morning, if you watched it. The Hot Shots jumped right in, but the fire had spread so much it'll be hard for even them to slow it down. More are coming in today."

"Both Steve and I watched the update. Thank goodness we're getting some help. Plus a water tanker plane. He said one was coming in today. Poudre Canyon residents were evacuated, and the road's closed from Ted's Place store at the intersection with the main highway, all the way west into the canyon up near Rustic."

Kelly's smartphone that lay on the table beeped with a text message. She picked it up and read. "From Lisa. She said . . . Oh, no. Wildfire has spread over Soldier Canyon Ridge. Greg spotted the fire blazing in the trees from his office windows at the university." Kelly looked up at Burt; his surprise mirrored hers.

"Good Lord," Burt said, then tossed down his coffee and pushed back his chair. "I'd better get those supplies over to Landport, then see what else I can do."

Kelly rose and pushed her laptop closed. Spreadsheets could wait. "If it's spread over the top of Soldier Canyon Ridge, that means it's burning on the ridge right above Horsetooth Reservoir. There are bunches of mountain homes all along there."

Burt pulled his cell phone from his pocket as he walked toward the back door of the café. "They're gonna have to get those folks out of there. I'm calling Dan to see if the department needs any help with directing traffic away from that area. Talk to you later, Kelly." He was out the door and down the steps quickly.

Kelly headed for the front door and down the steps, then out the curved stucco archway entrance to the front parking lot near the busy city street. Walking away from the shop, she aimed for the edge of the golf course, hoping she could glimpse something from there. Peering westward in the hot, hazy midmorning sky, Kelly thought she spotted a new plume of smoke, but buildings in Old Town blocked a clear view.

Her phone beeped again, and it was a message from Marty, sent to the group. He could see the fire from the tall bank building where his law offices were located, west of Old Town. Flames were burning hot red orange.

Kelly's gut squeezed. *Oh, no.* So many people had made the foothills near Horsetooth Reservoir their home, building some grand but mostly modest houses in the shallow canyons and on the gently rolling ridges. She felt compelled to jump in her car right now and drive to the west side of town to Overland Trail. It hugged the western edge of the city right beside the foothills. There was no way she could concentrate on spreadsheets now with the wildfire burning on the other side of the reservoir, in the midst of beautiful hiking and biking trails.

She walked swiftly back toward the café and noticed several customers gathered on the balcony and standing on the black wrought-iron chairs. Everyone was gazing westward. News of the wildfire's spread was clearly being passed from person to person. Without frequent news alerts on radio or television, nowadays people notified each other via e-mail and text messages and tweets. Information was immediate now. So were rumors.

Now that this wildfire was classified as serious enough for a national response, Kelly hoped the fire incident commander could give citizens even more accurate and updated information. All they knew was what their own eyes told them: The wildfire was growing, igniting more areas. More plumes of smoke were evidence of that. Plus the news that the fire had spread from eight thousand to over twenty thousand acres now. Dry forests and pine bark beetle–killed trees ignited quickly, practically spontaneous combustion.

Reaching the café patio garden, Kelly saw Pete on the deck staring westward with his customers, pointing. Noticing Kelly, Pete gave her a half-smile and a wave. "Hey, Kelly. Mimi was looking for you," he said as she paused beneath the balcony. "She went back into the shop, I think."

"Thanks, Pete. I bet you've been baking extra to make up for all that private catering you guys did this weekend," she said, smiling up at him as she walked along the flagstone pathway that led through the garden and around to the front entrance of the knitting shop.

The bright hardy red geraniums and yellow zinnias were holding up well in their sunny spot of the garden. Thank goodness most of the patio garden was shaded a great deal of the day. Only the midday sun really bathed the front third, which suited the gardenias, zinnias, and honeysuckle bushes just fine, she noticed.

Kelly yanked open the heavy wooden front door and looked around the foyer for Mimi. Only two customers were browsing the bins in the foyer.

Walking through the central yarn room, Kelly scanned around the main knitting room. No Mimi. The room was unusually empty this morning, so Kelly figured there must be a class going on, and headed for the adjoining workroom.

As she turned the corner, she nearly ran into Mimi. "Ooops, I'm still taking those corners too fast. Sorry, Mimi."

Mimi didn't even smile like she usually did. Instead, she grabbed Kelly's arm and leaned closer, her voice dropping. "Kelly, I've been looking for you. I just had a phone call. Andrea's dead!"

FIVE

Monday afternoon, June 11

Kelly drew back, shocked. "*Dead!* How? Did she get caught with the fire in the canyon?"

Mimi shook her head. "I don't know. Curt called a few minutes ago and said Dennis called Jayleen earlier. Told her he found Andrea lying on the ground behind her house in Poudre Canyon Saturday night. Nobody was around. Jim Carson wasn't there. Dennis said he took her in his car down the canyon road to get to a hospital. He believed she was still alive because he thought he felt a weak pulse. Then he flagged down paramedics driving into the canyon and the guy checked Andrea. He said she was already dead. No heartbeat. No pulse."

"Good Lord! I can't believe this! She was healthy and strong on Saturday. How could she be dead? Did she have some disease, Mimi? I mean, did she get seizures?"

Mimi gestured helplessly. "I don't know anything about Andrea's health history, Kelly. She was one of our regular fiber suppliers, that's all. I didn't know her personally like Jayleen. I'm simply repeating everything Curt told me. Curt had another call coming in, so he couldn't talk more."

"How horrible," Kelly said, staring out into the yarn room colors. "Andrea seemed so vibrant and alive. How could she suddenly be dead . . . ? It doesn't make sense."

"A lot of things in life don't make sense, Kelly," Mimi said, wistfully. "Let me know if you learn anything. You may get a chance to talk to Jayleen later." Mimi's cell phone started ringing. "Oh, I have to take this. It's the vendor I've been trying to reach. I'm placing an order with a new supplier."

"Talk to you later, Mimi."

Kelly watched Mimi walk through the workroom into the office and storage space behind. Mimi had given her an idea, and Kelly headed back to the café. Noticing some customers still standing on the café balcony staring westward, she shut down her laptop and loaded it into her over-the-shoulder briefcase. She looked around for Jennifer and saw her loading two soup and salad selections onto her tray. Early lunchtime had already started.

She walked over to her friend and spoke softly. "Don't tell anyone but Pete. Mimi just heard that Andrea Holt, Jayleen's alpaca rancher friend in Poudre Canyon, was found dead at her ranch. No other details yet."

Jennifer looked shocked. "Whoa, I think I met her a few times at the café. Didn't she come in here to sell Mimi alpaca wool?"

Kelly nodded. "Yeah. And we all took six of Jayleen's alpacas to her place up the Poudre on Saturday. Who knows what's happening with them now. I'm going to drive over to Curt's ranch and talk with them to see if they've learned anything else. I wish we could help. Who's going to feed those animals now?"

Jennifer frowned. "I know you want to help, Kelly. But you guys can't go into Poudre Canyon. I don't care how many alpacas are there. Police and firefighters closed the road."

"I know." Kelly sighed. "That was wishful thinking. I wonder how long the canyon road will be closed. They were able to stop the fire."

"For now. Who knows what will happen? Look at it now, coming across Soldier Canyon. New spots are popping out all over. Remember the police chief on TV last night saying there was no hope of containment. The wildfire was spreading in every possible direction.

"It's a good thing more Hot Shots are on their way. They should be on the ground tomorrow. Thanks to that wind, this wildfire has gotten way out of control. We've never seen anything this bad around here. We've seen it near Denver — like when the Haymarket Fire happened, but not here. Listen, I've gotta take care of customers. Catch me up later on anything you learn, okay?"

"Will do," Kelly promised, then headed toward the café's back door. Noticing Cassie wiping off a table, Kelly gave her a wave as she left.

Turning her car onto Curt's long ranch driveway, Kelly detected the increased smell of smoke in the air. East of town, at Lambspun, it wasn't as noticeable as in the western part of Fort Connor. Burt's ranch was southwest of town, far enough away from the Bellevue Canyon and Buckhorn Canyon areas where the risk of fire was higher. Only the far edges of Burt's ranch bordered the lower Buckhorn area.

The fact that the smoke smell was evident here meant only one thing: The wildfire had spread closer and was moving southwest.

Kelly thought she spotted her alpacas in the midst of Jayleen's herd as she got closer to the ranch yard. As she pulled her car to a stop, she saw Jayleen walk out of the corral and head her way.

"Lord, Kelly, what brings you out here through this God-awful heat?" Jayleen asked as she strode up, her tee shirt damp and already clinging to her skin.

Kelly slammed her car door. "Two things, actually. First, I had to see that fire over on Soldier Canyon for myself."

Jayleen wagged her head. "Lordy, Lordy, that was a frightful thing to see. Right there across from Horsetooth."

"I know. I deliberately drove over on Overland Trail so I could see how bad it is. Awful." Remembering the fearful feeling when she saw for herself the red orange flames licking the tops of trees just over Soldier Canyon ridge. Gray, black, and white smoke billowing up. "But I did see firefighters working on it. Greg texted us that he hoped it wasn't his imagination, but he thinks he spotted less flames than when it first started. I hope he's right."

"Lord, yes. Of course, you folks in Fort Connor aren't in any danger. There's no way a wildfire is gonna cross over Horsetooth Reservoir. That's for damn sure."

Jayleen gave a purposeful nod, then eyed Kelly. "I imagine I know what the other reason is. Mimi told you about Andrea."

"Yes. And I couldn't believe it, Jayleen." Kelly gestured. "I . . . I mean we were all together in Bellevue and at Andrea's ranch up the Poudre . . ." She looked at Jayleen, bewildered.

"I know, Kelly. It was hard to make sense of what Dennis was telling me when he called. Poor man, I felt sorry for him. He was crying all the while he was talking. It was hard to understand what he was saying."

"Mimi said apparently Dennis found Andrea lying on the ground behind her house. Is that right?" Kelly swatted away a fly.

"That's right. Dennis said he drove to Andrea's place as soon as the orange glow behind the south wall of the canyon ridge got brighter. It was dark by then, after nine o'clock at night. He saw all her lights on, but she wasn't inside the house. Jim Carson wasn't there either. Dennis said he was concerned so he walked around the back and that's when he found her lying on the ground. Right below the steps. She's got a flight of steep steps up to the balcony around the back of her house. So he figured she must have fallen. Dennis swore he felt a faint pulse, so he was convinced Andrea was still alive." Jayleen wagged her head with a sigh. "But some paramedics he found coming into the canyon checked her and didn't find a heartbeat. She was already dead."

"You know, even though Mimi already repeated everything Curt told her, hearing it a second time still sounds unreal. What a freakish accident. And right in the midst of all this wildfire chaos." She swatted away another fly as it buzzed close to her face.

"I feel the same way, Kelly. Why don't we go inside the ranch house and get out of this heat? I don't know about you, but I need some ice-cold sweet tea."

Kelly fell into step beside her rancher friend. Jayleen Swinson was what Kelly called a Colorado Cowgirl. Despite her sixty-plus years and the silver taking over her long blonde curls, Jayleen displayed the same hardworking, can-do spirit she had since Kelly first met her years ago. Fourteen years sober, Jayleen had created success in her life by building her alpaca ranching business slowly, step by step. As her accountant, Kelly had offered financial advice along the way, but Jayleen had taken the risks necessary to make success a reality.

Now, all that hard work might be in jeopardy. The wildfire still blazed around

Bellevue Canyon, the wind whipping it here and there, no telling how much had burned. Way over twenty thousand acres by now. Smoke still billowed upward like it did Saturday. Manpower was stretched thin right now. Firefighters were flying in, according to news reports, but not fast enough. The wildfire was faster than all of them.

Kelly had also not forgotten Jayleen's alpacas that she and her friends had rescued from Bellevue Canyon and taken to Andrea's ranch on Saturday. How could they rescue them now?

"Jayleen, what about your alpacas at Andrea's?" Kelly asked as she followed her up the steps to Curt's wide front porch. She and her friends had spent many an enjoyable hour relaxing on that porch over the years at countless barbecues and potluck suppers. "We can't drive up into the canyon to get them out. Who's going to take care of them now that Andrea's dead?"

Jayleen held open the screen door for Kelly to enter the homey ranch house kitchen. "Well, Dennis is taking care of them for me, but you can't breathe a word. He's laying low at Andrea's place. Staying out of sight, keeping the lights off at night so no one can spot him. He's even sleeping in the barn with the animals to make sure no big cat comes a-hunting. He hikes back to his place up the river when he needs supplies."

Kelly stared at her friend in surprise. "You are kidding? And the cops haven't spotted him?"

"Nope. Dennis is a mountain man. He knows how to stay out of sight in the bushes and trees. He stays off the road and moves around at night. When he has to go to his place, he hikes back at night, sleeps some, then goes back to her ranch before dawn. And, frankly, the police are too damn busy to care. The firefighters are volunteers who live up there, and they're off fighting the fire or keeping watch so it doesn't come into the Poudre again. Besides, everybody up there knows Dennis. And they all must have heard about Andrea, or will soon. Word spreads around police and firemen." Jayleen opened the refrigerator and took out a large glass pitcher of iced tea. She grabbed two glasses from the nearby cabinet and poured both glasses full. "I'll bet they all figure that Dennis is taking care of Andrea's livestock, and they're leaving him the hell alone."

"Wow," was all Kelly could say as she pictured Dennis Holt hiking a few miles at night in the dark and back again. Taking care of his ex-wife's alpacas . . . and Jayleen's.

"Besides, police can't force anyone to evacuate. If you stay you assume the risk, knowing firemen won't put their forces in jeopardy to rescue you."

Kelly gratefully accepted the icy glass, condensation appearing already on the warm surface. Even in air-conditioned homes, the heat crept inside. Normally she didn't drink iced tea. But a couple of years ago, she'd tried Jayleen's sweet tea and found it was delicious, much to her surprise.

"Thanks, I need this." Kelly drained the glass, the icy cold sweet tea flavor quenching a thirst she'd ignored all the way from Lambspun.

Jayleen smiled and refilled her glass. "That's a long drive over here in the heat. Drink up."

Kelly did as she suggested, draining half the glass this time. *Ahh.* "Boy, that hit the spot. I didn't know how thirsty I was."

She glanced around the warm, inviting Stackhouse kitchen, with its sunshine yellow walls and wide counters.

"Wow, sleeping in the barn, keeping watch over the herd at night. That means he must have his shotgun with him. The first time I saw Dennis Holt was when Jennifer and I discovered the body of Jennifer's client Fred Turner in his cabin up the Poudre. I was standing on the cabin front porch while Jennifer was in the yard calling police about finding her real estate client dead. Shot in the head. I glanced around and spotted this shaggy-looking guy hiding in the bushes beside the cabin, obviously eavesdropping. And he had a shotgun over his arm."

Jayleen grinned and pulled out a chair at the rectangular kitchen table. "That would be Dennis, all right. Have a seat, Kelly girl."

Kelly responded to the familiar nickname that Jayleen had started using years ago. It always made Kelly feel good inside for some reason. "I figured. Boy, that's devotion to duty. And you said Andrea divorced him, right? So their relationship must have stayed amicable."

"Oh, yeah. Dennis used to have a drinking problem, and when he drank he'd pick a fight with Andrea and yell. Well, she finally had enough and divorced him. That was the shock Dennis needed. I offered to take him with me to AA meetings. And thank the Lord, he agreed. And he's been sober for over three years. Once he stopped drinking, Andrea would at least talk to him again." Jayleen lifted her glass in salute and took a drink of tea.

"I love to hear stories like that," Kelly said with a smile, raising her glass as well. "To Dennis. Not everyone can change their lives like that. It takes courage and determination."

"And prayer." Jayleen raised her glass again. "That's one of AA's mottoes. One day at a time. Hand it over to a Higher Power."

"I'll drink to that," Kelly said with a wink.

"Yeah, Dennis was hoping he'd eventually be able to convince Andrea to give him a second chance. I didn't have the heart to tell him that Andrea had already kind of moved on, you could say. Of course, once he saw her with Jim Carson, well, that gave Dennis quite a jolt." She sipped. "Dennis and I talked the day before the Wool Market, and he asked if I needed any help bringing animals up to the Estes Park fairgrounds. I asked how he was doing, and he admitted he was having a hard time getting over seeing Andrea with another man. Dennis still had that dream he and Andrea would get back together."

"Now you've made me sad. Poor Dennis." Then something she remembered Jayleen saying earlier came back into her mind. "You said that Dennis thought he felt a pulse and drove Andrea down the canyon where he met up with some paramedics. And they confirmed that she was dead. What happened then? Did they take her to the hospital? Did Dennis go with her?

Jayleen shook her head. "Dennis said the paramedics took all his information, then told him they'd call an ambulance to take her body to the hospital. They were already on their way up the canyon. Someone was having a problem breathing with all the smoke and they had emphysema, so it was critical."

"Could Dennis take her?"

"He offered, but they told him not to. They said the ambulance would be there soon, and it was. Dennis said he only waited ten minutes. Andrea's place is not far from the mouth of the canyon. Dennis said the ambulance guys practically ordered him to get back to his property in the canyon in case the fire spread. He'd be of more use there. Sure enough, flames crossed over the ridge from Bellevue Canyon a couple of hours later." She gave a crooked smile. "Turns out that was good advice. There was nothing Dennis or anyone could do for Andrea. So he said he went back to his place and gathered his things so he could stay at Andrea's ranch and take care of the animals."

"He's lucky he took their advice. Otherwise he might not have gotten back into Poudre Canyon. Cops started evacuating people later that night once the fire started down the ridge."

"That's right, and they closed the road. Dennis said he left his car parked at his house and took off with a backpack, going in the dark through the trees along the river. It's a couple of miles down the river from his place to Andrea's. By the time he got there, he saw the fire crest the south ridge into Poudre Canyon. He dumped his gear in the brush, then rushed back to Poudre Park to help any way he could. Water brigades, whatever. Ran most of the way back, if you can believe." Jayleen wagged her head then took a sip of tea.

"Good Lord," Kelly said, amazed by Dennis's stamina. "He really is a mountain man."

"Then just before dawn, he disappeared into the brush and hiked back to his place. Laid low outside in the bushes far enough away from the house, so he could watch when cops came to search for people. Once they cleared out and headed down the road, he was able to creep back and let himself into his house. When it turned dark later that night, he hiked over to Andrea's."

Kelly leaned her chin on her hand, listening to this adventure story. "How far away was the wildfire? Wasn't he in danger of it spreading toward Andrea's place?"

Jayleen shook her head. "No, Dennis said the fire swept over the ridge about a mile west of his place and didn't get near his place or Andrea's farther down the river. Thankfully, the flames also stayed on the other side of the road and didn't cross over. So their side of the canyon was untouched." Jayleen wagged her head in familiar fashion. "Lord, Lord. Those poor folks who were evacuated told me they were so scared. Forced out of their homes just before midnight Saturday night. Most weren't even given time to grab more clothes or anything. Police ordered them out to save their lives. Nobody wanted people getting trapped by the fire. So they had to run with nothing, just the clothes on their backs." Jayleen rose to fetch the pitcher of iced tea, then poured some more into Kelly's glass and hers.

Kelly took a long drink. "That really does sound like something you'd see in a movie. They must have been scared to death."

"Oh, they were. They didn't have any time to save things. I was lucky. All of you folks and other friends showed up to help Curt and me load things from the house. I swear,

I think the entire contents of my file cabinet are downstairs in Curt's basement. But that was when the fire was first starting in Bellevue Canyon. It got out of control fast, so firefighters weren't taking any chances with people's lives."

"What will happen with Andrea? Did she have any family around?"

"No, Andrea had lost both her mom and dad years ago. Dennis will have to make any decisions about a funeral and all that. But anything like that will sit on the back burner because of the wildfire."

"How's he contacting you? Cell phone?"

Jayleen shook her head again and took a sip of tea. "No. Andrea's ranch house has a landline which is reliable. As opposed to all those fancy smartphones." She grinned.

"Well, that's true. We're always losing the signal every time we go up into the canyons."

At that moment, Kelly's phone started buzzing with another text message. She dug it out of her cutoff jeans pocket. "Message from Greg. He's been keeping track of the Soldier Canyon fire from his university office window. Oh, thank goodness. He says that the wildfire that spread over the ridge into Soldier Canyon is out. No more flames.

Yay, firemen!" Kelly raised her arms in victory.

"Praise be," Jayleen said, closing her eyes for a second. "Let's give those folks a toast." And she raised her glass of sweet tea high. "To the firefighters!"

"Oh, yeah!" Kelly joined, glass held high. "And keep 'em coming!"

Steve took a bite of pizza and closed his eyes, clearly enjoying it. After swallowing, he said, "I can't tell you how relieved I was to see only a little smoke coming up from that Soldier Canyon spot as I drove back into town." He sank into the lawn chair and took a drink of Fat Tire ale.

Kelly grabbed another slice of pesto pizza from the box on the glass table in the center of Lisa and Greg's patio. The entire gang plus Cassie had gathered for a quick dinner to compare wildfire stories they'd each heard during the day. Kelly wished she could tell Dennis Holt's dramatic adventure but she was sworn to secrecy.

"You and me both," Marty said. "I had to go over to Greeley this afternoon and the fire was still burning as I crossed over I-25. But they'd put it out by the time I drove back. Hallelujah!" He raised his bottle of craft beer. Everyone was toasting whatever small wildfire victories they could.

"A few people on our floor in the IT labs live up the Poudre, and they said firefighters literally woke them up knocking on their doors late Saturday night. They could only grab their laptops and wallets. One girl grabbed her tablet, of course. Oh, and cell phones. Everybody took those." Greg devoured the slice of pizza in his hand, then reached across the table for another, rustling in the cardboard box.

"Isn't it amazing how the first thing we think about taking is our computers and devices?" Lisa said

"It's the world we live in," Megan said, sipping her ale.

"I agree. My laptop would be the first thing I'd grab. And my wallet. Gotta keep track of clients' money." Kelly grinned as she leaned back in her chair.

"Ever the accountant," Pete said with a smile.

"It's a dirty job, but —" Kelly started, then everybody chimed in to finish.

"— somebody has to do it." They all laughed, causing Cassie to look over from where she was lying on the shaded area of grass beside the patio reading a book. The canopy threw a fair amount of shade.

"Why's accounting a dirty job?" she asked

with a smile. "I've seen Kelly's spreadsheets, and they're all super neat and clean."

"Out of the mouths of babes," Kelly said with a smile, saluting Cassie with her glass.

"We love accountants in my business, Cassie," Marty announced, with his trademark smile. "They know where the money is and keep track of where it's going. And most people don't pay attention. That's why people who decide to steal other people's money often get away with it. For a while, anyway. Then, someone gets suspicious and calls in the accountants. They're the bloodhounds who find out what the thieves are up to. And that's when they're caught."

"And that's when you guys get to earn exorbitant fees to represent those sleazeballs in court," Greg said.

"Hey, it's a dirty job, but . . ." Marty paused as everyone groaned.

Cassie giggled. "Are any of those bloodhounds related to the ones in this book?" She turned several pages at the front of the book she was reading. "What are Baskervilles?"

"Beats me," Steve said with a good-natured grin, taking another sip of ale.

"I think it's named after someplace in England," Kelly offered.

"Cassie has discovered Sherlock Holmes,"

Jennifer said.

"Ooh, great!" Megan enthused. "So you're reading *The Hound of the Baskervilles*? Excellent."

"It's really good so far. I love Doctor Watson. Holmes is totally weird, though."

"I think Holmes is supposed to be weird," Lisa said. "It helps him solve cases."

"The guy's a freaking genius," Greg intoned. "That's what solves those cases. Just keep reading."

"Are those your books, Pete?" Marty asked, peering at Cassie, who had already returned to 221B Baker Street.

"She'd really enjoyed some of the other mysteries she was reading, so I thought she might like Sherlock." He grinned. "She's had her nose in the book ever since."

"Are those some of your engraved editions?" Steve asked, clearly incredulous.

Pete gave a genial nod. "Yeah. She's good with books."

Kelly and her friends simply laughed quietly in the still bright light of a summer evening, while Cassie disappeared into Victorian England.

Six

"Look, Carl. Squirrels are on the run," Kelly said to her Rottweiler as he dashed across the cottage backyard.

Carl raced to the fence just as Brazen Squirrel, the leader of the bunch, landed and scampered like mad along the top rail. The low-hanging branch of a nearby cottonwood tree beckoned several feet away. For a minute, Kelly thought her dog might actually get to Brazen before Brazen could get to the cottonwood branch. She was wondering how to handle that occurrence, fairly certain Carl would be so surprised that he caught Brazen he'd probably drop the wily creature in shock. More likely, Brazen would sink sharp squirrel teeth into Big Dog's nose — such a tempting target — and Carl would yelp in pain and, once again, drop Brazen.

Kelly needn't have worried. Brazen turned

on his after-burners and shot down the fence rail in a blazing burst of squirrel speed. Impressive, she thought with a smile, watching Carl resort to his usual behavior when Brazen had escaped his clutches — again. Carl stood on his hind legs, front paws on the fence rail, and barked doggie threats at Brazen, who dangled just out of reach on the cottonwood branch and fussed in chattering squirrel-speak to his nemesis.

"He was just too quick for you, Carl. Next time," Kelly promised as she slid the patio door closed to keep the hot air outside. The heat was starting to build, so she would spend the day inside working in Lambspun's comfortable temperatures.

Finding her coffee mug, Kelly drained the last drop of morning coffee. Then she loaded her laptop into her shoulder bag, checked to make sure Carl had enough water in his bowls, then grabbed her empty mug and headed out the cottage front door. She could get some client work done before leaving for the softball fields to teach her clinic for young teenagers.

Once outside, Kelly walked across the parking lot and gazed westward across the golf course greens. Like many of the golfers who were out in the early morning already, she couldn't resist the frequent temptation to gaze at the foothills to make sure she didn't see where another fire had broken out, whipped by that ever-present wind. Thank goodness, she didn't see any. But the wind was still gusting every now and then.

Kelly walked toward the outside patio garden of the café wondering when that wind would die down. Firefighters from all over and teams of Hot Shots were pouring into Fort Connor. But if that wind didn't die down, they would all be fighting a losing battle. As soon as they contained one hot spot, the wind would fling more flames and cinders to a new area and it would ignite. It was almost as if Nature was working against them. The wildfire had grown to forty thousand acres.

She spotted waitress Julie serving breakfast to a foursome at a shaded table outside. Kelly waited until Julie had finished with her customers before calling her name.

"Hey, Julie, I'm glad to see you made it back," she said, hastening along the flagstone path. "You really had a long journey to get to Fort Connor."

"You can say that again," Julie said, rolling her eyes. "It took forever. My friend drove and we had to go all the way from Steamboat on Route 40 to Kremmling then east to Granby. Then we took Route 34 into

Estes Park, then back into Fort Connor." She started clearing dishes off a nearby table, empty of customers.

"How long did it take you?"

"Seemed like forever," Julie said with a laugh. "We left Steamboat Sunday afternoon and got to Granby late that night. We were exhausted, so we bunked in a motel, then headed out Monday morning."

Kelly walked beside her as Julie started toward the café back door. "That must have cost a lot more in gas, too."

"Ohh, yeah. I had to hit the ATM as soon as we got into town."

Julie sped up the back steps to the café, and Kelly followed her inside. As soon as she entered, Kelly inhaled the familiar and enticing aromas floating through the air. *Breakfast.* Kelly's favorite meal. Even though Kelly knew she'd regret it, she followed Julie toward the grill and the kitchen. She saw Eduardo flipping cheesy scrambled eggs over and under, his spatula somehow keeping them creamy rather than turning them into an omelet. How did he manage that? Whenever Kelly tried it, it became an omelet.

Fried eggs popped on the griddle beside round pancakes, which were browning perfectly. And sizzling away on the farther side of the grill was the most tempting item of all. Kelly's favorite. *Bacon.* She inhaled the wonderfully delicious scent and closed her eyes. *Ahh.* Yummy.

That settled it, she decided. Her light breakfast of fruit and yogurt wasn't strong enough to fight off a full-frontal assault of bacon and eggs and pancakes. She had to have some. But maybe a smaller portion this time.

"Look out, Eduardo," Jennifer warned as she approached the counter. "Kelly's got that lean and hungry look."

Eduardo grinned, revealing his gold front tooth. "I've seen that look before. It doesn't scare me."

"What can we get you, Kelly?" Jennifer asked as she loaded two full platters of tempting breakfast food onto her tray.

"How about one slice of bacon and one small pancake and just a little scrambled eggs. I thought I'd practice portion control."

"Good for you," Jennifer said. "Join the rest of us. Right, Eduardo?"

"Awwww, you two girls are always talking about your weight. You look fine the way you are," he said, flipping the pancakes over.

"I bet you'd say that even if we had to waddle away from the table, Eduardo," Kelly teased.

Eduardo laughed. "Crazy Kelly." His regular admonition.

"Hand me your mug and I'll fill it. Meanwhile, you can have a seat over there in the alcove. There's that smaller table in the corner."

"Yes, ma'am," Kelly said obediently, handing over her mug. "Did you guys see the wildfire update this morning?"

"Yeah, it's gotten to be a morning ritual for all of us, I'm afraid," Jennifer said, pouring a black stream of coffee into Kelly's mug.

"It looks like a bunch more firefighters have arrived from all over. That's good." Kelly plopped her bag onto a chair at the smaller table. "And lots more Hot Shots. Bless those guys and gals. They really jumped on that Soldier Canyon fire so it wouldn't spread. But the fire is spreading north now, close to Colorado 14."

"I know. It's only 10 percent contained. They're trying to establish fire lines to the south, so the fire won't spread to the other side of Poudre Canyon," Jennifer said, returning Kelly's mug. "But watching the news this morning and seeing all those firefighters streaming into town made Pete and me feel a whole lot better. Surely we can get ahead of this fire with all those extra hands at work."

"If only that blasted wind would die down." Kelly took a drink of Eduardo's black nectar. *Ahh. Caffeine.* She'd need it.

Neither she nor Steve had had a restful night's sleep, even though the house was air-conditioned and they weren't subjected to the draining heat. The whole wildfire situation had everybody on edge, it seemed to Kelly. The entire city was on alert. People had one eye on their jobs and one eye on the mountains.

She settled at the table and checked her watch. She had an hour and a half before she needed to gather Cassie and drive to the softball fields at Rolland Moore Park on the west side of the city. It would be smokier there, hopefully not too much.

"Today's my softball clinic. Is Cassie around? I figured we could head over there about nine thirty."

"She's in the workroom helping Mimi organize yarns and stuff. I have to admit, the shelves are looking a lot neater now that Cassie's started to help Mimi."

"Well, Mimi and Rosa and Connie have so much to do already with customers, there's not much time left over for shelf organization. By the way, have you seen Connie? Did she show up for work today?"

"Yeah. Mimi told me Connie came in early today. But I haven't had time to go over and see her. We've been super busy this morning. Thank goodness Julie is back." Jennifer picked up her coffeepot. "Gotta check the customers."

"See you later," Kelly said as Jennifer scurried off. Noticing movement out of the corner of her eye, Kelly saw Burt enter the café.

He burst into a smile. "Hey, Kelly, good to see you. This is getting to be a regular morning occurrence."

"Hi, Burt. Pull up a chair and catch me up on what's going on in wildfire central, Landport."

Burt settled in across from her. "Traffic is still a nightmare going through town, for one thing. No surprise with one main road. All the extra firefighters and Hot Shots have set up a tent city at the Armory on West LaPorte Avenue. The big supply store is letting them park some of their vehicles in the back parking lot. But all those big trucks and firefighting equipment really tie up the road. Can't avoid it, though." He took a sip from the takeout cup he had with him, which had a familiar logo.

"What about the disaster shelter there? And the one at the Ranch out on the interstate? Do they have enough room?"

"Well, the shelter at Cache La Poudre middle school is full already." He caught Kelly's eye. "Apparently only twenty homes were lost in Poudre Canyon so far, thanks entirely to those brave firefighters who faced down the flames in Poudre Park."

"What have you heard about Bellevue Canyon?"

"Everyone up Whale Rock Road had to evacuate. Word is the fire's swept through that whole area. No telling if any homes survived. We'll have to wait and see."

"Oh, no!" Kelly pictured the great views from that more remote location high atop a ridge in Bellevue Canyon. "All those people may have lost their homes? How awful!"

Burt nodded. "Yes, it is. Many of them had friends or relatives in the area they could go to, but a lot of folks didn't. They'll have to go to the shelter at the Ranch."

"Are you going to help with running supplies like yesterday? Do they have enough people to serve meals and take care of things in the shelter?"

"I hope to, if they need me. They're going to need a lot more supplies, the way I figure. There are going to be more folks affected. The Poudre Canyon residents in Poudre Park were evacuated late Saturday night, as you know, and they've ordered evacuations in Livermore and the Glacier View subdivision north of Colorado 14. Also Pingree Park, west of Poudre Canyon. People have scattered all over town. Some to friends and some to the shelters. Plus some churches have taken in people, too."

"Sounds like they need all the help they can get. Let me know if we can do anything, Burt, okay?"

He smiled. "Don't worry, I will." He sipped from his cup. "So far it looks like they have enough hands on deck. I even saw Jim Carson serving meals at the shelter. At least I think it was him. He had a scruffy beard growing, but it looked like him."

That surprised her. Kelly recalled Jayleen saying that Dennis Holt had found Andrea lying all alone in the backyard. The house was empty. No sign of Jim Carson. "Did you speak to him? Did he say anything about Andrea?"

"Naw, I was too busy at the time. If I see him again, I'll speak to him. If it really is Jim. As I said, this guy had a scruffy beard growing."

Kelly pondered that. "I wonder why he wasn't there with Andrea. The two of them were acting like a couple on Saturday. Funny, that he'd leave."

Burt shrugged. "Who knows? Maybe something called him back to town and he had to leave."

"Yeah, probably. Well, if it is Jim Carson, he must have heard about Andrea. Maybe this is his way of handling it. You know, helping other people." She shrugged. "Maybe."

Burt smiled. "You could be right. I'll make it a point to check the shelter this afternoon at that same time and see if he's there. Hopefully he may know something about how the accident happened. I mean, I assume it was an accident. It sounds like it was."

"What will happen now? Will the medical examiner take a look? Police are swamped right now, so they won't have any manpower to spare."

"You're right about that. But I imagine the medical examiner will have a chance to examine her and rule on cause of death. It will all take longer than usual, though." Burt frowned. "That reminds me. I forgot to ask Jayleen about her alpacas up at Andrea's ranch. I'm hoping there are some residents who live higher up the canyon who could come down and feed the livestock for her. Did she say anything when you talked to her yesterday?"

Kelly nodded, glad she could answer truthfully. "Yes, she indicated there was a resident up there who was taking care of them for her."

"Well, that's good." Burt checked his watch. "I'd better get in that line of traffic going into Landport and see how I can help." He rose and started toward the café front door. "Oh, by the way. Connie came in this morning. Make sure you go in and say hi. Mimi talked to her this morning and told her about Andrea. Connie hadn't heard a thing, naturally. The wildfire has dominated the news. Connie looked dazed and didn't say a word, just stared out the window. She was acting real subdued when she first came in this morning and didn't talk much. Now, she's barely saying a word at all. Just to the customers."

"She's probably still trying to adjust to everything that's happened. Saturday was beyond traumatic. Yelling and accusations. You're lucky you didn't have to witness it like we did. And the wildfire on top of everything. Chaos in the midst of chaos." She rolled her eyes. "I'll go over now and give her a hug. That's all I could do on Saturday. Hug her and tell Connie that she had friends there. Meanwhile, keep us updated on wildfire news. You're closer to the front lines than any of us."

"Will do," Burt said, walking away just as Jennifer brought Kelly her breakfast.

Kelly headed for the hallway leading into the knitting shop, hoping to find a quiet moment with Connie. She turned the corner into what Kelly called the Loom Room because it was dominated by a large loom. Weavers called it the Mother Loom. There they created beautiful scarves, table runners, and all manner of finely woven fiber wonders. Kelly often marveled at the beauty of the woven stitches.

Connie was on the other side of the room replacing several cones of fine fibers and threads that filled the shelves lining two walls. She glanced toward Kelly then looked away, mumbling, "Hi, Kelly."

Kelly walked over and placed an arm around Connie's shoulders, giving her a hug. "How're you doing, Connie?" she asked softly. Connie gave a little shrug in reply, without words. "We're here for you, Connie. You know that."

Connie's lower lip curled and her face started to flush, then she nodded. Kelly didn't want to make Connie cry, so she gave her another hug then walked into the adjoining central yarn room. She spotted Mimi in the main room, pattern folders spread on the table around her.

"Hey, there," Kelly said in a lower voice. "I just saw Connie and gave her a hug. Told her we were here for her, you know. She looked like she was about to tear up so I just gave her another hug and left her alone." Kelly pulled out a chair across the table from Mimi.

"That's all we can do, Kelly," Mimi said with a sigh. "She was acting so subdued and not talking to anyone when she came in, I assumed she'd already heard about Andrea." Mimi glanced over her shoulder, then said in a lower voice, "But when I mentioned what a shock it was to hear about Andrea's death, Connie just stared at me wide-eyed. Like she was dazed or something. All she said was *'How?'* I told her Andrea must have fallen down the outside steps because she was found lying on the ground. That's all I knew. I swear Connie turned white as a sheet. She just sat at the winding table and stared out the windows for a long time." Mimi shook her head, her face revealing her concern. "I left her alone with her thoughts. Thank goodness some customers came in and she started to answer their questions. I was beginning to worry."

"Sounds like Connie is kind of suffering from the shock of everything that happened this weekend. All the trauma. Yelling and stuff. Believe me, Mimi, you and Burt were lucky you weren't around to see it. It would have upset you too much."

Mimi closed her eyes. "You're right. It sounded awful just hearing you tell me about it on the phone."

Cassie rounded the corner from the workroom with several plastic-encased patterns in her hands. "I found the patterns you were looking for, Mimi. Hey, Kelly."

"Hey, Cassie. Are you going to softball today? I'll be leaving in about an hour." Kelly checked her watch.

"Sure thing. I've got my stuff in my backpack in the workroom."

"Good deal." She pushed back her chair. "Maybe I'll bring my laptop in here and work for a while. That way you can help me keep track of the time. In case I get lost in the numbers."

"Only accountants get lost in numbers and seem to enjoy it," Mimi said as Kelly headed toward the café again.

The alcove was empty now, Kelly noticed. That quiet time in the café between breakfast and lunch. Grabbing her shoulder bag and coffee mug, she walked down the

126

hallway and through the workroom. More pattern books were opened on the work table.

"Are you reorganizing the pattern books or something?" she asked, admiring a pattern for a sleeveless sweater that lay on the table. "That's pretty. I need a new knitting project. Maybe I'll make that one. Is it hard, Mimi?"

"Not at all."

"Wait a minute. Why am I asking you?" Kelly said as she withdrew her laptop from her bag and settled into a chair. "Everything's easy for you."

Cassie giggled. "She's right, Mimi. Every time someone asks about a pattern, you always say, 'It's easy.' "

Kelly gestured to her accomplice. "See? It's not my imagination. Cassie says it, too. I've got backup."

Mimi gave a dismissive wave of her hand. "Well, it is easy. And you would enjoy making it, Kelly. But it might be more helpful if you tried one of the easier sweater patterns. A lot of us are starting to knit sweaters for the wildfire evacuees who've lost their homes and possessions. They could really use anything we can make for them."

"But it's so hot!" Cassie exclaimed, eyes wide. "They wouldn't wear a woolen sweater in the summer!"

"You took the words right out of my mouth, Cassie," Kelly said, taking a deep drink of coffee.

"Well, they wouldn't be using them now, but in a few months they will be needing those sweaters. And those poor folks are not going to be able to buy all new clothes. That's expensive. So anything we can knit for them will be appreciated, I promise you."

"I heartily agree with you, Mimi," a deep contralto voice sounded from the central yarn room behind Kelly.

A voice she hadn't heard in a long time. That of Hilda von Steuben. One half of the pair of spinster sisters and knitters extraordinaire. Kelly turned in her chair and saw Hilda and sister, Lizzie, standing in the archway between both rooms, smiling. Tall and big-boned Hilda, and shorter, dainty, round-as-a-dumpling Lizzie.

"Hilda! Lizzie!" Kelly cried in delight and leaped from her chair, giving first Hilda then Lizzie a hug. "How wonderful to see you both! It's been a few weeks since you've been in."

"Kelly, my girl, it's so good to see you," Hilda said, as Kelly kissed her on the cheek.

"Oh, my, yes! You look wonderful, dear!" Lizzie said, her bright smile revealing her dimples.

Mimi was right behind Kelly. "Oh, you two, how marvelous to see you both!" She gave them each a hug as well.

"Oh, such a fuss," Hilda protested mildly, holding on to Mimi's arm with one hand. Her other hand rested on her cane.

"We'd have come in sooner, but we both had a terrible stomach flu bug. We'd recovered from that by last week, but then this heat has been so bad, and then the smoke," Lizzie explained as she flounced to the end of the table, pink and white ruffles in full bloom. "We have to run two filters to clear the air in our home. We're in the middle of town, you know." She pulled out a chair. "Here, Hilda, this will be easier for you at the end."

"Come in and sit down," Mimi said, taking Hilda's arm as she slowly walked the elderly woman to the chair Lizzie had indicated.

Kelly quickly pulled out the chair at the other end of the table. "Here, Lizzie, why don't you take this one. That way we'll have von Steuben sisters anchoring both ends of our knitting table. It'll be like old times."

"Old times, eh?" Hilda said. "Well, Lizzie and I are experts on all things old, aren't we, Lizzie?"

"Oh, my, yes," Lizzie said, settling into the chair Kelly held out. Rearranging her ruffles, Lizzie gave her silver hair a pat in its tidy twist at the back of her head.

An old familiar gesture Kelly hadn't seen in a while.

Feeling a pang of nostalgia, she said, "I have really missed you two. It seems every time you made it over here, I was down in Denver with one of my clients."

"As well you should be," Hilda intoned, setting her tapestry knitting bag upon the table. "We've kept track of your career progression, my dear. Thanks to Mimi and Burt, of course. I take it Burt is out on one of your many errands, Mimi. I'm sorry to miss him."

"Well, I'm going to call him and tell him to make sure he stops by to say hello. He's over in Landport now, volunteering to drive supplies back and forth to the various shelters and such."

"Oh, my, that awful, awful fire!" Lizzie's hand fluttered up in a trademark wave that Kelly loved. "That is simply dreadful, isn't it? I'm so glad Burt is helping." She opened her multicolored embroidered knitting bag.

"He's a good man," Hilda said, withdrawing the light blue silky yarn from her knitting bag. It looked to Kelly like a half-

130

finished baby sweater.

Glancing to the side, Kelly noticed Cassie standing back, watching the two elderly ladies at the table. As if she read her mind, Mimi quickly walked over to Cassie's side and placed her arm around Cassie's shoulders.

"And I'd like both of you to meet the newest addition to the Lambspun family. This is Cassie Wainwright. She's Pete's niece who has lived in Denver most of her life. But now that her grandfather's health has deteriorated, Cassie's moved up here to live with Pete and Jennifer." Mimi gave Cassie a big smile.

"Ah, yes, I remember your telling us about this young lady," Hilda said, gazing at Cassie over the top her spectacles. "I'm pleased to meet you, Cassie."

"I'm . . . pleased to meet you, too . . . ma'am," Cassie said softly.

"Oh, and so am I, my, dear!" Lizzie gushed, her hand fluttering to her lacy bodice. "And what beautiful blue eyes you have!"

Cassie ducked her head, murmuring a soft thank-you as a flush spread across her cheeks.

Kelly shoved her laptop aside, leaned back into her chair, and watched as two lifelong schoolteachers began to draw a bashful Cassie into conversation.

SEVEN

Kelly leaned against her kitchen counter and sipped her early morning coffee, all the while listening to her real estate investor client Arthur Housemann on the other end of the phone.

"I tell you, Kelly, it's hell, not knowing what's happened in Poudre Canyon. I've gone to every single briefing the fire commandant has held. I've met with the police department. And no one, not one of them, will let us know the extent of the damage up there. They won't even give us a hint. I mean, it is frustrating beyond belief!"

Kelly could recognize the sound of carefully controlled anger in her client's voice. She'd only heard it once or twice since they'd started working together. The first time was a year ago when Arthur had been involved in a real estate transaction with a landowner who had a rather shady reputation.

Usually Arthur Housemann was the model of experienced restraint. Measured. But his property in the Poudre Canyon, right on the river, was dear to Arthur's heart. He'd built his dreamhouse there. Consequently, anything that might threaten it was met with fierce resistance. However, none of the canyon residents had any defenses against wildfire. It was the most powerful of all adversaries.

"I hear you, Arthur. My friend Jayleen Swinson told me the same thing. None of the Bellevue Canyon residents have heard anything about their homes, either. Of course, firefighters are still putting out fires up there."

"That's understandable, up in Bellevue Canyon. They've had fires breaking out around Whale Rock and Davis Ranch roads. But our brave crew was able to beat back the flames near Poudre Park. Only a few places were lost, thankfully."

"It's incredible what that small crew did, Arthur," Kelly said, pouring more coffee into her mug. "I heard that there were only a handful of volunteer firefighters on duty that night because everyone else had gone to fight the fire in Bellevue Canyon."

"They were truly heroic, Kelly." Emotion was evident in his voice. "That fire swept down the ridge in a horseshoe and they had to fight two prongs. Just a handful of them. Someone said they literally put their bodies between the wildfire and people's homes. Not just once, but over and over again, in order to save them. I tell you, they deserve medals in my book."

"I agree with you. Whenever this horrible wildfire is finally put out, the entire community should hold a celebration for those brave firefighters." She glanced toward her desk in the corner of what was now her cottage-turned-office. Several files lay open on the top of her desk. "I'm afraid the wildfire has thrown a wrench into my normal everyday work schedule. So those mid-month projections I usually give you may be a little delayed."

"Don't even bother with them, Kelly. I've put almost everything on hold at the office while this fire is still threatening. I have a feeling no one is going to be showing land parcels to anyone for a while. At least not in Bellevue or Poudre canyons."

"I understand, Arthur. You and your wife were uprooted in the middle of the night and evacuated from your home. I swear, I don't think I would have handled that well at all. I would probably have argued with them."

Arthur Housemann laughed, the first laughter she'd heard from him in days, ever since she'd first contacted him after the wildfire broke out. It was good to hear him laugh. Like her two father-figure mentors, Curt Stackhouse and Burt Parker, Kelly thought of Arthur Housemann the same way. He reminded her a lot of her own father. Smart, soft-spoken, and a savvy businessman.

"I imagine you would have, Kelly. At least, you'd have tried." He chuckled. "But those firefighters don't take much backtalk, so I'm pretty sure you wouldn't have changed their minds."

"You're probably right, Arthur. Listen, I'll wait to send you the financial reports at the end of the month then. After all this is over. I swear it's disrupted everyone's life, even if they don't live in the fire zone."

"Yes, it has. My daughter and her family in Loveland have taken in some friends who have property around Stove Prairie, near Paradise Park. I tell you, people are displaced all over." The sound of an incoming call beeped on his line. "Sorry, Kelly. I have another call coming in. I'll talk to you another time."

"Take care, Arthur. And I'll be sending good thoughts about your Poudre Canyon home." Kelly clicked off her phone and shoved it in her pocket.

The heat was already building, and it was only midmorning. She had client spreadsheets waiting. Work to do. But once again, it would not be comfortable working here in the cottage. There was no air conditioning. Normally, Kelly had been able to get around the few hot days in July by escaping into the knitting shop to work. But this summer was different. Hot weather had started in May and didn't let up. Now Kelly spent more days working at Lambspun either in the café or around the knitting table. Clearly, today would be the same.

Kelly closed the file folders, loaded them and her laptop into her shoulder briefcase bag, refilled Carl's two big water dishes, and gathered her coffee mug. "Keep an eye on those squirrels, Carl," she called to her dog, who was snuffling around the bushes at the side fence. Carl glanced at her briefly then returned to snuffling, having picked up the elusive scent of squirrel feet. Or, perhaps, a raccoon. Kelly knew raccoons visited her yard at night as they made their nocturnal rounds, checking garbage cans for loose lids, eating grapes from people's grapevines and arbors, then spitting the seeds all over the patios. Adding insult to injury.

Heading out her front door, Kelly checked the bright annuals that were blooming because of her faithful watering. Pink, white, and coral impatiens proudly flaunted their colors beside the hardy purple and white petunias. Miniature purple petunias snuggled next to the others, vining through the flowers. And the shade-loving violas in another container danced in the breeze beside the pansies — yellow and purple.

She started across the driveway, but she couldn't help walking over to where there was a break in between the cottonwood trees. There, she stood and gazed westward toward the mountains, searching for any new signs of smoke. Smoke could be seen billowing up from behind the foothills, indicating that there were still fires breaking out.

Last night the wind had gusted strongly, starting in early evening and going into the night. And sure enough, Kelly spotted some new plumes of smoke rising. She'd heard on the news that fire crews were worried about wind from the southwest spreading fire north of the Poudre Canyon Road. Fires were already burning west of Stove Prairie, but fire crews were not as worried because that area was unpopulated and filled with beetle-killed pines.

Turning toward the knitting shop, Kelly spotted both Jennifer and Julie serving breakfast in the garden patio area of the café. She deliberately steered clear of the tempting favorite foods and hastened up the brick steps and into the front door of Lambspun. The cool air-conditioned air felt good.

Kelly took her time walking through the foyer, checking for new fibers displayed. Some of Mimi's special hand-dyed yarns sat out on the tables, luscious blends of colors twining together. Now, delicate open-weave tops were dangling from the cabinet doors of a dry sink.

She wandered into the central yarn room where wooden bins lined the available walls. Each bin spilling over with various combinations of Mimi's hand-dyed yarns — pinks and purples, blues and turquoise, as well as the pastel shades of bamboo yarns and silky cottons.

Brilliant summer colors tumbled out of an antique trunk on the floor — Popsicle red, lemon candy yellow, lime rickey green. Kelly couldn't resist touching, enjoying the soft brush of delicate cotton yarns.

"Hey, Kelly, how're you doing?" Rosa

asked as she walked from the main knitting room, her arms filled with magazines.

"Okay, I guess, considering what's going on in the mountains." Kelly dumped her mug and her shoulder bag on the long library table.

Rosa's cheerful smile disappeared. "Oh, I know. My next door neighbors had to take in their parents because they were forced to evacuate their place in Bellevue Canyon. They're not that far away from Jayleen's ranch. And no one knows if their house is still there. It's terrible."

"I was just talking to one of my clients who built his dream house up the Poudre Canyon. He and his wife were chased out at midnight Saturday night. They have no idea if they'll have a house to return to or not." Kelly settled into a chair at the table and pulled out her laptop and files.

Rosa plopped the pile of magazines at the end of the table and began removing the older editions from binders and replacing them with newer ones.

"You know, I love going up into the canyons, but I tell you, I don't ever want to live up there. I mean, it's too risky. Wildfires can start anywhere. Even without a campfire. They're saying that this fire started with a lightning strike." She gestured in aggravation. "All it takes is one strike in these dry woods, and we have hundreds of lightning strikes every spring and summer."

Mimi suddenly rushed into the room, eyes wide. "I just had a call from Burt. He's in Landport, helping the Red Cross folks. They're hearing that fire has spread farther into the lower Buckhorn Valley. The wind whipped it over there last night."

Rosa gasped, hand to her mouth. *"Madre de Dios!"*

Kelly stared at Mimi. Curt's ranch bordered one far edge of the Buckhorn Valley. "Oh, no! There are scores of people and ranches in the Buckhorn. They're spread all over."

"Did he say anything else, Mimi?" Rosa asked.

"No, he simply wanted me to know and tell everyone." Mimi's concern was revealed clearly on her face. "I'm going to tell Jennifer and Pete in the café." She hurried away.

Kelly dug her cell phone from her pocket and scrolled down the directory to Jayleen's number. She listened to it ring and ring then switch to voice mail. Not surprised, she said into the phone, "Jayleen? Kelly, here. I just heard that the fire has spread more into the lower Buckhorn Valley, and I was concerned about Curt's ranch. I know he's not actually in the Buckhorn, he's south of it. But I was worried anyway. When you get a chance, please let us know what's happening. Take care."

With that, Kelly clicked off and glanced up at Rosa, seeing her own concern reflected on Rosa's face. Friends, so many friends, were being put in danger, and their properties were in the path of the wildfire. The capricious, devastating wildfire. Kelly couldn't think of a worse enemy to face. More dangerous and relentless and unpredictable than any human.

"Have you heard anything else?" Jennifer asked Kelly as she refilled her glass of iced coffee.

Kelly pushed her laptop to the side. One of Arthur Housemann's spreadsheets on his real estate properties was open on the screen. "No, Jayleen hasn't returned my call. But I'm not surprised. I'm sure they're out trying to see exactly where the wildfire spread to. Outside with all that noise, neither of them would even hear their phones."

Jennifer stared out into the lessening mid-afternoon lunch crowd. "Yeah, but the wind has whipped those hot cinders around, so who knows what might happen. Thank goodness Curt's ranch isn't right in the Buckhorn. Poor Jayleen must feel like she's cursed. Wherever she's taken her alpacas to for safety has become a target for the wildfire."

"I know." Kelly glanced around. "I didn't see Cassie. Isn't she with Lisa this afternoon at the Rehab Clinic? I know she was at tennis with Megan this morning."

Jennifer smiled as she gathered Kelly's almost empty lunch plate. Only two shreds of lettuce remained. "She was in and out again in a minute. Megan was going to take her to lunch then drop her at the Rehab Clinic to meet Lisa."

"That's right. It must be Wednesday. Tennis in the morning and watching physical therapists in the afternoon."

"I swear, she comes back with stories about all sorts of injuries people have and how they're rehabbing. She tells Pete and me everything at dinner. She even demonstrates some of the therapy Lisa and the others use. Pete and I are getting a kick out of it. Gotta get back to my other customers. Talk to you later." Jennifer walked toward the grill counter.

Kelly returned to the accounting spreadsheets, sipping her iced coffee. Temperatures were going to reach ninety-eight or ninety-nine today, even with occasional wind gusts. Nothing affected the wind. And it created its own weather system within the wildfire. That was another reason these wildfires in the mountains were so hard to overcome. Two weather systems were in play: Mother Nature's and the wildfire's.

Her cell phone rang as it lay on the wooden café table. Burt's name flashed on the screen. "Hey, Burt, I'm glad you called. Any more news on the fire spreading farther into the Buckhorn?"

"Firefighters moved even more men into those hot spots that opened up last night and early this morning. I tell you, it seems they're throwing everything they can at it. There're over twelve hundred firefighters on the ground now, from all over. You should see that tent city at the Armory. I glimpsed it from a distance. Guards don't let anyone in without fire credentials."

"Man, we can't catch a break with this fire, can we?"

"I know it appears that way, Kelly. But these fire crews are working like crazy, twelve-hour shifts in that inferno heat, two-hundred-foot walls of flames, they've told me. And they're trying to build fire lines so the fire can't spread beyond where it's burned. The water tanker plane helps but

144

this fire is so strong, that's like spitting into it."

Kelly remembered watching the small plane make numerous trips from the Horsetooth Reservoir where it lowered its bucket-like container to refill with water, then fly out over the wildfire again to dump the water where it could help the most. "I agree with you, Burt. At least those water dumps made a difference when the fire spread to Soldier Canyon. Of course, that was a smaller outbreak."

"And they could jump on it right away, too."

Kelly heard noise in the background. "Where are you? Running errands?"

"Yeah, I'm picking up stuff for the volunteers who're out at the Ranch. Oh, that reminds me. I finally heard from my old partner Dan at the department. He's taking over Andrea's case. I'm glad. He told me the medical examiner took a look at her and made his report. Cause of death was a broken neck. That's what we all figured. I mean, that's what would happen to any of us if we fell down a flight of wooden steps and landed on the rocky ground. Examination indicates she landed on her back because that's where the major tissue and bone damage were. The department is treating it as an accidental death. No doubt caused when Andrea was trying to evacuate her home when the wildfire started in the canyon."

"That makes sense. I mean, we would all be rushing about trying to grab things to take with us. I saw those steps, and they were steep."

Kelly pictured Andrea tripping then falling and hitting the rocky ground. She screwed up her face at the brutal scene. "Poor Andrea. I surely hope she lost consciousness as soon as she hit the ground. That sounds like an awful way to die. I'd hate to think of her lying there in pain, dying." She involuntarily shivered.

"She probably died right away, Kelly. Her neck would have snapped."

Not wishing to picture Andrea's broken body lying on the ground anymore, Kelly switched subjects slightly. "You know, I've wondered about something, Burt. Everyone, including the medical examiner, has decided this was a terrible accident. Does that mean the police won't question anyone who was with Andrea that day? There were actually a lot of us who saw her on Saturday."

"Oh, no. Police will definitely question everyone who was with her that day, including you and the gang. But it could take a while. Police are stretched thin with this fire, so there's simply not enough manpower to spend investigating this death. The department may assign a community service officer to do the preliminary questioning. There're a lot of people involved, and that will take some time."

"Yeah, it certainly will. There were the six of us, then Jayleen and Curt, and Dennis Holt, and Jim Carson. And who knows the other people she met with while in the canyon. By the way, did you see that guy who looks like Jim Carson again?"

"No, I didn't. So maybe he was helping just that one day. And I wasn't sure it was Jim, anyway. Hey, how's Connie doing today? Is she still acting quiet?"

"Yeah, I went to the front to see her right before lunch. She still looks withdrawn and doesn't talk except to the customers. Totally different from her usual lively self."

Burt's sigh came over the phone. "She needs counseling badly. She needs to talk to someone. Not us. We're involved somehow because we know all the players. She needs a trained therapist."

"I agree, Burt. Has Mimi suggested it to Connie? I think she'd listen if Mimi said it."

"Mimi mentioned it briefly yesterday, but

Connie kind of drew back and shied away. Maybe we should wait another day and suggest it again. I don't know." The sound of a beep on his phone interrupted. "That's another call. Talk to you later, Kelly."

Kelly clicked off and shoved her phone into her pocket. She needed something to take her mind off those images of Andrea Holt falling to her death and the very real sight of a Lambspun friend sinking into a deep depression.

Once again she shoved her laptop into her shoulder bag, grabbed her iced coffee, and headed back into the knitting shop. Maybe she would take a few minutes to choose a yarn to use for that sweater project Mimi suggested. That would totally divert her thoughts. Nothing like luscious fibers and colors to distract a person.

Mimi stood at the knitting table in the main room, paging through one of the binders that held patterns.

"Ahh, perfect timing," Kelly said as she walked into the room and dumped her things on the table. No one else was at the table. "I thought you could help me start that sweater pattern you suggested the other day. You said it was easy."

Mimi sent her a warm smile. "It certainly is, Kelly, and it would be a perfect choice for you to make for the evacuees clothing project."

"I hope so. You know I've stayed away from sweaters ever since I tried one a couple of years ago and one side wound up longer than the other." Kelly made a face. "I figured they were beyond my skill level."

"Pshaw," Mimi said with a dismissive wave of her hand. "You've definitely become a more skillful knitter over the years. I'm sure this will turn out perfectly."

Kelly deliberately made a shocked expression. "Mimi! You know you cannot have my name and the word 'skillful' or 'perfect' in the same sentence. They cancel each other out."

Mimi laughed lightly. "Silly. You come into the workroom and take a look at some of these yarns while I make a copy of this pattern." Mimi had already removed the sweater pattern from the binder.

Kelly dutifully followed her into the adjacent workroom; three sides of this room were also lined with yarn bins. But knitted children's clothing also dangled from the shelves and ceiling, precious little dresses and baby sweaters with hoods, tiny baby hats and larger children's stocking caps. Some had crocheted flowers attached. Adorable, all of them, Kelly thought.

But how in the world did they manage to work on those teeny tiny needles they use for the smallest garments? Size one and two needles. Kelly was always amazed at how easily some knitters worked with those tiny needles. Kelly couldn't even hold them without dropping them. Particularly the shiny metal ones. They slid right off her fingers. The smallest size Kelly had comfortably worked with were size four needles, which she would use to make children's hats.

Mimi came out of her office where she'd disappeared while Kelly was admiring the delicate work all around her. "Here we go. Now, let's find a yarn that would work." She walked toward another bank of shelves in the room, the bins brimming over with both bold primary and subdued colors. "The pattern gauge suggests using a yarn that will give ten stitches per four inches, so let's take a look."

Kelly watched Mimi pick up one skein of yarn after another and read on the label if the gauge would yield what they needed, then she would either hand it to Kelly or replace it into a bin again.

"Thanks again for helping me with this, Mimi," Kelly said, holding up a bright royal blue yarn. She checked the label. Lamb's

Pride. One hundred percent wool. Then she read the label on a skein of shamrock green yarn. It felt softer, actually. And the label had confirmed it was alpaca wool. Oh, yes. Soft, soft. To-die-for soft was alpaca wool.

"Okay, here's a yellow to go with those. So, does any one yarn strike your fancy? I figure we can make this pattern in the small size so a child could wear it. And kids love primary colors."

Kelly compared the yarns in her hands and held up the shamrock green alpaca wool. "Can't resist the alpaca, plus it's a great rich green."

"Okay, shamrock green alpaca it is. Good choice, Kelly," Mimi said, and replaced the rest of the yarns in their proper bins. "Now, let's return to the table and get this started. Oh, do you have the right size needles? This pattern says to use number nine."

"Let me check my bag. I deliberately tossed several needles into my bag last night before I forgot about it. I knew I was going to start this sweater sometime. Hate to keep buying needles when I've got so many at home."

"All right, let's take a look," Mimi said, beckoning Kelly back to the main room. "You check your bag while I go wind this skein into a ball for you up front."

Kelly dug into her shoulder bag, fingers scrambling around the bottom, until she felt the needles. Pulling out a handful, she checked the ends for the size markings, and found the number nine needles.

Okay, I have the tools, now let's take a look at this pattern.

EIGHT

Thursday, June 14

"Hey, there, Cassie. Looks like you're on magazine detail this morning," Kelly said as she walked into Lambspun's main room.

Cassie stood beside the floor-to-ceiling bookcases that lined two walls of the knitting shop's gathering place. She looked over her shoulder and smiled. "Hi, Kelly. Rosa is needed up front with Mimi, so I'm finishing the magazines for her."

Kelly set her bag and coffee mug on the table. "Is Connie in today?"

"No, she has the day off. Mimi thought she needed to take it easy after this last weekend." Cassie picked up another magazine from the long library table then looked over at Kelly. "Maybe Connie is catching a cold or flu or something. She sure doesn't act like she feels good."

Kelly settled into a chair at the table and sipped her coffee, wondering how best to

153

approach the subject of Connie's abrupt change in behavior. Mimi had told Kelly that she, Burt, Jennifer, and Pete had not told Cassie the details of what happened last Saturday when Connie confronted her straying husband and Andrea Holt. All Cassie knew was that Connie had gone to Jayleen's ranch in Bellevue Canyon to help. That was technically true. The fact that Connie's presence proved more of a hindrance than a help was something else again.

"Maybe she is catching a cold," Kelly offered. "Or, maybe she's still tired after last weekend. Steve and I felt wiped out. We woke up exhausted Monday morning."

"Yeah, maybe so." Cassie slipped another magazine into its holder. "Connie's usually so cheerful and funny. But she's acting really weird. She doesn't smile or make jokes anymore. And she barely talks. I mean, she talks to the customers when they bring stuff up to the counter, but then she just sits at the winding table and winds yarn. She's gone through two whole bags of that lambspun alpaca wool already."

"Boy, that's impressive," Kelly said lightly, trying to deflect Cassie's obvious concern. "I know Mimi's been trying to work her way through those large bags. Since Connie's being so efficient, that means you'll have piles of new yarn skeins to find places for. Frankly, I don't see any available space, do you?"

Cassie glanced around at the full yarn bins. "Nope. I guess I'll have to start taking more yarns down to the basement for storage."

Kelly reached into her bag and withdrew the beginnings of her new knitting project. She figured that was guaranteed to catch Cassie's attention. "Hey, I finally decided which yarn and sweater pattern to use for my evacuee project. I settled on the shamrock green wool from those bins in the other room. You know, the alpaca yarns. They're all such pretty colors. I've only got a few rows started."

Cassie's eyes lit up and she leaned over the table, fingers reaching out. "Oh, that is so pretty. I love greens. Let me touch."

Kelly shoved the knitting needles containing ten rows of stitches and the fat ball of yarn closer to Cassie's wiggling fingertips.

"Ooh, so soft. I love alpaca. And their coats are just as soft, Jayleen says, before they're shorn. Hers had already been shorn when I saw them."

"She's right about their coats being soft. I love to pat them. Of course, they also pick up stickers and other stuff in those long coats, too. That's why their blankets have to be cleaned of trash and stuff before they go to the Wool Market to be sold."

Cassie looked at her in surprise. "Blankets?"

Kelly smiled. "That's what their coats are called after they're shorn from the animals. It's really fascinating to watch. I've seen it done several times at Jayleen's and at other ranches. I always try to get up to her place when she's shearing my alpacas."

"Oh, yeah. I remember Jayleen telling me you've got alpacas at her ranch, too. How many do you have?"

"Only six now. She took them to Curt's ranch last Saturday. I used to have more, but I sold them to breeders. I always take Jayleen's advice." Kelly retrieved her knitting needles and yarn and checked the beginning rows before she picked up her stitches where she left off. "But I kept the ones with the prettiest coats."

"What colors?"

"Ohh, let's see, there's a blue gray that's my favorite, a soft caramel brown, a lighter gray, a warm chocolate brown, a creamy beige, and a black." She smiled at Cassie. "That's just about the entire spectrum of alpaca colors."

Ignoring the small stack of magazines, Cassie continued to lean over the table, clearly intrigued by the subject. "What's it like when they shear them? I mean, how do they do it? Alpacas are kind of skittish. Those big eyes stare at you if a loud noise goes off. I remember last weekend when Eric and I were taking care of them, some firecrackers went off close by the livestock stalls, and the animals really got spooked. They clustered together and looked scared. Eric said to keep stroking them and talking to them. It calmed them down. That's why they cluster together like that."

"You're right, Cassie. Since the animals are so skittish, ranchers have to handle them carefully. And they have to separate them from the others to shear them." Kelly slipped the left knitting needle into the left side of the last stitch on the right needle, wrapped the yarn around the tip of the left needle, then slid the stitch off onto the right needle. Slip, wrap, slide. Slip, wrap, slide.

"Boy, I bet they don't like that."

"You're right, so you have to be careful not to frighten them. Handlers get them to lie down on the ground and restrain them, secure their legs so they don't try to get up or kick. So it takes two people to restrain each one while they're being shorn. Thank goodness the shearing doesn't take long. You'd be surprised how fast those shearers work."

Cassie frowned. "Does it hurt?"

Kelly started another row of shamrock green. "Jayleen told me that shearing doesn't hurt because the razor only cuts off the long blanket of fleece and doesn't cut into the skin. It leaves a nubbly short coat so it can start growing again." She slid another stitch from the left needle to the right one. "The shearer tries to cut off the blanket in one piece on each side. Apparently, it's more valuable like that. So, they can start at the back of the alpaca, beneath their tail, then move in a really smooth motion to finish off at their neck and shoulders. Or, they can do it the other way around. Whatever the shearer chooses. The fleece beneath their necks and lower around their legs isn't as long, so they shear that separately and put it in a separate pile. That way the complete blankets can be shown and sold separately at places like the Wool Mart. The whole blankets get top dollar. The other pieces of fleece are sold separately for less."

"Wow," Cassie said, clearly fascinated by Kelly's explanation. "I'd love to see it being done. Jayleen said they do it in the spring. Is it April or May?"

"I'll bet you will be able to watch Jayleen's shearings next spring. She usually does them in May. So they had all been shorn by the time you got up here to Fort Connor." Kelly looked up from her needles and smiled "You know, you've only been here in Fort Connor for three weeks, Cassie. But it feels longer, don't you think?"

Cassie stared out into the room. "Yeah, it does."

Kelly chose her next words carefully, wanting to tread lightly on a delicate subject: Cassie's staying with Pete and Jennifer and her grandfather's health.

"How's your grandpa Ben doing? You and Pete were down there last week, I think. He's still in pretty serious condition from everything I hear."

"Yeah, he is," Cassie said quietly, tracing an invisible pattern on the table. "Pete just talked to the doctor yesterday. Grandpa is doing the same. Stable, the doctor says. He's still in the hospital."

"I'm not surprised. He had five blocked arteries, so that was serious surgery. Grandpa Ben will probably be in the hospital for several more weeks, I bet."

"Yeah, Pete says the same thing. Then he said Grandpa would probably be moved to some other kind of medical place where there'd be lots of nurses around."

"That sounds exactly like what Lisa told Steve and me. She said your grandpa had to become stable for a good time before he could be shifted to another facility like a nursing home. A skilled nursing facility, she called it." Kelly wrapped the yarn around the needle, readying another stitch. More stitches appearing on the row, more rows accumulating. "Lisa's had a lot of experience with recuperating patients. She's even worked with patients in the hospitals doing their therapy. So she knows a lot about what's involved in serious medical conditions like heart attacks."

Kelly deliberately didn't add that Lisa informed them that she didn't think Grandpa Ben would ever leave a nursing home, judging from his condition.

Cassie kept tracing an invisible pattern on the table, a slight frown on her face. "How long do people have to stay in those nursing facilities? How long does it take them to get better?"

Uh-oh, Kelly thought. She didn't want to tread on ground that properly belonged to Pete and Jennifer, but she had to give Cassie some sort of answer. So she decided to approach it gradually.

"Well, it depends entirely on the patient,

Lisa says," Kelly answered truthfully. "Patients who are in good physical shape before their heart attacks can recuperate really well because they'd been exercising regularly and keeping their weight in check. Patients that were not in good physical shape before the attack, well . . . that's another story. Some can recuperate slowly with a lot of work, but it takes quite a while. Other people have a harder time recuperating."

Kelly paused, hoping smart Cassie would catch the drift of what she said and draw her own conclusions. Cassie knew what kind of shape her grandfather was in.

Cassie looked up and caught Kelly's gaze. Kelly could almost see Cassie making the connections. "Pete kind of said the same thing. We'll have to wait and see. But he said it looked like Grandpa Ben wouldn't be going back home for a long time. And maybe never."

Kelly exhaled an inner sigh of relief. *Whew.* Thank goodness Pete had already covered this ground. "That makes sense, Cassie. I'm sure that's why he registered you for school here in Fort Connor. Pete and Jennifer wanted to make sure you know you have a home here with them while your grandfather is recovering." Kelly grinned. "And we're all really glad they did because we love having you here with us, Cassie. I can speak for the whole gang. And Mimi and Burt. And Jayleen and Curt."

"I am, too," Cassie said, her smile returning. Then, to Kelly's surprise, she came over and wrapped her arms around Kelly's neck in a big hug.

Kelly dropped her knitting and gave Cassie a big hug in return.

Kelly popped a cherry tomato into her mouth as she mixed the rest of the salad ingredients in a large mixing bowl. Hearing her cell phone's jangle, she saw Steve's name on the screen.

"Hey, how long before you get here? I don't want to grill those steaks until you're back."

"I'm passing Longmont now. Have you been listening to the news? Wildfire just exploded on the south side of Poudre Canyon. Those wind gusts again. Radio news guy said flames were hundreds of feet in the air."

"Oh, no!"

"It's burning through a stand of beetle-killed lodgepole pines. That's why it exploded. Those dead trees light up like torches."

"Good Lord! When is it going to stop?"

"No time soon. It's only been six days. Turn on the news. I'll be there in a few minutes." He clicked off.

Kelly did as Steve suggested and turned on the television to the news channel and watched some of the scenes Steve described come to life on the screen.

NINE

"Well, I don't have to ask if you enjoyed the grilled cheese or not," Julie teased as she removed Kelly's empty lunch plate from the café table. "It looks like you licked the plate clean. We won't have to wash it."

"Tell Eduardo that cheese combination he uses ought to be against the law. It is irresistible." Kelly held out her empty mug for Julie to refill with her pitcher of iced coffee. "Spinach salad was delish, too. That's a new dressing, isn't it?"

"You can blame Eduardo for that as well. He calls it Colorado Cilantro. Too yummy. I had some yesterday."

Kelly rose from the table. Time to return to the quiet of the shop and her spreadsheets. "Tell Eduardo that new dressing is definitely a winner. He'd better make a gallon of it, because I predict it will be popular."

164

"Will do, Kelly. I'll leave a carafe of iced coffee on the counter for you when we leave."

"You're a doll, Julie," Kelly said as she walked toward the hallway leading back into the knitting shop.

Her cell phone rang in her pants pocket. Jayleen's name flashed on the screen. *At last!* She'd been dying to hear how things were going at Curt's ranch. Kelly stepped back into the café alcove to talk. "Jayleen! It's so good to hear from you. What's happening there?"

"Sorry I didn't call before, Kelly, but we've been out riding the range ever since yesterday. That wind really whipped up, and firefighters told us the wildfire is leaping around like crazy. So we've been watching for any sparks that might blow over and ignite the dry grass on the far side of Curt's land. Some of those flames reached the other side of the valley, but the Hot Shots jumped on them right away. There're a whole bunch of people who live out there near Buckhorn Creek, and we were worried about them."

"The national incident commander said the fire had spread farther into the Buckhorn area, so we were all biting our nails, scared it might ignite near the ranch."

"Well, yesterday afternoon and last night were scary. All of us were out there. Curt and me, Curt's daughter Cindy, her husband John, Marty's parents, even Eric was riding with us. Keeping watch on the far edges of Curt's land and his neighbors closer to the Masonville crossroads. We all had walkie-talkies because our cell phones don't work well out there sometimes. That way we could stay in touch. We split up and rode the perimeter. Just about all night. Thank the Lord, the wind shifted early this morning. So we could take turns grabbing some shut-eye."

"Whoa, you guys must be exhausted if you've been riding out there most of the night," Kelly said as she slowly walked back toward the grill counter. Jennifer was unloading dirty dishes into a plastic container in the back area.

"We're pretty dang tired, you're right about that," Jayleen said. "We've been staying in touch with the fire crews so we could hear right away if any new breakouts flared up near us. We'd been keeping them updated about what we saw, too."

Kelly pictured Curt and Jayleen, out there in the devastating heat and smoke, riding the range and scouting for fire flaring up on the mountainsides. "Have you heard anything more about what's happening with the fire in Bellevue Canyon? Have they contained most of it? Is it still burning?"

Jayleen's long sigh came over the phone. "It's still burning, they say. As soon as they put out one area and build a fire line around it, the wind whips embers and cinders to another spot, and it starts all over again. Lord knows when they'll finally put it out completely."

Kelly wished she had something re-assuring to say to her dear friend, whose home and ranch were still at risk in Belle-vue Canyon. But no words could help Jayleen now. She knew how much all of her friends cared. Kelly decided actions could speak louder than words. Just like last weekend when she and the gang showed up to rescue Jayleen's alpacas, Kelly figured Curt and Jayleen could use their help now.

"Listen, Jayleen, you and Curt and the family are exhausting yourselves out there in this heat. Why don't we bring over some food for you guys. That way you can take turns coming in from the range, grab some food, and rest a bit before you go back out."

"Aww, Kelly-girl, you folks don't have to do that. We've still got some leftovers."

"Well, they'll be getting pretty old by now. Let me see what Pete has left over from lunch, and we can come over and set it up for you guys. My workload is pretty light right now, so I've got the time."

"I hate to see you go to the trouble . . ."

"No trouble, Jayleen. We do food runs for each other all the time," Kelly joked. "Let me get together with Jen and Pete and we'll drive there. And you don't have to wait around for us. You guys get back to riding the range, cowgirl."

"You're an angel, Kelly, you know that," Jayleen said, then laughed lightly.

"Hardly, Jayleen. I flunked my angel exams years ago, but I'm a great helper. So are Jen and Pete. Let us do our part, okay? I'll see you later this afternoon."

"Kelly, I learned a long time ago that it doesn't work trying to argue with you. Take care, and I'll see you later."

Kelly shoved her phone into her pants pocket as she walked over to the grill counter and beckoned to Jennifer. "Hey, is there any way you and Pete could help me take food over to Curt's ranch later this afternoon? I just talked to Jayleen and she told me they'd been out riding the perimeter of Curt's ranch all yesterday, last night, and today so far. I was worried when she hadn't returned my phone call. Now, I see why. Their whole family is out there. Curt,

Jayleen, Curt's daughter Cindy and her husband John, their son Eric, and Marty's parents, Curt's sister and husband."

"Good Lord!" Jennifer's eyes popped wide. "They were out there all night, too?"

Kelly nodded. "Yeah, most of it. Jayleen said the wind finally died down early this morning so they could take turns sleeping. And they're back out there again today. So I figure we could help them out. I was gonna buy some barbecue and buns and drive it over. Do you want to come along?"

"I sure will. And Pete will, too. He's downstairs now, so let me tell him and start gathering some food together. I know we had extra chicken salad left after lunch. Also, several salads, potato salad." Jennifer turned toward the section of hallway which led toward the doorway downstairs. "Oh, yeah, Cassie will want to come, too. So let her know and she can help us load the cars."

"Will do," Kelly said, and hurried down the hallway toward the knitting shop.

"Whoa, look at all the trucks," Cassie said, as Pete pulled his car to a stop in Curt Stackhouse's large ranch yard.

"Most of those belong to Curt's relatives," Kelly said, sitting in the backseat of Pete's car with Cassie. She was cradling a big container of hot barbecue beef in her lap. The lid didn't fit tightly, and consequently delicious and tempting sauce kept dribbling down the side of the container onto the bunch of paper towels she'd placed in her lap. Hopefully, the paper towels would hold up under the barbecue's assault. Otherwise, her new white summer pants would be history.

"Okay, everyone. I've popped the trunk so let's load up. Maybe we can carry everything in one trip," Pete said as he pushed open his car door.

Jennifer was already out of the car and scanning the fenced pastures surrounding Curt's sprawling ranch house. "I don't see anyone, so they must still be out there. Alpacas are all clustered near the corral."

Cassie jumped out of the car and sped around to open Kelly's door. "Thanks, Cassie," Kelly said, carefully balancing the barbecue as she climbed out of the back seat.

Pete held out several plastic containers. "Here, Cassie. These aren't too heavy."

Cassie reached for them. "I can carry something else under my arm. How about those plastic cups?"

Kelly looked up at the haze-covered sun above, beating down even through the haze.

Sweltering heat. Smoke-caused haze. Kelly could smell that acrid smell from last weekend. She'd never forget that smell. Her eyes smarted from the smoke.

"How in the world can Jayleen and Curt and the others stay out here, breathing all this smoke all day? This can't be good," Jennifer said, slowly walking toward the ranch house as she balanced several large plastic containers.

"Well, it sounds like they didn't have much choice," Kelly added. "There was only one way to know what was happening out there and that was to ride out and see it."

"It's been nearly a year since we were out here at Curt's summer picnic, but I think I remember how the kitchen is laid out." Pete carried containers in both arms.

"I can show you where everything is, Pete. I was just here a couple of weeks ago," Cassie said, scurrying ahead of the adults. "Here, I'll get the door." She skipped up the wooden steps to Curt's welcoming wide front porch. She pulled the screen door open and stood in front of it. "Hello?" she called into the house.

"Nobody home," Jennifer said as she crossed the porch. "Good. That will give us time to get everything set up in the kitchen and put out paper plates. Then we can put all the food on the counters, so everyone can go through buffet style."

"Oh, darn, I forgot the buns," Kelly said, turning around as she stepped inside the cheerful inviting Stackhouse kitchen.

"I grabbed them, Kelly," Pete said, following after her. "We've got everything. Any condiments, I figure they already have."

Jennifer walked over to the counter beside the sink and set down the plastic containers, then turned and looked around the kitchen. "Wow. A lot of memories in this kitchen."

"Ohh, yeah," Kelly said, setting the heavy barbecue container on another counter. "Lots of memories. Like meeting Marty for the first time." She grinned.

Cassie's eyes lit up. "Really? What happened?"

"What *didn't* happen," Jennifer said with a snort. "Marty was a disaster."

"You remember, Cassie, I told you Megan didn't like Marty when she first met him? Well, she met him here at Curt's in the living room when we were trying to decorate Curt's Christmas tree."

"What happened? Tell me!" Cassie begged. "It sounds really funny."

"Does the name Spot the Wonder Dog

ring a bell?" Jennifer said, laughing.

Cassie burst into giggles as Kelly and Jennifer took turns setting up the buffet supper and retelling Marty and Megan stories at the same time.

Curt leaned back into the cushioned kitchen chair. "I have to admit that was mighty tasty barbecue beef, even if it was store-bought."

"Well, it's not exactly store-bought," Kelly admitted. "I bought it at one of the specialty barbecue places in town. Steve and I really like it."

"Delicious. Pretty dang close to Texas good," Jayleen proclaimed, taking a drink of iced tea. "Jennifer, did you make this sweet tea? That's almost as good as mine." She winked as she smiled across the kitchen table.

"Dee-lumph-shus," Eric managed around a big bite of barbecue sandwich.

Cassie's giggles started everybody laughing as Eric's ears turned red. He didn't seem to care; he simply grinned around the bun and kept on eating.

"This boy is starving," Jennifer said, offering Eric a napkin. "That's his third barbecue sandwich. How long have you folks been out there riding?"

"Quite a spell," Curt said, sipping from

his cup of hot coffee, even in the midst of a summer heat wave. Kelly had to take her hat off to him. Even she switched to iced coffee these hot afternoons.

"His mom brought along some of those power bar snacks, but that doesn't do much for a growing boy's appetite," Jayleen said.

"Good thing you bought the super size, Kelly," Pete joked.

"If you've still got an empty spot, better switch to the chicken salad," Curt said to his grandson. "Otherwise your mom and dad and aunt and uncle won't get any. And I know how much your dad likes barbecue." Curt gave him a smile.

Eric nodded and managed "Yeth sup" around the barbecue. That only made Cassie giggle again, and the sound of that laughter sparked more adult chuckles.

"Ahh, young 'uns." Jayleen leaned back in her chair and grinned. "I can't wait to take all the kids out riding once this wildfire is finally put out. I sure hope we'll have something to show them back in the canyon."

"We're gonna keep thinking there will be," Curt decreed, giving a "that's that" kind of nod. "Firemen tell me that fire jumped around in the canyon like a grasshopper on a hot griddle. Burned some places and left other places untouched. So, keep picturing the ranch in your head, Jayleen."

Kelly was marveling at Curt's encouraging statement, which bordered on the metaphysical, when Cassie spoke up, eyes wide. "Did you *really* put a grasshopper on a griddle, Uncle Curt?"

This time everybody laughed out loud, including Eric, who had luckily just swallowed his last bite of sandwich. And this time, it was Cassie's turn to flush red. Kelly rose from the table and took her plate toward the trash, stopping first to give Cassie a hug.

"Welcome to my world, Cassie. Usually everyone's laughing at something I say. It's good to have company," Kelly said, then dumped the used paper plate into the trash can nearby.

Jayleen beckoned to Cassie. "Come over and give me one of those hugs, Cassie. I can use some of that before I go back out on the range."

Cassie eagerly complied, settling in on Jayleen's lap. Kelly leaned against the counter while Jennifer washed up several empty plastic containers. Pete pulled up a chair at the table as well.

Kelly lowered her voice even though conversation around the table had already resumed. "When did Cassie start calling him Uncle Curt?"

"Petty much since she came over here to the ranch the first time a couple of weeks ago. All of Curt's grandkids and nieces and nephews either called Curt 'Grandpa' or 'Uncle Curt.' So Cassie picked it up right away. In fact, she was saying it that night when she was telling Pete and me everything she did over here." Jennifer smiled. "I think it's great, because Grandpa Ben may never leave his hospital bed again. So it's good that she has kind of an 'extra' grandpa."

"And a grandmother." Kelly nodded toward Jayleen and Cassie, laughing at something someone had said. Eric had two of Pete's chocolate brownies on a paper plate in front of him.

"Yeah, that's true. You can tell how much she and Curt have taken to Cassie. They started treating her like one of their own."

"Well, Cassie makes that easy. She's a great girl. Easy to love." Glancing toward Jayleen and Cassie again, Kelly added, "And it looks like she's filling a big hole in Jayleen's heart. Missing grandchildren."

"Cassie, why don't you pull up a chair for Jennifer?" Pete said, pointing toward an extra chair by the door. "C'mon over, Jen. Those plastic tubs aren't going anywhere."

He beckoned her to the table.

"Here, Jennifer, you can have my chair," Jayleen said, as Cassie jumped up. "I've been sittin' in the saddle ever since yesterday. I need to stand up." Jayleen rose from the chair and stretched.

"My butt is sore," Eric said, then took a big bite of brownie.

Curt patted his grandson on the back. "Aww, it'll toughen up over time, boy."

Eric swallowed. "Well, it oughta be tough as leather now. We've been riding ever since yesterday." He rolled his eyes before taking another bite.

"Leather butt," Cassie teased as she brought over the extra chair. "That's funny."

"Don't laugh. Wait'll we go for an all-day ride sometime," Eric said between bites. "You'll see. You won't be able to sit for a couple of days."

"Don't let him scare you, Cassie," Curt said. "Your butt will toughen up this summer. Soon as this fire gets behind us and put out, we'll start riding every weekend."

"Every weekend?" Cassie squealed. *"Awesome!"*

"Better start sitting on concrete steps now," Eric teased.

Cassie looked at him. "Really?"

Curt took his hat and used it to playfully

swat his grandson on the back of the head. "Don't let him pull your leg."

Eric just laughed, and Cassie jabbed him in the ribs with her elbow. Everyone laughed then.

Jennifer settled into the chair beside Cassie. "Well, the last time I took a ride with you and Jayleen, Curt, I wished my butt was made of leather. I was sore for days."

Everyone laughed again, including Jayleen, who walked near the sink then stretched both arms over her head. "Wooee! It feels good to stand up. No lie."

Kelly waited for conversation at the table to pick up again, then leaned toward Jayleen. "What have you heard from Dennis? Is he still laying low in Poudre Canyon taking care of the alpacas? Or has he been busted?"

Jayleen leaned against the counter beside Kelly. "He's still there, thank goodness. He says nobody hassles him because they know him and know the animals would starve without him. But he's gonna have to come into town sometime. He's the only next of kin Andrea had, so Dennis is the only contact the hospital and medical examiner's office have. He told me yesterday he had to arrange for a funeral home to come and take Andrea's body from the hospital tomorrow."

Kelly's only experience with funeral

homes was with her father's death and Aunt Helen's death. Neither of those brought good memories. "I remember having to do all that for Aunt Helen years ago. I was working in Washington, DC, then. Boy, it was stressful having to handle all of that long distance. At least for my father, I was there in the same area."

Jayleen looked over at Kelly and smiled. "Lordy, Lordy, has it been all those years since Helen died? Hard to believe, Kelly-girl. That's what brought you out here to live with us years ago. You liked it so much, you stayed."

Kelly nodded. "Yep. I fell in love with those mountains, I guess. Of course, all you good folks kind of helped that decision to stay."

"Well, we're all mighty glad you did."

Remembering her conversation with Burt, Kelly asked, "What's going to happen when police start questioning people regarding Andrea's death? Burt told me the cops would probably assign a community service officer to question everyone. There were a whole lot of people who saw Andrea last Saturday. Including Dennis. What'll he do when they contact him?"

Jayleen stared out into the kitchen. Everyone around the table was indulging in Pete's brownies, even Curt. "You know, Kelly, I'm glad you told me that. I'm gonna call Dennis tomorrow and leave him a message. He'll have to plan for that. The local volunteer firemen and sheriff may have cut him some slack, but the police department won't. He may have to sneak into town at night or something, meet with the officer at the department, then wait for nightfall to sneak back up the canyon."

Kelly pictured Dennis Holt hiking out of the canyon at night and then back up again. "Boy, that would be one heckuva long hiking day."

Jayleen shrugged. "Dennis is tough. He's a mountain man. Rugged. He can probably load up supplies in a backpack while he's in town. The animals will just graze so they'll be okay."

"I hope you're right. I kind of liked the idea of Dennis hiding out in the canyon, taking care of the herd. Staying beneath the radar. Maybe it's the rebel in me." She laughed.

"Well, let's hope they'll open up the Poudre Canyon so residents can get back to see their properties. Their canyon fire was put out. Fire is still burning in Bellevue Canyon. Who knows how long it'll take to contain. I know those firemen are working as hard as they can. Bless their hearts."

Just then, the ranch house kitchen door opened and Curt's daughter Cindy and her husband John walked in. Eric leaped up from his chair and went over to give his mom and dad a hug.

"Come on in, folks, and fill your plates and sit down. You deserve a break," Jayleen said to them.

TEN

Saturday, June 16

Kelly tabbed through the spreadsheet on her laptop screen, entering expenses for her Denver client Don Warner's development company. She'd spent most of yesterday morning in phone meetings with Warner's Denver office, and today was the day to catch up on accounts. Warner was considering a new project, so he was curious how much cash he could spare to start. Kelly had promised him some early numbers mid-month as guesstimates.

As she looked up from her spot at the end of the knitting table, Kelly noticed another woman had joined the sole knitter who was working on a lacy summer tee at the other end of the table. The newcomer was obviously helping the other knitter and murmuring encouragement as she continued her efforts.

Cassie walked into the room, a large

plastic cup with a fast-food logo on the side. "Hi, Kelly. Megan says to be at the field tonight at six thirty. You guys can practice before the game."

Kelly leaned back in her chair. "We're gonna have to have gallons of water there. It'll be brutal in that sun."

"Don't you guys bring water bottles?" Cassie said, taking another gulp of something cold.

"Sure. But we'll go through tons of those. We need to go back to using big containers. The world is filling up with empty water bottles."

"Are you playing some sport tonight?" one of the women asked.

Kelly didn't recognize either woman and figured they were newcomers who'd probably found Lambspun through one of Mimi's wonderful classes, All Things Fiber. "Yes, several of us who show up here at Lambspun also play on softball and tennis leagues. We're playing over at Rolland Moore Park fields."

"In this heat!" the other newcomer exclaimed. "You're going to get heatstroke."

At that, Cassie started to laugh. "What's heatstroke? Did you just make that up?"

"Oh, no! It's real!" the first lady said. She was middle-aged with short dark hair. "It happens when people are outside and exposed too long to the heat of the sun. In this kind of weather, you have to be careful."

Cassie looked over at Kelly with wide eyes, clearly weighing whether to believe that statement or not.

"Well, that's true, but all of us on the team are athletes and are used to playing ball outside. Plus, we make sure we keep ourselves hydrated. You know, drink lots of water. In fact, that's what Cassie and I were talking about. Taking big containers of water to the field rather than all those water bottles."

"You know, that's a good idea," the other woman offered, looking up from her knitting needles. There were several neat rows of bubblegum pink cottonlike yarn. She was clearly making progress. "It wasn't that many years ago when we took big containers of water to sports events. You know, like thermos things. Then all of a sudden we started using the smaller water bottle. Now we're up to our butts in plastic." She shook her head.

At that image, Cassie lapsed into another peal of giggles. Kelly had to laugh, too. "I agree with you, but how do we stop using them? We're spoiled by the convenience."

"Indeed, we are," an authoritative contralto voice decreed from the archway.

Kelly looked up and burst into a grin. "Hilda! I'm so glad you came in!" She jumped up from her chair and ran over to embrace the older lady, who definitely looked thinner than she had a year ago. Kelly could feel more bones as she gave Hilda a careful hug. "Where's Lizzie?"

"Coming, dear." A familiar birdlike voice came from the foyer, and Lizzie's shorter, round-as-a-dumpling self appeared in the central yarn room. "I was checking on one of those lacy yarns Mimi has out here in the foyer."

Kelly went to embrace Lizzie, giving her a firm squeeze. "So good to see you both again. I'm glad to see you two getting out, even in this heat."

"The air is so much better over here in the east part of town," Hilda said as she slowly made her way to the knitting table. Kelly scurried over to pull out a chair for her, helping the frail older woman settle into it.

"Doesn't your air conditioner filter out that smoke? I thought you said you also had two filter units or some thing."

"Well, we did, but one's on the fritz," Lizzie said, bustling around the table. Cassie immediately vacated her chair, but Lizzie waved her back down. "No, no, stay where you are, my dear. I'll sit right here between you and Kelly and catch up with you both." She carefully settled into the chair and set her tapestry knitting bag on the table.

"Cassie, you look like you'd be in middle school, am I right? Which grade will you be in this fall?" Hilda inquired, as she pulled out pale blue froth from her knitting bag.

Kelly wasn't sure, but it looked like one of those silky angora yarns that had come into the shop.

"I'll be in seventh grade," Cassie said, her gaze drifting to the blue froth. "Pete registered me at Baxter Middle School."

"Ohh, Baxter," Hilda said, nodding as her tiny needles started to work the blue froth. "I started there ages ago, when I first began teaching. You remember, Lizzie?"

"Indeed, I do," Lizzie said, removing a lacy white collar from her bag. The needles were so tiny, Kelly could swear they were straight pins instead. "And I started teaching at Wayne Junior High School that next year."

"It was different then," Hilda added. "There were junior high schools with grades seven through nine. Now we have middle schools with grades six through eight. After

186

that, there's high school with grades nine through twelve. Lizzie and I started teaching high school shortly afterward."

"What grade did you teach?" Cassie asked, glancing from Hilda to Lizzie.

"We taught mathematics and English literature for sophomores, juniors, and seniors," Lizzie said, a devilish smile appearing. "Can you guess who taught what?"

Cassie's eyes darted from Lizzie to Hilda and back again, then she smiled and pointed to Lizzie. "You taught English lit, and you taught math." She pointed to Hilda.

Lizzie's smile turned delighted. "Everyone says that."

"In fact, it's the opposite." Hilda looked over at Cassie with a smile. "I taught English literature. And my sister taught algebra, geometry, and calculus."

"Really?" Cassie looked amazed.

"I made the same assumption you did," Kelly said, saving the spreadsheet on her screen and closing her laptop. "I might as well join the rest of you," she said, reaching into her shoulder bag for her sweater project.

"Mimi told me you were making a sweater for the evacuee project. That's wonderful, dear," Lizzie said, looking at Kelly, while her fingers magically worked a lace pattern with the tiny white threads. "The wildfire survivors will appreciate those sweaters when cold weather comes this fall."

"Is that yarn or thread?" Cassie asked, leaning closer to Lizzie and gazing at the lacy collar she was creating.

"Well, it's a combination of both, actually," Lizzie said. "It's called lace yarn. And we use it to make delicate lacy things like collars."

Kelly picked up her stitches where she'd left off. Another ten rows at least had appeared on her needles. And amazingly, they looked fairly even. Maybe she was much better than she thought.

Hilda peered over the top of her glasses at Kelly's green sweater-to-be. "Very good, Kelly. Your stitches are much more even than before. Your progress is definitely noticeable."

Kelly gave an exaggerated sigh. "Thank you, Hilda. I was afraid it was my imagination."

"Nonsense, my dear." Hilda's fingers moved smoothly, considering her age. "Tell me, how is Connie doing? Mimi explained her recent change in behavior. Such an unfortunate situation. I believe you were there, correct?"

Kelly glanced toward the central yarn

room to make sure Connie wasn't there, then lowered her voice so the women at the other end of the table wouldn't overhear her. "Connie seems to be acting a little more like her normal self. She's been more talkative today, I noticed."

Hilda glanced over at Lizzie explaining the stitches to Cassie, then she leaned a little closer, obviously following Kelly's lead. "I vaguely remember meeting Andrea Holt a few years ago. But I do recall meeting Connie's husband Jim at several of Lambspun's Christmas parties. Tell me, is the bond between them irrevocably broken? It sounds as if it was, since he was living with Andrea. Or am I mistaken?"

"You know, I'm not sure, but I don't think he had actually moved in with her. But they definitely acted like a couple when I met them last Saturday."

"Ahh, relationships between men and women are such a minefield," Hilda said with the world-weary tone of a lifetime observer, not a participant.

"They are, indeed," Kelly said from the perspective of a participant who had been in the battlefield along with the land mines. She lowered her voice. "By the way, how is Eustace doing in the State Correctional

Facility? Lizzie is still able to visit him, isn't she?"

Lizzie and scholarly historian Eustace had found each other late in life. Devoted soul mates, their love had survived Eustace's sentencing in the killing of a manipulative investor who cheated Eustace's mother out of her family's centuries-old land. "Frontier justice," Eustace had called it. First-degree murder, the courts decreed.

"Oh, yes." Hilda nodded. "She's allowed to visit twice a month."

"How is he doing? How's his health?"

"He's doing well, according to Lizzie. Fortunately, he enjoys his duties in the prison library and he's even started writing again. So Lizzie and I are very pleased. We must have work to keep our minds sharp."

Kelly smiled. "I agree, Hilda." Then, over Hilda's shoulder, Kelly noticed Mimi standing in the central yarn room beckoning to her. She placed her finger to her lips in a shushing manner. Kelly nodded and placed her knitting on the table. "Excuse me for a moment, Hilda. I'll be right back. I think I'll get a refill on my coffee." She grabbed her mug as she rose from the chair.

Mimi stepped back into the foyer and beckoned Kelly to follow as she walked toward the café. "Let's go outside where we can have privacy," she said over her shoulder as she headed toward the café door. Kelly followed Mimi outside under the shade of the tall cottonwoods. The midday heat hit Kelly immediately.

"What's the matter, Mimi? You look worried."

Mimi glanced around and gestured toward the parking lot. "See that white car parked beside the red one? That belongs to the community service officer. She just came into the shop to question Connie."

"Oh, boy. How's Connie holding up? She looked a little better this morning."

The worry lines on Mimi's face deepened even more. "Not very well. When the woman came in and identified herself, Connie turned white as a sheet. She could barely speak at first. I felt so bad, Kelly. I went over to Connie and gave her a hug, then told the officer that they could use my office in the back to talk."

"How long ago was that?"

"Over fifteen minutes ago. And they're still in there."

Mimi started chewing the side of her lower lip, something Kelly noticed she did when her worry level ratcheted up. "Poor Connie. I have a bad feeling she's not going to hold up well under questioning," Kelly said. "What's the officer like? Does she come across as brusque or friendly?"

"Oh, definitely friendly. She's middle-aged and has a nice smile. Warm and sociable. She introduced herself as Officer Warren."

Kelly sighed. "Well, that's good. I remember how badly Barb did when police officers were questioning her a few weeks ago."

"I do, too. And Connie is in worse shape than Barb. Barb has a spine of steel, and she crumpled. Poor Connie, she's a marshmallow compared to Barb."

"Where's Burt? Have you told him that an officer is here?" Kelly glanced around the driveway between the shop and her cottage. "I don't see his car."

"He's out on errands, like usual. I left him a message on his cell phone, but he hasn't returned my call yet."

The large dark wooden door to the shop opened then, and a woman dressed in a navy blue Fort Connor police uniform stepped out. Mimi's observation was correct; the woman appeared to Kelly to be in her sixties, with her graying brown hair pulled back into a bun. She had a nice face.

"I've finished speaking with your clerk, Connie, Mrs. Parker. She also told me that a woman named Kelly Flynn lives across the driveway at the cottage. I knocked on the door, but no one answered. Would you know when Ms. Flynn would return, by chance?"

Kelly stepped up before Mimi opened her mouth. "I'm Kelly Flynn, Officer Warren. You wanted to see me?"

Officer Warren smiled. "Yes, your name was on my list to contact tomorrow, but we can talk now if you have a few minutes?"

"No problem at all, Officer," Kelly said. "Would you like to have a seat here in the café patio? That way we wouldn't be in the way of customers coming and going." She gestured toward the walkway leading around the shady tables of the black wrought-iron fenced garden.

"That's fine, Ms. Flynn. Lead the way," Officer Warren replied.

"I'll see you later in the shop, Mimi." Kelly gave her a reassuring smile before she headed toward an empty table. Finding one in the shade, Kelly pulled out a chair and settled in. Officer Warren did the same.

Kelly decided she would see if she could get some information while Officer Warren was questioning her. "Are you planning to interview everyone who saw Andrea Holt last Saturday? If so, I bet that's a long list. There were a lot of us who helped our friend Jayleen Swinson move her alpaca herd from Bellevue Canyon to safety."

Officer Warren gave Kelly a warm smile. "Well, there are a lot of names on my list. You're right about that. Tell me, Ms. Flynn, how long have you known Andrea Holt?"

"Well, I didn't really know Andrea. I had met her briefly here at Lambspun a few times when she brought in bags of alpaca fleece to sell to Mimi or put on consignment. Mimi knew her better."

Officer Warren scribbled in her small notebook. "You mentioned helping rescue Ms. Swinson's alpacas from Bellevue Canyon last Saturday. Was Andrea Holt already there when you arrived?"

"Yes, she was. She was loading two of Jayleen's alpacas into a horse trailer. My boyfriend, Steve Townsend, and I each drove trucks with trailers up into the canyon so we could get those animals out as quickly as possible."

"I've been told there were several people at Ms. Swinson's. Did you recognize anyone else there?"

"Yes, a lot of the people who came to help were my friends. There was Jayleen Swinson, of course, and Curt Stackhouse, who owns a ranch near the Buckhorn. My Fort Connor friends Lisa Gerrard and Greg Carruthers brought a truck as well. As did

Megan and Marty Harrington. Andrea Holt was there. And several people that I didn't know who were friends of Jayleen's. Oh, yes, and Andrea's husband Dennis Holt was also there helping."

"How did you know Dennis Holt?"

Kelly carefully chose her words. "I met him when I was going up into Poudre Canyon last year with my friend Jennifer Stroud. She's a real estate agent here in town, and she had a property up there she wanted to show me. Dennis Holt was a neighbor on the adjoining property."

"Have you had occasion to meet him since then, before last Saturday, I mean?"

Kelly peered at friendly Officer Warren, wondering at her question. "No, I've had no reason to meet him. In fact, it took me a while to recognize him last Saturday when we were at Jayleen's."

"Were you aware that he and Andrea Holt had divorced?"

Kelly deliberately took a sip of iced coffee from her mug, curious about all the questions regarding Dennis. "Yes, I believe Mimi told me."

"Was Connie Carson there when you arrived?"

"No, she drove up a few minutes after Steve and I loaded the alpacas."

"Did she also bring a truck and trailer so she could help move alpacas?"

"Uhh, no. I don't believe she has a truck. Connie drove up in her car."

"Did you see a man helping Andrea Holt that you didn't recognize?"

"Yes . . . yes, I did. I believe his name is Jim."

"Were you aware that he was Connie Carson's husband?"

"My friend, Lisa, told me while I was at Jayleen's. I asked her who he was."

"You mentioned that Connie Carson brought a regular car to Jayleen Swinson's. Did you get the feeling that she came to help move some of Ms. Swinson's belongings or did she come to speak to her husband and Andrea Holt?"

"Uhh . . . that's hard to say," Kelly dodged.

"Did you witness an argument between Connie Carson and her husband and Andrea Holt?"

Kelly released a sigh. "Yes, I did, and it was very unpleasant. Connie was extremely angry and accused Andrea of stealing her husband."

"Were all three of them engaged in the argument?"

"Well, all three of them spoke up and had

something to say, if that's what you mean."

Officer Warren nodded. "So, all three of them participated in the argument."

"Yes. All three of them. They were all visibly upset."

"Did the argument get physical? By that, I mean did any person put their hands on another person?"

Kelly took another sip of coffee. Friendly Officer Warren was a damned good interrogator. So much for friendly looking older women. Like a pit bull, she didn't let go.

"Yes. Connie Carson pushed Andrea Holt in the heat of the argument. Andrea stumbled but didn't fall."

"Did Jim Carson do or say anything after that?"

"Yes . . . he said something like they hadn't been together for months and he couldn't stand being around her." Kelly glanced away. "Pretty harsh."

"How did his wife Connie respond to that comment?"

Kelly sighed. "She burst into tears, started crying. Jayleen Swinson came over and put her arms around Connie then. Andrea and Jim drove off. Steve and I drove off after that, too. Police were going to evacuate the canyon."

"Was Dennis Holt present during all of

this? Did he say anything?"

"He was there, but he just watched like the rest of us."

"Did he load any alpacas into a trailer?"

"Yes, he loaded two alpacas and was going to take them to Andrea's ranch up the Poudre. That's where my friends and I were taking our trailer loads as well. Jayleen and Curt and their family took the rest to Curt's ranch near the Buckhorn."

Officer Warren paged back through her notes, then looked up at Kelly again. "Did you and your friends drive up to Andrea Holt's ranch that same day, Saturday?"

"Yes, after we got out of Bellevue Canyon, we took a short break for some fast food, then we all trekked up into Poudre Canyon to her ranch. We transferred all the animals into her corrals."

"Can you tell me who you saw at Andrea's ranch?"

Oh, brother. Here we go again. "Well, Andrea, Jim Carson, Dennis Holt, and all my friends, Steve, Lisa, Greg, Megan, and Marty."

"Those were the only ones when you arrived?"

"Yes . . . then Connie arrived," Kelly said reluctantly.

"And what happened when she did? Was

there another argument?"

"Ohh, yes. More shouting and accusations. Then my friends and I got Connie away from there and took her with us when we left the ranch. We sat with her for a while, then she left with us when we drove out of the canyon."

"Did you see her drive out of the canyon? I mean, did you notice her car on the road along with you and your friends?"

Damn. Friendly Officer Warren was relentless. "I did not actually see her car, but Steve and I were in the middle of our little caravan. Marty and Megan said that Connie was behind them until a rest stop where they saw her turn off and park at the restroom."

Officer Warren scribbled away for a couple of minutes. Then gave Kelly that deceptively friendly Mom-smile. "Well, I think that's all of my questions, Ms. Flynn. You've been very helpful. Thank you so much." She rose from the table. "Do you have any suggestions as to when would be a good time for me to contact your friends?"

"Actually, we'll all be together this evening playing softball at Rolland Moore fields. We're on a co-ed softball team. So, you could come out to the ballpark." Now it was her turn to give Officer Warren a winning smile.

Office Warren's eyes lit up and she laughed lightly.

ELEVEN

Later that Saturday, June 16

Kelly tabbed through Warner Construction's spreadsheet, entering various expenses and watching the numbers calculate at the bottom of each row. Updating data was a never-ending job. Settled at her favorite small table beside a café window looking out on the garden and golf course beyond, she took a sip from the newly filled mug of iced coffee.

"Hey, Kelly." Burt's voice cut through her concentration on the demanding numbers. "Mimi said you were in here working." Burt pulled out a chair across the table and settled in.

"I was hoping you'd show up before I had to leave." She looked up with a smile. "I wish Connie was still here, but she took off the moment Officer Warren pulled out of the driveway."

Burt's smile disappeared. "Yeah, Mimi

told me Connie looked awful after the interview. Her face was white and Mimi thought she was going to actually get sick."

"I only caught a glimpse of her, but she certainly didn't look happy. In fact, we haven't seen the old Connie since last week. And I have to admit, Burt, that bothers me." She closed her laptop and shoved it to the side of the table.

Burt's face clouded. "I know what you mean, Kelly. And the same thing bothers me, too. Connie acts, well . . . for want of a better word, guilty. You can't miss it." Burt leaned both arms on the table, his big hands clasped together in what Kelly recognized as his talking position. "You know, I'd left a message with Dan at the department the first of the week, asking him to keep me updated about any new information on Andrea Holt's death. He called me today. Officer Warren questioned Jim Carson first, which I found interesting."

"Really? Well, that explains why Officer Warren asked me so many questions about who was there at Jayleen's and who took alpacas to Andrea's ranch. What happened at Jayleen's and at the ranch, and all that. It was clear she already knew about the argument between Connie and Andrea and Jim because she asked pointed questions." Kelly gave Burt a crooked smile. "Boy, for a sweet-looking older lady, she was one heckuva relentless interviewer. A barracuda in disguise."

Burt laughed softly. "Ohh, yeah. Diane spent twenty years as a detective on the force. She just cut back to part-time this year and has worked mostly as a community service officer these last few months. And considering how short-handed the department has been with the wildfire, Diane was the perfect one to handle the interviews. So you were questioned by one of the best."

"I believe it. Now I understand why I needed a big mug of Eduardo's coffee afterward. I was exhausted." She stared off into the foothills.

Thankfully, no more plumes of smoke were visible from this vantage point. The continuing influx of firefighters from all around the country had made a big difference. The fire commandant had announced last night on the news that the fire was 20 percent contained after this first week. Over 54,000 acres were burned and more than 112 homes lost so far. The Whale Rock area alone, up a steep slope from Bellevue Canyon road, lost forty homes. People loved those remote locations with their beautiful views. Unfortunately, those homes on hard-to-reach roads were only accessible by four-by-four vehicles. That meant fire equipment could not get up those roads. Manpower alone was the only thing between the fires and people's homes.

"I wonder why she spoke with Jim Carson first," Kelly said. "You'd think she would have spoken to Jayleen first."

"Maybe she couldn't get in touch with Jayleen. Remember, the fire moved into the Buckhorn around that time."

Kelly nodded. "You're right. By the way, have you seen Jim Carson helping at the disaster shelter lately?"

"No, but I did remember to ask my friend who works for the Salvation Army about some of the volunteers. He said several of them signed up to help weekly, so he'll make it a point of checking the list and give me a call if Jim shows up. That way I can drop by and have a chat." Burt stared down at his hands for a moment then looked up. "There is one other thing Dan told me. Apparently, Connie admitted to Officer Warren that she drove back to Andrea Holt's ranch after she was with you guys on Saturday."

Kelly drew back, shocked. "You're kidding? *Dammit!* Why did she do that?"

Burt wagged his head in that world-weary way of his. "I don't know, Kelly. It sounds to me, after listening to you and the others describe those confrontations, that Connie was reacting purely on emotion. Fear, most probably. Fear of losing her husband Jim to Andrea. Mimi and I had seen Connie and Jim go through several breakups over the years. Connie has a hot temper and was jealous of her good-looking husband. Somehow, they'd usually find a way to patch over things and get back together. I guess this time it was different. For Jim, at least. He'd met Andrea."

Kelly stared out the window at the golf course. Only a very few hardy — or crazy — people were actually playing in the heat of this afternoon sun. Mornings were busy on the course. Early mornings particularly. Kelly was glad she didn't golf. With tennis you could always play on air-conditioned indoor courts in the summer. Softball leagues had already changed their schedules to include only evening games.

"If only Connie had left the canyon when we all did. But Marty said she turned off at the rest stop." She looked into Burt's eyes. "I hate saying this, Burt, but do you think Connie pushed Andrea or caused her to fall down the stairs? I saw how angry Connie was at Jayleen's when she shoved Andrea. She was beyond angry, Burt. Connie was hysterical."

Burt's gaze turned sad. "I hate to think that, too, Kelly, but I've learned over a lifetime that anything's possible when someone becomes enraged. Particularly a jealous rage. That's why there are so many cases of spouses killing each other when they catch them cheating with someone else. That kind of rage is like a temporary insanity. And that's why the law has the classification of murder in the second degree. That's unpremeditated murder, not planned. Often a crime of passion."

Kelly stared off at the mountains without seeing them this time. "Good Lord . . . if that's what happened, then it would explain why Connie's acting the way she is." She closed her eyes. "I don't want to think about it."

"Neither do I, Kelly. That's another reason I'm glad I'm no longer on the force. It would break my heart to have to arrest Connie."

"Officer Warren said she'd be questioning Steve, Lisa, Greg, Megan, and Marty, so I told her they'd all be at Rolland Moore ballfields tonight if she wanted to find them." Kelly shrugged. "She just laughed, so she probably thought I was kidding."

"Well, it's Saturday afternoon, so she may

try to contact them this weekend."

"Good luck. The guys will be playing in Greeley. And we've got another game in Loveland on Sunday."

Burt glanced at his watch. "Speaking of the weekend, I'd better check the class schedule and make sure everything's ready. I'm teaching a spinning class later today."

Kelly's cell phone sounded from where it lay beside her laptop. She spotted Jayleen's name flashing as she reached for it. Burt was already out of his chair. Kelly gave him a wave as she clicked on. "Hey, Jayleen, I'm glad you called. How is it going over there? We've been paying close attention to news reports and it looks like the fire's been contained in that area of the Buckhorn Valley."

"We can thank the firefighters for that," Jayleen said. "They've been working night and day to build fire lines and beat out any hot spots. Not just here but in Bellevue Canyon, too."

Kelly heard sounds in the background so she guessed Jayleen was outside. She left her chair and hastened outside to escape the café noise. "That's the best news I've heard in a week, Jayleen. On this morning's fire updates on TV, the reporter said firemen thought they'd turned the corner. Do you guys think so? I mean, do the guys on the ground you talk to think so?"

"We're all keeping our fingers crossed up here, Kelly. The guys I talk to all say they're 'cautiously optimistic.' Lord, I hope they're right. Twenty-seven homes lost in Bellevue Canyon so far, and seventeen in Poudre Canyon. I've been saying prayers, I swear I have."

Kelly hadn't said prayers in years, but decided she just might start now. This was as good a reason as any to start up communication with Higher Powers.

"Well, I might break down and send up a prayer as well. Your welfare and your ranch are as good a reason as any."

Jayleen's low laughter sounded over the phone as Kelly leaned against the café balcony. No customers were at the nearby tables. The lunch crush was over and closing time was drawing closer. "I'm honored, Kelly-girl. Oh, I got a message from some community policewoman. She wants to come over and ask us questions about last Saturday. God knows, I'll try my best to answer, but everything's just merged together in a blur that day. So much was going on. Talk about chaos. I'm hoping Curt has a better memory of it all."

"Her name's Officer Warren and she came

over to question Connie today, then she asked me questions. Apparently she talked to Jim Carson first, so she had a good rundown about what happened up at your place Saturday. Connie's outburst and all that. So she asked lots of questions. Be prepared for a grilling."

"Well, I'll do my best. But this wildfire has burned away anything that wasn't absolutely essential for me to focus on. So I may not be too much help. I bet she'll be trying to question Dennis, too. I'd better call him and see when he plans to meet with her."

"Wow, how's he going to handle that? He's still hiding up in the canyon taking care of the animals. Is he going to hike down at night, like you mentioned?"

"Yep. He's gonna have to come into town at night in order to meet her the next day. Then, he'll hike back that next night. I thought I'd help him out and drive him over to the interview from Ted's Place at the mouth of the canyon."

Kelly got a little buzz inside. "Jayleen, do you think Dennis would mind if I met him while he's in town? I'd be curious to hear what kind of questions Officer Warren asks him."

"That should probably work. Maybe we

can meet for lunch. I'll tell him you're helping me with some bank business and all.
Account stuff. So bring along your briefcase
so you'll look all professional."

Kelly could hear the smile in Jayleen's
voice. "Sounds like a plan, Jayleen. Why
don't you give me a call when you hear from
Dennis so you can tell me where and when
you want to meet."

"Will do, Kelly-girl. You take care. I've
gotta get back out there and meet up with
Curt. We're still checking the land, if you
know what I mean. Can't take any chances."

"Take care, Jayleen. Say hi to Curt for
me." Kelly clicked off at the same time as
her friend.

Steve turned his truck into the entrance to
Rolland Moore park. Kelly was about to
grab her dad's USS *Kitty Hawk* baseball hat
from beside the seat when her cell phone
rang in her shorts pocket. She pulled it out
and spotted Jayleen's name as Steve pulled
into a parking space.

"It's Jayleen. You go on and tell them I'll
be there in a minute, okay?"

Steve nodded and grabbed his water
bottle, then climbed out of the truck.

"Hey, Jayleen. Did you hear from Dennis
already?" Kelly pushed open the truck door

and climbed down from the front seat.

"Yeah, I sure did. Dennis said Officer Warren wants to meet with him on Monday morning at ten o'clock at the Justice Center. You can join us for lunch afterward. Are you going to be in town then, or is that one of your Denver client days?"

"No, Monday's good. I don't go to Denver for another week or so. So that will work fine. Is Dennis planning to hike out of the canyon Sunday night, then? Are you going to take him to the interview?"

"I plan to. Dennis said he'll have his backpack with him, so he'll go to one of those little motels on the edge of Landport and see if he can find a place to sleep Sunday night. If they're all full, he'll use his bedroll and sleep outside the shelter. He just needs a place to clean up so he won't look too scruffy when he meets that police-woman Monday morning."

"Well, that's gonna be hard, considering Dennis looks pretty scruffy to begin with," Kelly said, slipping on her baseball hat and grabbing her first baseman's glove.

Jayleen laughed. "I'm afraid you're right, Kelly. Well, why don't we meet you afterward at that all-night diner on North College at noon? I figure Dennis should be finished with his interview by then so I can pick him up and drive him over."

"That works for me. I'll see you then. Oh, and Jayleen, good luck with Officer Warren this weekend. Burt said she spent twenty years as a detective with the department. And I can vouch that she's one helluva good interrogator. So don't try to hide anything," she teased. "She'll get it out of you."

Jayleen laughed out loud. "I wouldn't dream of it."

TWELVE

"So, how'd Dennis look this morning when you picked him up?" Kelly asked over the phone as she settled into a café booth at the all-night diner.

Jayleen chuckled. "Not too bad, considering. His jacket was a little rumpled but his shirt and slacks were clean, so that's something. Dennis is usually in jeans and work shirts. Of course, he still had his hiking boots on, but that's okay."

"Has he come out yet or will he give you a call?"

"He'll call. I'm doing some business over at a copy shop here on College Avenue near Old Town, so I can get over to the Justice Center in a jiffy."

"Okay, I'm already at the diner in a booth. I'm going to get to work and have some coffee until you guys show up. That way I'll look like a proper accountant," Kelly teased

213

as she pulled her laptop from her briefcase bag.

"Smart girl," Jayleen said. "We should be there in less than half an hour, I'm thinking. Meanwhile, I expect Dennis will let me know how the interview went."

"I'll be anxious to find out," Kelly said as she clicked off, at the exact moment a waitress approached with a coffeepot in hand.

"Hey, good to see you, again, Dennis," Kelly said with a bright smile as he slid into the booth beside Jayleen.

Dennis Holt looked across at Kelly and gave her a smile. "Good to see you, Kelly. I didn't know you did work for Jayleen."

"I'm the only one of Kelly's old alpaca clients she kept once she started taking care of those two real estate and developer clients she's got now," Jayleen bragged. "I'm a lucky dog."

Kelly smiled. "Well, Jayleen was my first independent client when I left the Washington, DC, corporate accounting firm and started my own practice here in Colorado years ago. So I'm kind of sentimental."

"Well, I wish I had enough business to hire an accountant," Dennis said with a half smile as he looked up at the approaching waitress.

"Hey, there, Sandy. I bet you folks have been swamped with customers this last week." Jayleen addressed the older woman as she passed out menus.

"We sure have, Jayleen," Sandy said with a friendly smile, pulling a small green order pad from her pocket. "Different people involved with the firefighters are here almost every night. Fire crews eat and sleep at their camp over at the Armory. The other folks like our burgers and steaks so much they come here before they head back to Landport or the Ranch."

"Well, the next time you see those people, please say thank you for me, okay?" Kelly said. "I drove through the edges of Bellevue earlier today and saw all those signs outside people's properties saying 'Thank You, Firefighters!' and 'We Love You, Firefighters!' and 'God Bless You, Firefighters!' "

"The whole city owes them a big debt," Jayleen said, scanning the menu. "If only that wind doesn't whip up today like it did over the weekend. Those dry, hot winds caused that fire to flare up again. We've got sixteen hundred firefighters on the ground, and it's still only 45 percent contained. Weather sure isn't cooperating."

215

"Yeah, it's that wind I'm afraid of," Dennis said, looking worried. "I've got friends up in Glacier View Meadows on the other side of the Poudre Canyon. And they've evacuated hundreds. That little section higher up is most at risk, I think."

"I heard that, too." Kelly said, glancing toward the windows. "The good news is they saved more than five hundred homes."

"I'm just grateful that fire didn't spread down the canyon near my place or my neighbors'. Firefighters were able to contain it around Poudre Park. I'm praying it doesn't flare up again."

"Amen," Jayleen said.

"It's all up to that blasted wind," Sandy said, brow furrowing. "Now, has anything struck your fancy or should I come back?" Her pen was poised over the pad.

"Well, I know how good those burgers of yours are, so I'll take the Philly cheeseburger," Dennis said. "With fries and a black coffee."

"I'll have my usual burger smothered in green chili," Jayleen said with a grin, handing Sandy the menu. "And coffee. Hold the fries."

That did it. Kelly had been trying to ignore the tempting burger aromas floating all around, but no more. She threw in the towel. "Okay, so much for watching my diet. I'll have the burger that's smothered in grilled onions. Lots of onions. And black coffee, hold the fries."

Sandy scribbled away with a contented smile. Another table surrendering all attempts at dieting. "You got it, folks. These will be out in a few minutes."

Kelly decided this was as good a time as any to try and pry information out of Dennis and was wondering how to broach the subject of the interview when Jayleen spoke up.

"You know, Dennis, Kelly was telling me that Officer Warren was a real tough questioner. Friendly looking but a bulldog beneath. And I gotta admit, when she came up to talk to Curt and me this weekend she came across the same way. Every time you thought she was finished, she'd start up again. What'd you think of this Officer Warren? Did she ask you a ton of questions?"

Dennis folded his arms and leaned forward over the table. "Ohh, yeah," he said, nodding his head. "I'd say bulldog isn't close. Pit bull would be better. She'd ask one question after another and didn't let up."

Kelly leaned forward, glancing first to

Dennis then Jayleen. "She kept asking me about the argument between Connie and Andrea and Jim Carson. Did she ask either of you about that?"

"She grilled both Curt and me about that as well. Wanted to know how long we'd known Connie and Andrea and Jim and all that." Jayleen wagged her head. "Curt was this close to getting testy, I could tell."

"She didn't ask me much about that. What she grilled me on was my relationship with Andrea. How long we'd been married. How long we'd been divorced. Had it been amicable. And, of course, she even went into my past drinking problems." He shook his head. "Boy, you'd think I was the one who'd threatened Andrea, not Connie."

"Oh, Lord . . ." Jayleen sighed.

"Yeah, I wasn't surprised, actually. It's part of the divorce record." He shrugged. "She also mentioned our divorce settlement. You know, dividing up our assets. The property and all. I mean, she didn't leave any stone unturned."

That got Kelly's attention. "Wow, that sounds more like an interrogation than an interview."

Dennis gave her a rueful smile. "Yeah, I kind of felt that way, too. But I think I know why. At the end, she mentioned that my address was in Poudre Canyon. Then she looked me in the eye and asked where I was staying in town since the canyon was still evacuated. I could tell she knew. She'd probably talked to the county deputy sheriff who knew I was hiding out at Andrea's place. So, I came clean. I told her I was staying up there to take care of Andrea's herd and my own and Jayleen's animals, too. I wanted to make sure the animals were all right. I'd kept out of the way of the firemen and cops and laid low. But I didn't dare lie to her. I figured it was a test."

"Well, I'll be damned," Jayleen said. "You know, Burt said Officer Warren spent twenty years as a detective and has just now cut back to part-time, so it's no wonder you felt interrogated.

"That was a good move, Dennis. I agree with you. She'd already checked with the local cops and firemen in the canyon and knew you were still there. She was trying to see if you'd lie to her. Tell me, what did she say when you admitted to staying in the canyon?"

Dennis looked down at the table. "Nothing, really. I explained about the animals and all, and she listened and wrote lots of stuff in that little notebook of hers. But she didn't say much, she just asked another question."

"What was the next question she asked?" Kelly probed. "After you'd explained about the animals."

"Uh, she wanted to know where I slept and how I made phone calls. And how I got food. I told her I slept in the corral near the animals, in case any big cats came hunting. And there was already plenty of food there, so I didn't need to come into town. Until today, that is." He gave a half smile. "Then she wanted to know how I got here. She kind of smiled when I said I hiked down at night. My car was still parked up there at my cabin."

"I hope she was impressed. I sure am," Jayleen joked.

"Well, she didn't act impressed. She'd smile, then ask me another question. She also wanted to know if I was the only next of kin Andrea had. I am, I guess. Andrea's mom and dad died years ago and she had no brothers or sisters back in Nebraska. I had the feeling she already knew the answer to that because I gave all that information to the hospital. And they'd called me to ask how I planned to handle her death. You know, her body and all that. I told her that I arranged to have a local funeral home take Andrea from the hospital and keep her there until I could decide what to do." Dennis stared at his folded hands, his voice softer.

"I reckon that Officer Warner could tell you were trying your best to handle everything," Jayleen said. "I mean, you're taking care of the herd at her ranch. And you're having to handle the arrangements for Andrea's death. Sakes alive, surely she can understand that."

Dennis shrugged. "I don't know. She would just listen and write stuff down. Every now and then she'd smile at me. So it was hard to know what she was thinking."

"That's probably why Burt said she was one of their best detectives." A thought wiggled in the back of Kelly's mind. "You said you drove to Andrea's that night because the wildfire was glowing brighter on the other side of the canyon ridge near the top, and you wanted to warn her. Did you see Jim Carson there? I would have thought he'd be there with her."

"Well, I thought so, too, and I called out his name when I found Andrea lying on the ground. But he wasn't anywhere around. He was there with her when I left a couple of hours or so earlier."

"Tell me, did you see Connie Carson? Apparently she told Officer Warren that she came back to Andrea's ranch after she left with us."

Dennis looked surprised. "No, I didn't. I wanted to get back to my place and feed my animals. Why'd she come back?"

"Connie refuses to talk with anyone at the shop about it. But I'm guessing that Connie went back again to try to convince Andrea to let Jim go. Maybe Connie thought he would come back to her if Andrea stopped seeing him. But judging from what we saw that Saturday, I think Connie's deluding herself."

Dennis nodded. "Yeah, I'd have to agree with you. That guy Jim sure didn't act like he wanted to get back together with his wife." He looked away. "People breaking up, that's always sad. Somebody always gets hurt."

"Lordy, Lordy," Jayleen said, shaking her head.

Kelly didn't say anything. There was nothing she could add. Out of the corner of her eye, Kelly noticed the waitress walking up to their booth holding a tray filled with the most scrumptious-looking burgers she'd seen in a long time.

Thirteen

Wednesday, June 20

Kelly walked into the Lambspun foyer, escaping from the building heat outside. There weren't any customers browsing in the central yarn room, so Kelly took time to check out the new arrangements of yarn and fibers. The Lambspun "elves," as she called Mimi and her staff, had been at it again. Rearranging, adding new colors, displaying new patterns. The elf population had increased by one, with the addition of Cassie.

She walked into the main room and set her briefcase bag and coffee mug on the library table. As Kelly pulled back a chair to settle in and start her accounts, Connie walked around the corner from the workroom. She held a pile of magazines in her arms.

Connie looked up at Kelly, clearly surprised to see someone. "Oh, hi, Kelly," she said softly, glancing down. "I have to switch these magazines, but I can do it later if it'll bother you." She started to turn away.

"No, no, it won't bother me at all, Connie," Kelly protested, settling into the chair. "Please keep up with your work. I actually like to have some human beings working around me. The cottage is absolutely quiet and sometimes you get tired of working alone."

"Okay, if you're sure," Connie said, pulling out the chair at the end of the table.

Kelly deliberately pulled out her laptop and popped it open and turned it on, then removed some of Arthur Housemann's file folders from her bag. She actually wanted to be able to chat with Connie a little to see how she was doing. But Kelly hadn't been able to since the tragic Saturday events over a week ago. Connie had not returned to her former talkative friendly self since that time. Consequently, no one except Mimi had been able to actually have a conversation with her. Even Burt said he hadn't had a talk with her yet.

It was clear that Connie was reluctant to talk to anyone. So Kelly figured the only way she could make an attempt would be to have an "accidental" chat, talking while something else was going on. Like it happened naturally.

Kelly noisily turned pages in Housemann's folder in an attempt to look busy. Connie had removed several binders of magazines and stacked them on the table.

"How're you doing, Connie?" Kelly started, breaking the ice. She looked over at the middle-aged woman with a big smile.

Connie didn't look at Kelly, nor return her smile. She gave a half shrug. "Okay, I guess." Then she didn't say anything else.

Kelly took a sip of coffee and tried again, deliberately keeping her voice gentle and quiet, even though there was no one in the adjoining yarn rooms. "We all care about you, Connie. We're your friends. You know that."

Connie slid one magazine out of the binder and replaced it with one from the new stack. "I know," she replied in a little voice.

Brother, Kelly thought. Normally talkative, vivacious Connie had been struck with a mute virus or something. Kelly had thought for sure that since Connie was talking to customers, she'd eventually return to her former self and start talking to friends again. But that hadn't happened for some reason.

Kelly clicked on the icons for her spreadsheets and watched them fill the screen. Meanwhile, she watched Connie continue to silently replace magazines. So Kelly decided to take another tack. She would become the Chatty Kathy and see if she could draw Connie into conversation.

"Officer Warren talked to Megan and Lisa over the weekend. She talked to Marty and Greg and Steve, too. She actually drove over to the guys' game at Greeley on Saturday and our softball game on Sunday. I had to laugh. Their impression of her was the same as mine. A smiling bulldog."

Connie didn't say a word, didn't look up at Kelly, smile or nod. She simply kept changing out magazines in the binders. Kelly got an uneasy feeling in her gut. Connie's behavior was really abnormal.

She tried once more. "Officer Warren was something else, I'll say that. She had one question after another. Didn't let up."

At that, Connie glanced up, and Kelly couldn't miss the concerned look on Connie's face. Then she glanced down again. But this time, she asked softly, "What sort of questions did she ask?"

Kelly weighed how to reply, wanting to keep the sparse dialogue going if possible. "Oh, she asked me if I knew Andrea personally. And I told her not really. I'd just met her here at the shop. Then she wanted to know if I knew Dennis Holt, so I had to explain that I had met him when Jennifer and I were up in Poudre Canyon a couple of years ago seeing a piece of property she had for sale. Dennis was the next door neighbor."

Kelly had settled back into the chair and deliberately stared off into the central yarn room, trying to appear as relaxed as possible. Connie was still watching and listening, which was an improvement over staring at the magazines and not saying a word.

"Of course, I didn't tell her that I saw Dennis Holt creeping around in the bushes spying on Jennifer and me. We'd just gotten up to the cabin and found her client, Fred Turner, dead inside. So we were already on edge. Jennifer was calling the police and I was on the porch and noticed Dennis hiding in the bushes. Kind of hard to hide that bushy dark beard of his. It really spooked me." She had to pause to draw in a breath.

"Did she ask about anybody else?" Connie asked in a quiet voice.

Kelly nodded. "Oh, yeah. She asked about everybody. Apparently she went out to Curt's ranch this weekend, too, and grilled them as well. Jayleen told me Curt was this close to getting ornery and aggravated. I also saw Dennis Holt in town yesterday and he said Warren wanted to know everything about his divorce from Andrea and their property settlement and his past drinking problems. Dennis said it was an interrogation more than an interview."

Connie glanced to the side. "What did she ask about me?"

Kelly paused before answering. "She wanted to know what happened on Saturday. I told her you came up to help Jayleen and saw your husband there. Then you guys had an argument." Kelly sensed Connie would fill in the unspoken words.

Connie looked down at the magazines again, sliding one out and replacing it with a newer one. Kelly felt like she shouldn't just let the conversation die out on that last statement, so she ventured in again.

"Did it feel like an interrogation to you, Connie? When Officer Warren was with you, I mean."

Connie's lips tightened together. Kelly spotted that and hoped she hadn't made her cry. Connie nodded her head. "Yeah, it did," she said in a tiny voice.

"I'm sorry," Kelly said softly, not knowing what else to say. Feeling bad that she didn't.

Mimi walked into the room then, glanced at Connie then Kelly. "Good morning, Kelly. I think you're the only person in the shop so far. It's feeling really empty."

"They'll start coming in to escape the heat, if nothing else," Kelly joked, deliberately adopting a relaxed tone of voice.

"If you're finished with the magazines, Connie, there're some skeins of that merino wool and mohair that need winding."

"I'm finished, so I can do the winding right now." Connie pushed back her chair and replaced the binders on the floor-to-ceiling shelves behind her. She started to take the stack of older magazines.

"You can leave them, Connie. I thought I'd put some in these empty spots I have on the turnstile in the corner here." Mimi pointed to the corner between the workroom and the spinning alcove.

"I was going to get some more coffee," Kelly said. "Would either of you like some?"

"None for me, thanks," Connie said, as she walked toward the central yarn room.

"I'll be up front as soon as I put these magazines away," Mimi called after Connie. Then she turned to Kelly. It was impossible to miss the concern in Mimi's gaze. "I heard you trying to talk to Connie a few minutes ago when I was going to my office. Did she actually talk to you, Kelly? She's only talked to me so far, and the customers, of course. Thank goodness for that."

"A little. It was like pulling teeth, I tell

you, Mimi. She didn't reply at first, then I started jabbering away, talking about how Officer Warren grilled everyone. And on and on. She actually looked up and asked what Warren wanted to know. What kinds of questions. So I told her in very general terms."

"Really? I'm surprised she asked. What else?"

"Well, I mentioned Dennis Holt and all the questions he said Warren asked him. So I went into lots of detail about what Dennis told Jayleen and me." Kelly shrugged. "At that point I would have recited the alphabet to her if it would have held her attention."

"Did she say anything else to you?"

"When I told her about Dennis, I mentioned that he felt interrogated more than questioned. Then I asked her if she had felt the same way. And she said kind of. I felt so bad for her, Mimi. It made me sad. I told her right off that we all cared about her. I didn't know what else to say."

"I know how you feel, Kelly. Burt tries to talk to Connie and she just mumbles one-word answers, then stops."

"Well, at least she's talking to you, Mimi. Jayleen and I were able to have lunch with Dennis Holt yesterday. He'd just been questioned by Officer Warren. And he said she wanted to know everything about his divorce and his relationship with Andrea, even details of their settlement. And she mentioned his past drinking problems."

Mimi's mouth opened, clearly surprised. "You're kidding. Good heavens! Is Dennis a suspect now?"

"Who knows, Mimi. Warren was one of their top detectives, according to Burt, so I guess this is turning into a full investigation. It makes me wonder if they have a reason to believe that Andrea's death wasn't an accident."

Mimi's eyes widened even more. "Well, Burt hasn't heard anything like that. He would have said."

"I guess they're simply ruling everything out. Which makes me wonder what they are thinking now that Connie admitted she went to confront Andrea a third time in the canyon that evening."

Mimi didn't reply, she simply stared off into the central yarn room. Her worried face said it all.

"Hey, Arthur," Kelly said into her cell phone as she walked across the driveway between her cottage and Lambspun. "I wanted to get on your calendar for next week so I could bring these financial statements over and let you take a look before the end of the month."

"Thanks for giving me a heads-up, Kelly," Arthur said. "I wanted to check that rental income. Hmm, let's see, how is next Tuesday morning for you?"

Kelly pictured her own calendar in her mind and saw no conflicts for Tuesday. "Tuesday morning is good, Arthur. Ten o'clock or earlier?"

"Let's do it at nine, Kelly. Now that we're living back in town, I'm at the office in a heartbeat it seems. Funny, we've only been living in the canyon for six months, so you'd think we'd adjust quickly to being back in town. But my wife and I have been complaining about stuff we used to take for granted before. Like the traffic."

"You're kidding," Kelly said with a laugh. "And Fort Connor traffic is nothing compared to Denver's. Or back East. Boy, I used to live and work there. Now, *that's* traffic!" She unlocked her front door and walked over to the corner desk and dumped her briefcase bag on the chair.

Arthur chuckled. "I know, we've gotten spoiled by the peacefulness of the canyon already."

"I'll say. I have no sympathy for you, only jealousy." She walked over to the patio screen door and looked across the backyard, shaded from the brutal late afternoon sun by the huge cottonwood tree. Nary a golfer in sight on the course, shimmering in the sun.

"Well, let's hope all that beauty and peacefulness will still be there when this wildfire is finally extinguished," Arthur's somber voice said.

Kelly opened her fridge and fetched a pitcher of fruit juice, then poured herself a glass as Arthur spoke. "Have you guys had any word yet about when you can return to the canyon?"

"Not yet, dammit," he said, clearly annoyed. "There was another of those meetings yesterday afternoon. They told us the wildfire was 50 percent contained. But they're still not allowing us to drive back into the canyon and get a look at our properties. That's what's so frustrating, not knowing where the damage is. They're expecting to make more progress today and tomorrow because of lower temperatures and not much wind. Firefighters are concentrating on the western side of the fire where there are a lot of fallen and beetle-killed trees. They said about seven hundred of the seventeen hundred firefighters are in a special camp on the western side."

Kelly leaned against her kitchen counter, wondering how she could share some information she remembered hearing from Dennis Holt at lunch the other day. At least Dennis wasn't breaking laws. She pictured Dennis hiking back into Poudre Canyon late at night, only the moonlight to light his way. She didn't want to reveal his presence, so Kelly decided to take another approach with her questions.

"I wonder if anyone has tried sneaking up there? Have you heard?"

"No, not that I know of. Police said anyone who refused to evacuate cannot use the roads or move to a neighbor's property. They don't want anyone in the firefighters' way."

"You know, Arthur, I think I remember hearing Jayleen mention that she'd heard from a guy this week who lives near you in the canyon. He said that the wildfire didn't come close to your house or his property because they were located farther away from Poudre Park."

"Who was he?" Arthur's voice sounded excited now. "Did Jayleen give you a name?"

Kelly paused for a minute. "I think she said it was Dennis somebody."

"Dennis? Dennis Holt? That has to be him. He's my neighbor on the north side, beside the river. How'd Dennis know what was happening up there, I wonder?"

Kelly dodged a direct answer. "She didn't say. He probably knows some of the firemen up there. I know that Jayleen and Curt are trying to keep track of what's happening in Bellevue Canyon by asking people who supply the firefighters' camp."

"Well, if it's Dennis, that makes sense. He knows everyone in Poudre Canyon, it seems, as well as the deputy sheriff."

Kelly debated, then decided to reveal more. "I think I've already met him," she replied cagily. "Does he have a beard by any chance?"

"Yes, yes, he does. A bushy brown beard. Looks like a real mountain man." Arthur chuckled.

"Then I met him that Saturday at Jayleen's when we were all driving up to rescue her alpaca herd. This Dennis Holt was there, helping, too. Several of us were taking some of Jayleen's herd to a ranch up in Poudre Canyon. Another alpaca rancher who was a friend of Jayleen's, Andrea Holt, owned the ranch. I think Jayleen said Andrea and Dennis were once married, but divorced."

"Yeah, Dennis told me he and his wife were divorced. She got most of the alpaca herd they had together. He's kind of struggling, just getting by. Sounds like a lot of money problems. I sure hope nothing happens to his little herd during this evacuation period."

Kelly deliberately switched the subject, slightly. "Well, his former wife had a pretty bad fall that same Saturday. We all brought Jayleen's alpacas up to Andrea's ranch that Saturday, and she's got a nice house there. But there's a set of real steep steps leading from the outside balcony in the back down to the ground. And apparently she fell down those steps that night and broke her neck. She died. At least that's what I heard."

"My Lord! That . . . that's awful!"

"Yeah, Jayleen told me that Dennis was the only next of kin, so he's had to take care of all the arrangements for Andrea."

"Where's Dennis staying? Did Jayleen say?"

Kelly had to think fast, not wanting to implicate Jayleen. "No, she didn't. She probably doesn't know. Jayleen's got her own worries, like you. Not knowing what shape her ranch house is in. Or if she even *has* one. Last week, she and Curt were riding the edges of his ranch near the Buckhorn to make sure they spotted any fire breakouts near their neighbors or any blowing cinders onto Curt's land. He's got a good-sized spread past Masonville."

"Bless their hearts . . . I know how they feel. Well, thanks to Dennis, maybe I can rest a little easier. Thanks for passing on that information, Kelly. I appreciate it."

"It's third-hand, but at least it's something. If I hear anything else, Arthur, I promise I'll let you know."

"Thank you, Kelly. I appreciate that more than you know. Are you and your friends playing ball tonight?"

"Matter of fact, we are. All the games start later because of the heat. So we grab a quick dinner at home then drive out to the ballpark. We're playing in Fort Connor tonight."

"Well, good luck, Kelly. Hit a home run for me, will you?" He chuckled.

"I'll do my best, Arthur," she promised.

"You can put those pizzas down right here," Greg ordered the waiter as he approached their table at the outdoor café.

"A pesto slice for me, please," Megan said, rising from her chair. "I'm going over by the statues and flowerbeds where there's less noise. Gotta check this text message. My biggest client."

"A client is texting you now?" Greg said, looking appalled. "Drop him."

"Ignore him, Megan," Lisa said, rescuing

a slice of pesto pizza and placing it on Megan's plate.

Megan gave him a dismissive wave as she walked away.

"Don't even think about eating that, Marty," Kelly warned as she took a slice for herself. "It's Megan's."

Marty was tearing into the sausage and cheese pizza. When he swallowed, he said, "It's safe for now."

Steve held a cheese and sausage slice that had a large bite missing already. He swallowed, then said, "You know, we all should run after this meal rather than going home and hitting the sack."

"Well, it would be healthier, that's for sure," Lisa said as she tipped back her bottle of craft beer.

Marty checked his watch. "Naw, it's nearly eleven already. I've gotta be up at six tomorrow morning."

Greg made a face and shook his head. "Don't need to run. I have a cast-iron digestive system. Nothing bothers it." He devoured the last of the slice in his hand and reached for more.

Kelly smiled, watching her friends as they all indulged in their post-game pizza party. She leaned back in her chair and sipped her Fat Tire ale from the bottle with the colorful label. At night, the brutal daytime heat was just a memory. Now, the air was balmy with a pleasant breeze. The moon was full and fat above Old Town Plaza. Summer at its best. Every café was packed, as other citizens were enjoying the summer night as much as they were.

Suddenly Megan ran up to them and gasped, as if she were out of breath. "A wildfire broke out in Colorado Springs! It's happening right now! There's a whole subdivision of homes that's starting to burn! My client just told me." She waved her smartphone.

Kelly and her friends stared dumbstruck at Megan for a second. Then, almost in unison, each one of them dug into their pockets or purses and pulled out their smartphones as they clicked on various icons and small screens until they all saw the oh-so-familiar photos of red-hot flames burning in the black night sky. Burning over hillsides, burning trees, and, sadly, burning houses.

FOURTEEN

Friday, June 22

"Hey, Burt, I was hoping to see you," Kelly called as she approached the café patio garden behind Lambspun. The late morning heat was building to unspeakable heights. It was only midmorning and the temperatures were in the high nineties. Forecasters predicted one hundred degrees today . . . at least. And it was still June. Colorado didn't usually experience those really high temps until July. But not this year. The Drought Year. All bets were off.

Kelly hastened to meet Burt, who was standing in the shade of the large cottonwood tree in the corner of the enclosed garden.

"Perfect timing, Kelly. I have a half hour before I teach a spinning class. Enough time for us to get out of this heat and relax."

"I bet you've been driving around doing errands all morning, right? Same here. I was out at the office supply store then picked up several other things. Even with the air-conditioned car and stores, I feel like I'm baking in the oven." She followed Burt along the flagstone path leading to the café's front entrance.

"I hear you. It's brutal. I've taken to wearing ball caps just to get some shade in between stops at stores."

"Gee, maybe I should wear my cap all the time. At my last checkup at the doctor, she warned me about sun exposure outside. You know, use sunscreen all the time. No excuses."

They both hurried up the steps and escaped into the air-conditioned café. Kelly let out a loud "Ahh."

Burt turned to her with a grin and doffed his cap. "Pay attention to your doc, Kelly. Otherwise, your face will wind up looking like mine." He chuckled. "Lots of wrinkles." He walked over to a small table near the entrance and beside the window.

"For the record, Burt, I like your face. But, point taken." She pulled out a chair across from him.

"Don't tell me. Iced coffee for both of you," Julie said, walking up to their table.

"You've got great instincts, girl," Kelly said with a grin. "Make mine extra large.

241

Light ice, more coffee."

Burt laughed louder. "You can make mine normal, Julie. Otherwise, I'll be pacing the floor tonight instead of sleeping."

"You got it." Julie was about to turn away, then she leaned over their table, her face concerned. "You know about that wildfire that broke out Wednesday night in Colorado Springs? The Waldo Canyon fire. It's gotten way worse than ours. Over three hundred forty-six homes have been destroyed already! Over thirty thousand people were evacuated in Colorado Springs!"

"Ohh, yeah. Steve and I were watching TV news way too late these last two nights. It's a really bad fire, and it's still blazing."

Julie's eyes went wide. "I know! And now I'm worried that most of our firefighters here will have to go there to help fight it. They've already sent a bunch."

"Well, our fire is getting under control —"

"What if our wildfire flares up again! It's done it before. Every time the winds start blowing."

"Don't worry, Julie. The fire authorities won't jeopardize the fire-fighting efforts here. Firefighters have been able to get a handle on this High Park wildfire at last. It's still burning, but those winds have died down here in northern Colorado. Now, the fire seems to be burning only in the western sections of Larimer County. Unpopulated forest areas. They'll keep on it until it burns itself out."

Julie made a face. "That means it'll burn some of our forests. I hate that. I hate losing trees."

"I do, too, Julie," Kelly agreed. "But remember, those forests were filled with beetle-killed trees. As hard as it is to accept, maybe this is Nature's way of clearing those dead trees out and letting new trees grow. At least people aren't in danger anymore. And animals have enough sense to run away from burning areas."

Julie brightened. "Ohhhh, did you read about that little donkey who led another donkey and three Percheron horses to safety away from the fire in Bellevue Canyon? They were found all clustered together around the donkey, all safe. Her name was Ellie."

Kelly smiled. "Yes, I did read that. See? The birds and animals, large and small, either flee or burrow deep into their holes belowground until the wildfire passes."

"Sometimes I think they're smarter than people," Burt opined with a wry smile.

"Let me get you guys that iced coffee," Julie said, then hastened off.

"I bet you've talked to some of the fire-fighting authorities, haven't you, Burt?"

He nodded. "Yeah, I try to touch base with them every couple of days. I've been making the rounds at the shelters and Salvation Army and Red Cross, helping any way I can. Running errands, whatever."

A stray memory wiggled from the back of Kelly's mind. "By the way, did you ever bump into Jim Carson again while you were assisting the helpers?"

"Yeah, I did. Just yesterday, as a matter of fact. And I learned the reason why I hadn't seen him. He's been working in the kitchens and serving at all of the shelters and doing anything that needs to be done. Our paths just never crossed before. I'm not much help in a kitchen, but Jim worked in restaurants before he became a sales rep."

"How's he doing? I mean . . . Andrea's death had to hit Jim hard."

"I asked him about that. Had to work around it, of course. And you could tell from the expression on his face, he was still broken up about it. I was going to try to see if I could find out why he wasn't there when Dennis discovered Andrea's body. Then, Jim just blurted out that he feels responsible somehow. Seems he and Andrea got into an argument. She was upset by Connie showing up and 'freaking out' as she put it. Blaming him. Anyway, Andrea was all upset and told him to leave. She needed some time to think."

That surprised Kelly. "What? She told him to *leave*?"

"Yeah, I told him that didn't sound like Andrea, then Jim admitted that the argument was about more than Connie's explosions and accusations. Jim said he'd seen Andrea kissing Dennis outside near the barn. Dennis was getting ready to go back to his ranch. Naturally, that upset Jim and he accused Andrea of lying to him. So, it sounds like they both kind of blew up at each other." Burt shrugged. "Jim said he stormed off. Just walked away from the ranch and down the road into Poudre Park. He said he hitched a ride from there into Landport."

Kelly leaned back into her chair, staring at Burt, still surprised by what she'd heard. "Good Lord, Burt. That is just bizarre."

"Yeah, I know. Jim said he stayed at the disaster shelter that night because he had no car. It was still parked at his home, because Andrea picked him up that Saturday. Of course that was when everybody was evacuated from Bellevue Canyon and people were all over, sleeping on cots and on the floor. Jim slept on the floor, too, and started helping out however he could right away."

"When did he hear about Andrea?"

Burt nodded. "He got visibly upset when I asked. His face got red and I could see tears in his eyes. Said he read about it in the paper and discovered the actual identity the next day. And in his words, he said he broke down. Jim blames himself for Andrea's fall. He's convinced if he was there, Andrea wouldn't have fallen. He was almost crying when he told me."

"Here you go," Julie announced as she walked up. "Two iced coffees. Now you both will be all set." She placed the coffees on the table and hurried off again.

"Have you talked to Dan at the department about this conversation? You said the other day that Officer Warren had talked to Jim Carson first. Do you think he told her all this?"

"I'm betting he did. He sounds like he's getting it off his chest. So, that's probably why Officer Warren knew so much about what happened last Saturday. She started off with Jim Carson, and he told her *everything.*"

"Oh, boy . . . drama, trauma, and melodrama. The good, the bad, and the ugly."

"Oh, yes." Burt nodded in emphasis. "Jim

said he'd also gotten a visit yesterday from the Fort Connor police detective investigating Andrea's death. And from some of the questions Jim told me the detective asked, it sounded like it was Dan doing preliminary investigation."

"Okay, well then, we'll know Andrea's death is being thoroughly examined. Dan's a smart, good guy. I trust him."

Burt smiled. "So do I. I trusted him with my life while he and I were partners. You can't say that about everyone you work with."

"I guess Dan will question Connie now, especially after she's admitted confronting Andrea a third time that Saturday."

"I'm sure he will." Burt's frown reappeared. "And I know Dan well enough after working with him for several years to know that he's probably put Connie at the top of his suspect list already."

"I hate to say it, Burt, but I agree with you. After these few years watching how Dan and other detectives approach an investigation, I'd be willing to bet on it." Kelly gave a wry smile.

Burt met her gaze. "I'm not a betting man, but I would definitely join you in that bet, Kelly."

Kelly chopped up ingredients for a large lunch salad while she glanced up every few minutes to watch the evening news on the small television on her cottage kitchen counter. She needed a break from juicy fattening burgers, delicious as they were.

The TV images of the Waldo Canyon wildfire in Colorado Springs were vivid and mesmerizing . . . and they brought back the awful images of the first days after their own High Park wildfire broke out. Plumes of dark smoke spiraled into the sky. Dark smoke meant the greedy wildfire was consuming trees and buildings. More plumes of white smoke were spiraling upwards as well, new fires breaking out. Kelly felt her heart squeeze, remembering.

As fast as the High Park wildfire had spread, Kelly could tell by the national fire commandant's nightly updates that Waldo Canyon was spreading even faster. And this wildfire had struck a more populated area, where many more houses were built in that forested area near Colorado Springs. There was horrific television footage of flames engulfing whole houses, devouring them, blazing high into the sky, consuming them in one fiery gulp. Not simply small areas of homes were being consumed, but whole sections of subdivisions fell prey to the greedy flames.

Kelly looked away from the devastating scenes on television and finished her salad. She tossed in some chicken she'd used for a lunch salad the other day to join the fresh spinach and tomatoes and olive oil. She was about to dive in when her cell phone rang. Lisa's name flashed on the screen.

"Hey, there, what's up?" she asked her friend.

"I'm watching that awful Waldo Canyon wildfire on TV. Good Lord! It's much worse than our wildfire. It's covered even more acres in one day than the High Park fire has in almost two weeks."

Kelly popped a cherry tomato into her mouth and savored it. "Well, Waldo Canyon is a more populated area and doesn't have the same hills and ridges that Bellevue Canyon or Poudre Canyon have. We're lucky for that. I wouldn't want to think what would have happened if our fire had devoured so much so soon."

"You're right about that. Are you at home?"

"No, I'm at the cottage taking a lunch break. Then I'm going to clear out old files and do some shredding this afternoon. Steve's working late and probably won't be home until nine."

"Better be at the field by eight o'clock so we can warm up."

"Thank goodness the games are starting later. I'll be glued to the television watching wildfire news until then, even though I'll be afraid to see Waldo Canyon updates on the news tonight."

"Yeah, I know. Did you hear that the national fire commandant said the Waldo Canyon fire is the number one wildfire in the entire country right now?"

"Really? Well, that's not surprising. I guess we'll lose even more of our High Park fire-fighters now."

"I heard that our fire has moved to the northwestern section of the canyons."

"I know. No people, but lots of forests. Several are pine bark beetle–killed, too."

"That's gonna make a heckuva bonfire."

"Oh, yeah," Kelly agreed, then popped another cherry tomato into her mouth as she continued to watch the mesmerizing images on the TV screen.

Kelly squinted against the setting summer sun as it kissed the tops of the foothills. Thank goodness the softball game times had been switched to later evening, otherwise they would all be forced to wear sunglasses while playing. Kelly didn't think she could throw straight, let alone bat, while wearing sunglasses. She wasn't used to having something on her face.

The Greeley team's batter swung at Lisa's sinking fastball. The bat whipped through the air with a swish as it missed the ball.

"Strike!" called the umpire, who was kneeling down behind home plate.

Cheers sounded from the Fort Connor team's section of the bleachers beside the ballfield at Rolland Moore Park. It was one of several parks that contained softball and baseball fields as well as a soccer field and basketball hoops. The popular city park was a mecca for all the city sports teams as well as offering walking trails that connected to the Fort Connor trail system. Three distinctively different walking and biking trails wound through the city and its edges. The river trail followed the Cache La Poudre River as it flowed diagonally through Fort Connor from northwest in Landport, tracing the river all the way until it left the city's southeastern edge. The Spring Creek trail ran westerly from its start in the foothills that edged the western side of Fort Connor all through the central part of the city until it joined the Fossil Creek trail in the far southeastern edge of the city. The Foothills trail started at the foot of the foothills surrounding the large Horsetooth reservoir and traveled along those higher ridges.

"Hey . . . batter, batter, batter, batter, *batter!*" rang out the familiar cry from the Greeley team's side of the bleachers.

Kelly watched the Greeley team's best batter stroll up to the plate. She paused, swung the bat a couple of times in practice swings, then stepped behind the plate and into the familiar crouch. Kelly's muscles automatically responded by going into her familiar first baseman's crouch, bent over, watching the batter. Catcher Peggy threw the ball to Lisa on the pitcher's mound, and Lisa eyed the batter. She'd played her before. Many times.

Oh, boy, Kelly thought. This was the Greeley team's best player. She could hit it outside the fence exactly like Kelly could. And she was a double threat. Not only could she hit long, but she could also run fast. Faster than most players. Faster than Kelly, even. She could hit a double easily, without breaking a sweat. If so, they'd have two players on base.

Kelly glanced toward second base where an earlier hitter had gained second when her hit to left field took a bad bounce as the fielder ran to retrieve it. If this batter hit a double, then that runner could easily gain third, if not try for home. That would mean her Fort Connor team could fall behind. They were ahead by one point, that's all. If another batter hit one into far right field, then the third-base runner would fly home. And the fast-footed batter could make a dash for home right on her heels. Kelly had seen this girl easily gain two bases on a play.

Lisa's first pitch to the batter fell outside. *Ball one. That's not good, either,* Kelly worried. It didn't matter how this girl got on base. Once she was there, she was a bigger threat due to her speed.

Lisa's second pitch was right in the zone, and Big Batter swung hard — and missed. *Whew!* Kelly glanced over her shoulder at her teammates who were also crouched and ready for whatever came. Lisa threw again, this ball moving faster and right in the zone. Big Batter swung and that sweet sound of bat hitting ball rang out. *Crack!*

Kelly watched as the ball sailed up, up, and far into right field. An easy double for fast-footed Big Batter.

"Nice hit," Kelly congratulated her as she rounded first base. Big Batter smiled and saluted while she jogged toward second base. Megan, as fast as she was, had just reached the ball. Her strong arm heaved the ball to the center field player, who threw it to second . . . two seconds after Big Batter arrived.

The Greeley team's fans loudly cheered the double and the tying run from the stands. Kelly watched the Greeley team congratulate their teammate after she'd crossed home plate.

The second baseman called out, "We're tied. Stay sharp!"

Kelly watched another batter take a couple of practice swings, then take position behind home plate. This batter was an average hitter. She'd hit a single one time, then struck out the next. Not as much power as Big Batter.

Lisa's pitch was high. *Ball one!* The next pitch was a little low, but the batter swung anyway. *Strike!*

Okay . . . one ball and one strike, Kelly thought, gently swaying side to side in her first baseman's motion, keeping her muscles loose and ready. The next pitch was high again. Ball two. The following pitch was wide. Ball three.

C'mon, Lisa, tighten up, Kelly silently counseled her friend. The next pitch was just in the zone on the edge. The batter swung and missed. *Strike two.*

Oh, boy . . . Kelly thought. Crunch time.

Lisa wound up and delivered, the pitch flying smack dab into the zone. The batter swung . . . and this time, she hit it. *Well, I'll be damned,* Kelly thought, watching the ball fly out then head downward and bounce in deep center field.

Kelly watched the center fielder race up and snatch the ball. Glancing to the side, Kelly saw the batter running as hard as she could toward first base . . . almost there.

"Here!" she yelled to the center fielder who was already aiming toward her base.

The ball sailed fast and Kelly reached high to snag it, just in time as the batter stepped out to touch first base.

"Got it!" Kelly yelled, ball firmly in her glove and her left foot solidly on base.

"You're out!" the base umpire called, pointing toward home plate.

Kelly quickly glanced toward third base and spotted Big Batter hastening back to third base for safety.

"Whoo hoo!" Megan yelled from right field. "Way to go, Kelly!"

Cheers from their side of the bleachers rang out, and Kelly looked over and spotted Jennifer and Pete and Cassie waving their arms at her and cheering. She threw the ball to Lisa, then grinned and waved back at them. She thought she noticed Burt and Mimi but she wasn't sure it was them, so she waved that way in case.

The sun winked its last bright glare over the mountain tops, then slid quietly behind. Shade, at last. The temperature would start to drop now and the evening mountain breezes would pick up. By nighttime it would feel cooler with no remnant of the day's heat. Except maybe the sunburned faces of tourists who didn't think they needed to wear sunscreen in the mountains. They only made that mistake once, usually.

The next batter that came up for Greeley was an easy out. She couldn't resist swinging at pitches whenever they were in her vicinity. Unfortunately, she usually struck out . . . as she did right now.

"Three outs!" yelled Coach Megan from right field as she jogged forward.

"That was close," Kelly said to the center fielder as they walked toward home plate.

"You got that right," the center fielder said, pointing to Big Batter. "She's always dangerous."

"Oh, yeah. She must have run sprints in college or something," Kelly joked.

"Hey, nice catch," Big Batter called over to Kelly as she retrieved her fielders glove and headed that way.

Kelly smiled and waved to her as she called out, "Thanks!" Now, if only she could hit a nice long drive into left field, maybe she could help her team break this tie. That would be really sweet.

FIFTEEN

Kelly watched the television in her cottage, saw the flames leap from treetop to treetop. Such a frightening sight. The hot dry wind whipped up and caused the wildfire to roar back to life from the smoldering hot spots north of Poudre Canyon and wiped out a week's worth of effort in that area. Glacier View residents to the north were completely evacuated, all the way to the small town of Red Feather Lakes. Kelly saw those red orange smoke plumes rising behind the mountains as she drove home from the game last night. Scary. And they all thought that the firefighters had turned a corner in the High Park fire. Julie's concern about the wildfire flaring up again was justified. Burt was convinced the winds had died down in northern Colorado. Unfortunately, they hadn't. Those wicked hot winds had a mind of their own. Wildfires created their own weather systems with the hot dry air and flames.

Carl's bark outside in the backyard brought her attention back, and Kelly checked her watch. She didn't have that much accounting work on her plate today, so maybe this was a good time to make some progress on that sweater. Plus, she wanted something to take her attention away from those horrible scenes of wildfires destroying entire subdivisions of homes and burning forests, whether it was in Colorado Springs or Fort Connor.

Kelly went onto the patio and refilled Carl's new water dish from the outside faucet. Carl came racing over to check if any food was involved in the procedure. Discovering that there wasn't, he galloped back to the fence, where he'd been keeping watch over a woman who was walking her dog along the edge of the golf course. Carl woofed a warning, just in case the pair might decide to venture into his territory.

As far as Carl was concerned, all the shade from the huge cottonwood tree belonged to him. He allowed the squirrels to share it because they provided entertainment value. And sport. But strangers walking small animals needed Big Dog's permission to intrude into Carl Territory. *Noblesse oblige.*

Carl ran back to the patio and slurped from his new water dish. Kelly gave him a quick head rub before Carl galumphed off to the fence again. "Super-size water dish, Carl. Enjoy," she called to him as she went back inside.

Grabbing her newly filled coffee mug and briefcase bag, Kelly headed out of her cottage. She hurried across the driveway, eager to escape the high-nineties-degree heat. How could it have built that high in mid-morning? Yesterday was ninety-nine degrees. Tomorrow would reach one hundred degrees or more. This was not typical Colorado weather. Once again, she blamed La Niña. La Bruja would be more like it, she thought, using the Spanish word for "witch." Kelly was thankful there were no softball or baseball games tonight. She and her friends would gather in air-conditioned surroundings.

Stepping into the foyer of Lambspun, Kelly felt the welcome cooler air brush against her skin. She spotted Cassie in the central yarn room, filling yarn bins. "Ahh, it feels so good in here. I was just out in the backyard with Carl, and it's in the high nineties already."

"I know, it's crazy," Cassie said, stuffing the last ball of yarn on the table into a bin.

"I'm glad we had softball clincic yesterday."

Kelly walked into the main room and set down her mug and bag. "You know, I wonder if I should call all the kids' parents and see if they want to move the clinic earlier in the morning or something."

Cassie followed her into the room. "Naw, I wouldn't try it," she said, wrinkling her nose. "It sounds like everybody's schedules are pretty full. I thought I had a full schedule, you know, like going to softball with you and tennis with Megan and university lab with Greg and therapy clinic with Lisa. But some of the girls have even more going on. It's crazy."

Kelly had to smile. Cassie and her friends were already confronted with scheduling problems. "I don't know whether to feel good about that or not," she said. "Some people say kids your age are over-scheduled with no free time. Others say it's good training for real life. I can see both sides."

Cassie's eyes went wide. "Oh, no, I *love* doing all those different things! I never had a chance to do all this back in Denver. Like yesterday, I was at the computer lab with Greg and the Geeks, and they were showing me how a motherboard works. You know, inside the computer. They showed me how everything is put together and which part does what. It was fun. They even let me take some stuff apart and put it back together. That's so cool."

Kelly settled at the table and pulled the evacuee sweater from her bag. "I've seen Greg's computer lab, and it is definitely filled with tons of stuff. So if you like messing with computers you'll find plenty there." Kelly picked up her bright green stitches where she'd left off. She was one row away from binding off the sweater bottom.

"Oh, yeah. I love going over there. Greg says the Geeks save up stuff for me to play around with. Plus, there's always some new software stuff to look at."

Suddenly Mimi stepped inside the main room and waved at Kelly. "Kelly, if you have a minute, can I ask you a question? We can go up front."

Curious at Mimi's suggestion, Kelly dropped her knitting onto the table. No wonder it took her so long to complete a project. So many interruptions. "Sure, Mimi," she said, joining her friend in the central yarn room.

"Oh, Cassie, I saw Carl looking over here, big paws on the fence," Mimi said. "He looks lonely. Why don't you go give him a pat?"

"Sure. Can I go into the yard and play

with him, Kelly?" Cassie asked as she headed toward the foyer, clearly eager to take Mimi's suggestion.

"Absolutely, Cassie. Carl loves to play with kids. They're way more fun than adults."

Cassie laughed that little laugh as she pushed open the front door. Kelly turned to Mimi and noticed a worried expression she hadn't seen before.

"Okay, Mimi, what's up? You've never needed me to come up front to ask a question."

Mimi's concern deepened. "You're right. Dan, Burt's former partner, showed up a few minutes ago to question Connie. They're outside at one of those far tables, away from the other customers."

"Oh, boy. I guess this investigation has moved into the official phase now. Officer Warren was pretty darn thorough, so I'm sure the detectives are using all her notes. She was always scribbling in that little notebook of hers. She reminded me a lot of Detective Morrison."

"What I'm afraid is Dan came because Connie told Officer Warren she went back to Andrea's ranch after she left you folks. That would have made a third visit to see Andrea. And considering everything you and the others have told me about that Saturday, and all those arguments, well . . . I can't help but worry about that third visit."

"You're not alone, Mimi. I've worried about that, too. Apparently, no one else was there to witness what went on at that third visit. Burt said that Jim told him he left Andrea's ranch and wasn't aware that Connie had returned. And it sounds like Dennis was already gone as well. That's what worries me. No one else was there." Mimi's worried expression deepened.

"What has Connie told you about that third visit? You're the only one she talks to. She barely speaks to me. I'm sure it's because I was there to witness the first two blowouts."

"She hasn't told me a thing about that last visit, Kelly," Mimi said anxiously. "That's another reason I'm so worried. I've tried talking to her about it twice, and each time she just looks away and says she doesn't want to talk about it. Well, you can imagine how that makes me feel. When I told Burt what she said, he got that worried expression of his. He told me it makes Connie look like she's hiding something." Mimi started chewing the side of her lip.

"I hate to say it, Mimi, but I agree with Burt. It does make Connie look guilty.

Heck, she looks guilty whenever I even mention that Saturday. Even if I'm saying we're all her friends and we all care about her. She still ducks her head and her face kind of screws up like she might cry, and she doesn't even answer most times."

Mimi wagged her head, another sure sign of worry. "You have to wonder what else would cause that guilty-acting behavior. And as much as I hate to even think it, I have to consider the possibility that she pushed Andrea or something. If she did, it had to be in a moment of anger. Connie has a hot temper. Burt and I have seen it flare up for years. Especially if Jim paid attention to another woman."

"Did he do that a lot?" Kelly asked, curious.

"Not when they were first married about fifteen years ago, but if truth be told, Jim did develop a wandering eye. Particularly these last few years. He's tall, dark, and handsome, and Connie was very jealous and possessive of him. Unfortunately, she's also got quite a temper. I've known Connie for a long time. She was one of my first employees when I had a little shop over in Old Town."

Just then, Burt beckoned to them from the loom room. "C'mon out to the café. I have a feeling that interview is winding up, and I think Mimi and I should go outside and talk with Connie after Detective Dan leaves."

"Good idea, Burt," Kelly said, ushering Mimi in front of her as they all three headed toward the hallway and into Pete's café. Burt beckoned them toward an empty table beside the large windows.

"See, Dan is standing up now. So I think this is a good time to talk with Connie. In case there's anything she wants to get off her chest."

Mimi took in her breath and drew back, hand to her breast. "Oh, my! Burt . . . do you really think she pushed Andrea?"

Burt wagged his head in that way Kelly recognized as his resignation to something he didn't like. "I wish I didn't Mimi. I don't know if she did or didn't. But I think we should offer Connie a chance to tell the truth about what happened in that third visit."

Kelly looked through the window, watching Connie's face. It was red as if she'd been crying. "Oh, brother. It looks like she's been crying. I don't know if that's a good sign or not.

"It all depends on what Connie has done and what she told Dan," Burt said solemnly.

Mimi didn't say anything, simply patted her hand against her chest and stared anxiously out the window as they all watched the end of Connie's police interview with Detective Dan.

"Hey, Jayleen," Kelly said into her cell phone as she stepped inside her cottage. "The fire authorities said they've got the Bellevue Canyon fire put out at last. Is that true?"

"Yes, Kelly-girl, firefighters have beaten down all the hot spots there, so, finally, we have no large outbreaks in our canyon. At last. Wildfire is only burning to the northwest in those remote forested areas."

Kelly felt a wave of relief wash over her as she dropped her briefcase bag on her desk chair in the corner. She sank into the comfy cushioned armchair, kicked off her shoes, and stretched out her legs to relax. "Oh, thank goodness. Steve and I have been watching the fire authority meetings on television every night. Thanks to all those firefighters, we made a lot of progress . . . until yesterday." She sighed loudly. "It shocked me to hear how fast that Glacier View fire moved. With the national commandant now moved to Colorado Springs, there's a whole different bunch of fire guys talking on TV. So I wanted to make sure I got the straight word from you."

"Well, Curt and I have been going out and talking to people every day, trying to get the straight word, as you call it. Some of them get to talk to the firefighters themselves when they're delivering supplies. One guy said he heard a fireman say the wildfire rolled over that upper ridge of Glacier View like a huge ball of flames. It ate up that newest development of houses in one fiery gulp."

Kelly pictured some of those homes and their pretty views and closed her eyes at the image of flames consuming that entire area.

"Curt covers Landport, and I go into Loveland and Fort Connor and over to the Ranch where the other evacuee shelter is."

"What else have you heard?"

"Well, containment dropped back to 45 percent because of that Glacier View outbreak. They expect hot, windy conditions to continue for a while, so priorities are containing hot spots and the unburned areas within the fire's interior."

Kelly sipped iced coffee from her mug, trying to cool off. In the late afternoon, the cottage was hot, even though the ceiling fans were moving, stirring the hot air. She wouldn't have braved being here now if she didn't have to go through some of her file folders in the desk drawers. "Well, that makes sense." A clanging bell sounded from Jayleen's end.

"Hold on, Kelly. A text just came in from Curt."

Kelly laughed. "That's the loudest text alert I've ever heard."

"That's so I'll hear it." Jayleen paused. "A wildfire broke out in Estes Park."

"Oh, no! Is it around the town, or did it go into Rocky Mountain National Park?"

"No, it's small and on the other side of town. They've jumped on it right away, so they should be able to contain it."

"Have fire authorities told you when you folks can return to Bellevue Canyon?"

"No, not yet. We're expecting to hear something this evening. Maybe."

"Okay, I'll keep my fingers crossed, Jayleen, that you guys can return to the canyon soon. And that your place is not on the fire authorities' list."

"We've been keeping track of everything we hear about. Burt has a big map of Bellevue Canyon, and we're putting black marks on places we hear rumored to have been lost. Keeping track. So far, there's no black mark right on my ranch, but there're others pretty close. We heard one rumor that there may be damage to the property but the ranch house is still standing. I can live with property damage. I'm praying those rumors are right."

"Well, I need some good news. So I'm going to take Curt's advice and picture your ranch house still standing."

Jayleen laughed softly. "Bless your heart, Kelly."

A thought darted into Kelly's mind. "By the way, you said you've been going over to the Ranch evacuee shelter. Have you seen Jim Carson? He told Burt he was helping out over there in the Salvation Army kitchens at the Ranch. Serving food, I think."

"No, I haven't bumped into Jim yet, but Curt has. Over at the Red Cross shelter. He looked like he was helping over there, too. He must have taken vacation or something to be working so much. Curt didn't get to talk to him at all because they were so busy, so he just waved. Seems he's grown a beard."

"That's what Burt said. He finally got a chance to talk with Jim the other day for a few minutes. And Jim told Burt that he and Andrea had an argument that Saturday after we all left. Dennis had left, too."

"You know, I saw Burt over at the Ranch yesterday, and he told me all about it. Sakes alive. I figure those two just weren't thinking straight after all that wildfire chaos. What with Connie coming up and acting like a jackass at my place and driving up to Andrea's to carry on again. *Lord a-mighty!* Then for Andrea and Jim to go have a blowup . . . and Jim goes storming off. Can you believe that?"

"I agree, Jayleen. It had to be all that wildfire chaos and confusion. Nobody who had a place in either of those canyons could think straight. Everyone was just trying to save themselves and their animals."

"I'm sure that's why Andrea fell down those steps. Poor girl. She was probably trying to carry things outside or for the animals. Who knows? But I'll bet my bottom dollar she was moving too fast and tripped."

"And it must have been dusk by then, so twilight makes things look different. Harder to see sometimes."

"How's Connie doing? Burt told me she's still not acting normal. Still not talking much. Which is certainly not like Connie."

"She's still the same, and maybe getting worse. She's refused to talk to Mimi about her third visit alone with Andrea up in the canyon. And today, the detective came to question her. And I tell you, Jayleen, Connie did *not* look good afterward. Her face was red, like she'd been crying. But she still refuses to talk to any of us, not even Mimi. Burt hates to admit it, but it seems like she's hiding something. And that makes us all feel terrible. Like she really did push Andrea or something. No one will ever know unless she talks."

"Lord have mercy," Jayleen said, shaking her head sadly. She said nothing else.

Kelly didn't either. She had nothing left to say. Connie's behavior spoke loudly.

Sixteen

Monday, June 25

Kelly tabbed through the columns of one of the files on Arthur Housemann's commercial rental properties, entering revenues received and expenses incurred that month. Comfortably settled in her favorite spot in Pete's café beside a large window looking out at the gardens and toward the mountains, it was easy to zone out all the café noise around her — even the sound of her name being called. Suddenly, she looked up from the laptop screen.

"Hey, Kelly," Burt said as he walked over to her table.

"Hi, Burt. I didn't hear you at first. Zoned out with the accounts. Numbers can do that to you."

"Well, I'm glad you enjoy it. Numbers can scare me sometimes when I'm doing accounts." He glanced over his shoulder. "Do you have a minute? I wanted to share a conversation with you, but we need more privacy. This morning the temps aren't as high as they have been, so it's actually not bad outside in the shade. Why don't we go find a table?"

"Sure, Burt. I'm on top of these accounts, so no problem." Kelly saved and closed out the spreadsheet, and shut down her laptop. "Save my spot, Julie. I'll be right back," she called over her shoulder as she followed Burt toward the café's front door.

"See, it's not bad," he said as they went down the steps into the gardens. "And my favorite shady table is still free."

He headed to a round table beneath the oldest and tallest cottonwood tree in the garden. Its branches shaded most of the patio tables and diners. Situated inside but beside the beige stucco wall that surrounded half of the garden area, Kelly often remembered that old cottonwood shading Aunt Helen, Uncle Jim, her father, and her during hot summers when they would get together for a supper outside. Kelly's childhood memories would pop up occasionally with a scene.

"This is one of my favorite spots, too," Kelly said as she settled into a chair across the table from him "I'm curious, Burt. Yesterday you said Connie didn't want to talk at all after the detective's visit. So I'm guessing you had a conversation with your old partner Dan at the department."

Burt smiled. "Right, you are, Sherlock. I left Dan a message yesterday after I'd tried to talk with Connie and she went mute like usual. I wanted to find out what Dan thought after his interview with her Saturday. Dan called this morning and said that Connie has definitely raised some suspicions in the department because of those angry episodes with Andrea earlier that Saturday, which all of the witnesses said were very threatening."

Kelly sighed. "I was afraid of that, Burt. And I know you were, too. Plus, Connie confronted Andrea a third time."

"Exactly. And after that, Dennis Holt found Andrea dead. It definitely raised their suspicions."

"Did Dan reveal what Connie told him about that third visit?"

Burt was about to answer when Jennifer walked up with two mugs of coffee. "It looked positively weird to see you two sitting and talking without coffee in hand. I figured I'd remedy the situation or the Earth would shift alignment or something." She set the glasses in front of them.

"You're clairvoyant, Jen," Kelly said, grinning up at her friend. "But I didn't feel the Earth move, so I think we're safe."

"Before I forget, Jennifer, ask Cassie if she'd like to join Mimi, my daughter and grandkids, and me this Sunday. We're going to help sort clothing donations for the evacuees and wondered if she'd like to help."

"Oh, that's good of you guys," Jennifer said. "I'll ask her. I know that this Saturday, Curt and Jayleen asked if she'd like to join up with his family's troops and help out some of the folks in the Buckhorn area who had burned land. They're going to cut back burned bushes and start cleanup."

"Oh, those are both great ideas. If they need any more help, I'll check with the gang and see who can help out with both these projects," Kelly said.

"Okay, I'll talk with you two later," Jennifer said, returning to her other customers.

"As I was about to say, Dan asked Connie about her last visit to Andrea. Connie told him she returned because she'd calmed down and she wanted to tell Andrea that she loved her husband and ask her to please break it off with Jim. Apparently Andrea listened to her then told her to leave. She'd had enough trauma for one day."

Kelly leaned forward, engrossed. A calm Connie begging Andrea to leave her husband alone? She had a problem picturing that. "That's a surprise. What did Connie do? Did she get angry? Did she leave?"

Burt shrugged halfway, which Kelly recognized as one of his skeptical gestures. "Apparently, she did. Connie told Dan that she could tell Andrea wasn't going to talk with her. So she asked Andrea to please tell Jim that she loved him. Since she didn't see him around, she figured he'd gone. Then she said she left."

Kelly pondered that, trying to picture it. "Wow. I hate to admit it, but that doesn't sound like Connie. Calmly, peacefully backing away and leaving. Tail between her legs."

"I hear you," Burt agreed. "So, naturally, I asked Dan if he believed her or not. He admitted he wasn't sure. Connie could be telling the truth. The medical examiner said he'd been able to determine that Andrea broke her neck in the fall. The ground was very rocky. So, her death was consistent with a fall under those circumstances. Most people would either die or would be severely wounded from a fall like that."

Kelly felt a little shiver inside. An accident like that could happen to anyone. Hurrying down steps, carrying something, perhaps. Too easy to trip.

"Dan mentioned that the medical examiner also said she landed on her back. He could tell from the injuries and tissue damage, indicating she fell backwards. He added that often when people trip and fall from steep steps they fall forward and hit the ground face down." Burt stared off into the garden.

Kelly peered at Burt. "There's something about that medical examiner's statement that bothers you, I can tell."

Burt caught her gaze and smiled. "You know me too well, Kelly. Yes, something does bother me because it bothers Dan. He said there was nothing else on the ground around Andrea's body. No boxes, no packages, no items of any kind. Dan said he found that curious. Usually, if someone trips on steps like that, it's because they're carrying something in their hands and they're not as careful. But Andrea clearly wasn't carrying anything or it would have been on the ground, too. Plus, Andrea had lived there for years. She rode horses and herded alpacas, so she was not a clumsy person. Dan said it made him curious. And anything that makes Dan curious makes *me* curious."

"You know, Burt, I don't have a very good feeling. It sounds like Detective Dan may be looking at this death in a new light. And, he may have moved Connie into another category. What do they call that . . . a person of interest?"

"Well, they use that term when there's definitely been a murder or crime committed. That's not the case here. Police still consider this an accidental death. But, I agree. Connie has gotten herself on their radar screen. And with the police, that's never good."

"Now that you've spoken with Dan, I'm curious. Did you ask about Jim Carson? What did Dan say about Jim's story of arguing with Andrea?"

"You know, I did ask him about that, and he didn't say much. Jim's story totally matched Officer Warren's notes. Sounded like they had a fight and Jim Carson stormed off. Left Andrea's ranch and didn't come back. He hitched a ride into Landport. Of course, he didn't get the guy's name."

"So, you can't tell what Dan thinks of Jim's story?"

Burt cocked his head to the side. "It sounds like Dan's inclined to believe him. He thought it made sense. Jim sees his girlfriend kissing her ex-husband. Most guys would get mad. Plus with that wildfire going on and everybody tense, it's no wonder things blew up. Happens easily, especially between men and women. I've seen enough over the years to testify to that. Plus, Jim's been really open and honest and forthcoming with both these interviews. He's even admitted he felt guilty about not being there with Andrea. He thinks their argument is the reason she fell."

"Yeah, I imagine he does. I wonder if that's part of Connie's guilt? Knowing that she upset Andrea with all of those explosive visits."

Burt gave a rueful smile. "The other possibility is that Connie really does have something to feel guilty about. That's the big question."

"I wonder if Connie has an attorney. It looks like she will surely need one," Kelly said sadly.

"Don't worry. Mimi and I will make sure she's got a good lawyer, if it comes to that." Burt took a sip of coffee. "Dan did say they're taking another look at Dennis Holt. A harder look. Apparently some information has come to light. He didn't give any details."

Kelly leaned forward over her coffee cup. "Oh, brother. I bet police are mad because Dennis has been staying up at Andrea's ranch in Poudre Canyon against police orders to evacuate."

Burt peered at her. "How did you know that, Kelly?"

She grimaced. "Jayleen told me but swore me to secrecy. She said Dennis made it look like he left, then he stayed to take care of the animals. Feed them, chase away mountain lions and stuff. He said he'd lay low during the day and moved around at dusk and at dark. He even slept with them in the barn. He walked into town at night in order to meet up with him."

"Did Jayleen tell you all this?"

"Most of it. But I was also with her at a diner in town and had lunch with Dennis. I wanted to meet him. My first encounter with Dennis had been up in Poudre Canyon when I spotted him lurking in the bushes beside the cabin Jen had listed for sale. He was eavesdropping on Jennifer and me. We'd just discovered Fred Turner's body. Dennis was a neighbor."

Burt nodded with a little smile. "And you never mentioned that."

Kelly shrugged good naturedly. "Hey, I wasn't about to squeal on a good guy like Dennis who's making sure all those alpacas were all right. He wasn't doing anything illegal, actually. Besides, he admitted that he'd told Officer Warren when she interviewed him."

"True, he can refuse to evacuate, but it's not a good decision. What if all those Bellevue Canyon residents decided to stay behind in their homes? Some of those homes went on to burn."

"I know, I know." Kelly held up her hand. "But still, my sympathies are with Dennis. Besides, Jayleen said most of those local firefighters and the sheriff know Dennis. They probably knew he was up there all the time. But they cut him some slack because he was doing a good deed."

"Well, now the cops all know what Dennis has been doing. Apparently good Officer Warren suspected something and put that in her notes. So Dan drove up into the canyon on official business and found Dennis at Andrea's ranch."

"I was wondering when they'd have that second interview with Dennis. I hadn't heard anything from Jayleen."

"I think they kept it quiet. They knew Dennis has a lot of friends on the force."

"They're not going to charge him with anything, are they?" Kelly didn't bother to hide her displeasure.

"No, they won't. But it wasn't a good beginning for the interview. Dan had several questions about Dennis Holt's financial situation. Some new information had come to their attention, Dan said."

Uh-oh. That didn't sound good for Dennis, Kelly worried. "Has Dennis done something wrong? Cheated on his taxes or something?"

Burt chuckled. "I don't know, Kelly. Dan didn't go into detail. Apparently he's just starting that harder look at Dennis."

"That doesn't sound good, Burt."

"Well, it all depends, Kelly, on what turns up. If Dennis has got something to hide, I'm sure Dan will find it. If not, then Dennis has nothing to worry about."

Kelly didn't reply. But her experience in the financial world had taught her that when it came to money, lots of people made mistakes. Good people and not-so-good people could succumb to cheating. Or lying. But like most mistakes in life, sooner or later they would come to light.

Kelly walked back into the knitting shop just as Jayleen stepped into the foyer. "Hey, Jayleen! Good to see you." She hurried over to her friend and gave her a one-armed hug, since she was holding her coffee mug in the other.

"Hey, Kelly-girl. I was hoping I'd find you here." Jayleen gave her a squeeze.

Kelly noticed even Cowgirl Jayleen had given in to the awful summer heat and abandoned her normal cotton or denim shirts with rolled up sleeves. While she still wore her trademark jeans, Jayleen had switched to a short-sleeved cotton tee shirt, like Kelly and her friends. Of course, they usually opted for sleeveless.

"Errands bring you into town?"

"Sure thing. That plus some business here with Mimi. She mailed an invoice showing I was due payment for some of my bags of fleece I'd put on consignment here. Then I figured I'd pick up some more groceries and swing by the hardware store and get some supplies. Curt's been helping neighbors repair fences where they had to cut through so firefighters could get to some of those fires close to the western edges of their ranches."

"Boy, I'll have to drive out and say hi to Curt. He's not even driving into town, he's so busy."

"You've got that right." Jayleen nodded. "The only place Curt has gone has been into Landport every day to talk to people who supply the fire crews. Of course, we both have to drag ourselves over to the Ranch for those landowner briefings. Lord, have mercy! They still haven't told us yet which properties were damaged. All of us are getting restless. We've been hauling ourselves over there for briefings that don't give us any real information. They've finally got the fire under control in the canyon. The only places where it's burning now are west of us in the forested lands with no people."

"Would you step outside for a couple minutes, Jayleen? I wanted to ask you a question." Kelly pushed open the shop front door.

"Sure, Kelly. What's up?" she said as she followed Kelly onto the Lambspun shaded front porch outside.

"It's about Dennis Holt. Burt talked to his old partner Dan at the department and Dan's investigating Andrea's death. Burt and all of us were concerned because Connie is still not acting like herself and it seems like she's hiding something. Then we learned she made a third trip to see Andrea, and of course, now we're all worrying about what happened."

"Did Dan tell Burt anything? Did Connie admit to something?" Jayleen peered at her.

Kelly shook her head. "All Connie said was she went up to talk to Andrea once she'd calmed down. She asked Andrea to break off her relationship with Jim because Connie said she loved him."

"Oh, Lord . . ." Jayleen rolled her eyes.

"What'd Andrea do? What did Connie say?"

"According to her, Andrea told Connie to leave and refused to talk with her. Connie told the detective she did just that. Which, of course, the rest of us find hard to believe. Hot-tempered Connie turning tail and leaving, not standing for another fight? I don't know."

"Ah, who knows, Kelly? People do the strangest things when they're in love with someone. I can testify to that."

"You sound like Burt." Kelly smiled.

"The voices of experience. Believe us."

"Burt also said that the department is taking a harder look at Dennis. That's the word Burt used. Apparently some new information has come to light. Some sort of financial information."

"Oh, yes. I was just about to tell you. I heard from Dennis this morning. That other detective paid Dennis a visit yesterday up in the canyon. Found Dennis at Andrea's ranch. Apparently he wasn't too happy that Dennis disobeyed the evacuation orders. But he did say that he understood why Dennis did it."

"That must have been Burt's former partner, Dan. Did Dennis say what kind of questions Dan asked him? What kind of financial information was he talking about?"

"That's what's got Dennis kind of spooked. This detective asked about loans that Dennis took out and his payment history. And he found out that Dennis was behind on the mortgage on his own property in the canyon. Dennis said from the way he talked, it sounded like he'd already gotten a look at Dennis's tax payment records from last year and the year before and his property tax record. All sorts of stuff. I tell you, Dennis sounded worried over the phone."

That worried feeling flared again in Kelly's gut. Property taxes. Income taxes. State and federal. There were all sorts of ways people could slip into financial trouble by not paying their taxes. Unfortunately, it was easy for people to forget about the taxman when they were behind on their mortgage.

"Did Dennis fall behind on his taxes, too? That's bad, if he did. Both state and federal tax men will jump on him. And they charge interest and penalties. That makes it even harder to catch up."

"You know, I think I recall his saying he'd paid his taxes, property and income. I think all of us are afraid of the tax man, so we don't want to risk getting into trouble."

"Well, that's good. I wonder how far behind Dennis is in his mortgage payments by now?"

Jayleen's expression saddened. "That I don't know. But I have a feeling it's a couple of months. That's enough to get the bank's attention for sure."

"Yeah, you're right." Kelly frowned. "Had he ever asked you for money . . . a loan, maybe? To help him get back on the straight path?"

She shook her head. "Nope. I wish he had, because I would have lent it to him gladly. But Dennis not only looks like a rugged mountain man, he is one. And he's fiercely independent. There's no way he would take a loan, even from a friend."

"Darn. People like Dennis confuse a loan with charity if it comes from someone they know. Loans are business arrangements. The lender earns interest. There are a lot of private lenders out there, willing to lend money to qualified people. And those loans can earn good interest for the lenders, too. No middleman. No corporation or bank taking the profits. I remember telling some of my self-employed clients that private lenders might be their best choice for small and medium-sized loans. With the banks' new rules, even customers who have W-2s and good credit scores sometimes get denied loans. Self-employed people don't have those W-2s to vouch for their incomes. They have revenues and expenses and profits, and only their tax forms can show what kind of incomes they earn. Nowadays, most banks aren't even granting those 'Stated income' loans."

Jayleen grinned. "I love to hear you talk about taxes, Kelly-girl. It reminds me of how it used to be and how far I've come. Years ago, I used to scrimp and save to come up with my tax payments. Now . . . thanks to your budgets, you've got me putting away money every month so I can pay those quarterly estimated payments without breaking into a cold sweat."

Kelly laughed softly. "Music to my ears, Jayleen." Then her grin faded. "Now, if only there was a way to get Dennis back on the straight and narrow budget path. Unfortunately, he's got some problems to solve first."

"Big problems," Jayleen agreed with a nod.

No more smiles. Money problems had a way of sobering everyone's conversation when they reared their ugly heads.

Seventeen

Tuesday, June 26

Kelly cradled her cell phone between her cheek and her shoulder as she placed file folders into her briefcase. "What did you hear at the fire authority's update briefing over at the Ranch last night?"

"Actually, we got a little bit of good news," Jayleen replied over the phone. "We may be allowed to go back up into Bellevue Canyon later this week, if conditions permit. Lord have mercy, I surely hope so."

"I'll keep my fingers crossed, Jayleen." Kelly picked up the last of the Arthur Housemann folders and shoved that inside her briefcase to join the others.

"You and all of us. No matter how many rumors said the ranch house is still standing, I won't believe it until I see it with my own eyes."

"I understand, Jayleen. But I've got a good feeling about your ranch. Have you been practicing what Curt said to do last week? You know . . . picture the ranch house intact? I never knew Curt had a metaphysical streak to him." She laughed lightly.

Jayleen hooted in reply. "I swear, that man is amazing. All sorts of things come out of his mouth. And, yes, I have been following Curt's advice. So this will be a good test, I guess."

"The power of positive thinking. Well, if anyone can make it work, it's you, Jayleen. You created that ranch out of your dreams and hard work. I'd say that was pretty powerful stuff."

"Why, thank you for saying that, Kelly-girl. That means a lot."

"Has Dennis had any more visits from Detective Dan? I have to admit, I've been worried over what you told me yesterday."

"Ah, me, I'm afraid he has. He called me earlier this morning right before you did. That detective called him first thing this morning and said that they'd gotten authorization to check Andrea's bank records. They found some cash withdrawals that were . . . what was that word they used? *Questionable,* that was it. I tell you, Kelly, I had a sinking feeling when Dennis told me that. I asked him if he had any idea what the detective was talking about, and Dennis admitted that he had taken some money out to pay for Andrea's expenses at the funeral home. He'd gotten a bill in the mail from the hospital for the ambulance and other charges. And he didn't want to risk having another unpaid bill on his record. His credit rating was sinking already, he said. Lordy, Lordy."

"Poor Dennis. I bet he didn't have enough savings to cover Andrea's expenses. Arthur Housemann lives next door to Dennis and mentioned that he was having financial problems." Kelly stopped what she was doing and stared outside into her backyard. Carl was lying in his sunny spot. Midmorning naptime. Brazen was balanced on the top rail of the fence, checking if it was safe to explore for seeds and tasty buds. Big Dog's territory was unguarded. She continued in a quiet voice, the better to not wake Big Dog. "I was trying to ease Arthur's worry about his Poudre Canyon property near Poudre Park, so I got a little creative and told him that I'd heard from a friend of a friend that those homes were still okay."

"Creative, huh?" Jayleen laughed softly. "Friend of a friend. That about covers it. Nobody can work around the truth like you, Kelly-girl."

Kelly wasn't sure if bending the truth

creatively was a good thing or not. She did know that it was useful, especially whenever she was sleuthing around a murder investigation. "I'll take that as a compliment, sort of. It's kind of a dubious ability, but useful."

"Well, Arthur Housemann is a good man, and he's put a lot of work into his new house up the canyon. I imagine he's been worrying as much as I have."

"He sure has." Kelly poured the last of her coffeepot's contents into her mug.

"Gotta talk to you later, Kelly. There's another call coming in."

Kelly heard the sound of beeping on Jayleen's line. "Later, Jayleen. I'll keep my fingers crossed about your ranch house."

"Bless your heart," Jayleen said before clicking off.

Kelly drained the last of the coffee in her mug and checked her watch. She had an hour before she needed to drive over to Arthur Housemann's office. That was just enough time to see if she could grab a few minutes of Burt's time. He was teaching a spinning class this afternoon, so maybe she could catch him.

Checking Carl's water dish to make sure it was still full, Kelly refrained from disturbing Big Dog as she gathered up her briefcase. Brazen Squirrel was having a grand old time checking for tasty morsels in her flower bed of sun-loving yellow zinnias, purple petunias, and red geraniums. Kelly pocketed her cell phone and stealthily left the cottage. She'd seen the drama many times before when Big Dog suddenly awoke and Brazen froze, unseen, amidst the greenery. It always amazed her how crafty the little squirrel was in managing to evade Big Dog. She figured Nature endowed the smaller creatures with an extra helping of cunning so they could survive.

The sun beat down on her as Kelly walked across the driveway, hastening to reach the shady café patio and escape from the heat. Maybe she'd better heed her dermatologist's advice and slather on more sunscreen, to be safe. "Never leave the house without it," the doctor had warned.

As soon as she reached the shade of the trees dotting the patio, Kelly could feel the difference. She also noticed Burt sitting at an outside table, finishing his breakfast. "Hey, Burt, I was looking for you, so this is perfect timing," she said as she approached. "May I join you?"

Burt wiped his mouth with the white napkin. "No need to ask, Kelly. Have a seat. I was about to flag down Julie for some more iced coffee."

"Oh, that sounds good. The heat is still brutal." She plopped her briefcase on a nearby chair as she sat across from Burt.

As if she were reading their thoughts, Julie suddenly walked up. "Hey, hey, I can spot thirsty people when I see them. Burt, that enchilada probably made you want another round of iced coffee. How about you, Kelly?"

"Absolutely. In fact, make a second one to go, would you, please? I'm going to see my Fort Connor client after I chat with Burt."

"Sure thing. I'll be right back, guys."

"Thanks, Julie," Burt said as she scurried away, then leaned back in his chair and smiled at Kelly. "I can tell you've got something on your mind. What's up?"

"I'm starting to worry about this transparency thing," she laughed. "You're reading me way too easily, Burt."

"Naw, we've learned to read each other's signs, that's all."

Kelly settled back into the metal chair. "I talked to Jayleen a little while ago, and she said that the police called Dennis and told him they had gotten access to Andrea's bank records and found some questionable withdrawals. Their word. Of course, that got my attention. Jayleen said that Dennis admitted to her yesterday that he had withdrawn money to pay the funeral home charges and a hospital bill for the ambulance and other charges. I'm guessing Dennis simply didn't have the money in his bank account to pay for Andrea's expenses. I'd heard he was having financial problems."

"Who told you that?"

"Arthur Housemann. He's Dennis's neighbor in the canyon, so they talk regularly, I guess. Anyway, Arthur mentioned that Dennis had admitted he had trouble keeping up with bills. So I imagine that's why he took money out of her account. Of course, that doesn't excuse it."

"No, it doesn't. And I'll be honest with you, Kelly. Dan updated me this morning and said Dennis has now moved onto the police radar screen, right behind Connie." Burt's bushy eyebrows argued with each other, a sure sign of displeasure.

"Won't the police take the circumstances into account? I mean, Dennis was in financial trouble already, so he told Jayleen he didn't want to risk having another uncollected bill on his credit rating, which was sinking." Kelly looked over toward the golf course, the greens empty now. The heat was intense. "I know, it sounds weird hearing me say that, accountant that I am. But this is still a recession, and people are having problems."

"Unfortunately, Kelly, the police cannot take someone's word for their actions. Dennis told Dan that he had to sign at the hospital as the responsible party, or they wouldn't release her body to the funeral home. Even though they were divorced, there was no other next of kin alive."

"How'd he do it? I mean, banks require a photo ID to withdraw from your account. And most ATMs have cameras."

"He admitted to Dan that he checked Andrea's wallet and found her account number and pin to use at the automated bank machine at night. He probably didn't know ATMs take your photo. Dan said Dennis acted really contrite and appeared convincing. But you know detectives. We have to keep our skeptical natures. Dennis's actions may have been well-intentioned but they are still illegal. He did not have legal access to Andrea's accounts, and he withdrew money. That's a crime."

"Yes, it is. *Damn.* No way he can get away from that, can he?" Kelly shook her head sadly.

"I'm afraid he can't, Kelly. And let's just hope that minor theft is all Dennis winds up being guilty of." Burt arched a brow in her direction.

Kelly simply shook her head sadly in reply, as Julie approached with their iced coffees.

"These numbers are looking pretty good, Arthur," Kelly said as she pushed the pages of the income statement across the mahogany table. Arthur Housemann sat across from her in his side office. It always looked like a law library to Kelly. Bookshelves lined three walls. Blessed air-conditioning sent cool air to counteract the blazing nearly one hundred degree heat outside.

Housemann studied the income statement for a couple of minutes, then compared it to the previous month's statement. "Actually, I'm surprised, Kelly. I thought some of my tenants close to the foothills might have left before the end of June lease date. Several of my older apartments and houses are right off Overland Trail Road. Right up next to the foothills like that, the smoke got really heavy. The fact that my renters stayed amazes me. Of course, some of them may be staying with friends in the city. So, these numbers are surprisingly good."

"I thought so, too, Arthur. I was pleased." She glanced toward the window in his library and stared outside. Lots of sunshine, but thankfully, no clouds of smoke hanging in the air. And no more spirals of smoke curling up into the sky from newly ignited pine trees or houses. "Thank goodness that smoke finally died down."

"All thanks to the firefighters' hard work." Arthur leaned back in his chair, following Kelly's example and gazing out the window toward the foothills on the other side of town.

Kelly sipped from her coffee mug. "I tell you, I'm glad Steve and I are living in his last development up near Wellesley. That's way to the northeast, away from the smoke."

Arthur smiled. "That's right. You two are staying in one of Steve's new houses that hasn't sold yet. Smart move."

"It was an easy decision. Greg and Lisa are renting there. Megan and Marty started out renting next door to them, then after a year they decided to buy. Steve gave them a good price as a wedding present."

Arthur chuckled. "That was one heckuva wedding present. Steve did a good job with those houses. I've been inside with real estate agents, so I've seen all the extras he included. Megan and Marty got a great deal. Those houses are going to appreciate fast once we get out of this recession."

Kelly grinned. "They were really happy, I'll say that. And we're all happy to be in the northeastern part of town, away from the smoke. I've driven over to the western edge of the city several times that first week and last week, too. Keeping track of the wildfire's progress judging from the smoke that's spiraling up from the mountains. That first week was really scary. I pulled over to the side of Overland Trail Road each time I went, just so I could watch the wildfire. It's mesmerizing in a way. A fearful way. Kind of like looking at a monster or something from farther away."

"Yes, indeed, that wildfire was a monster, all right. I remember how worried we all were in the Poudre Canyon that night, wondering if the fire would jump the ridge from Bellevue Canyon. We could smell the smoke getting worse. That's always a bad sign. So when we got the word it had crossed into our canyon, it was like all our nightmares come to life."

"That must have been scary, trying to quickly gather some of your belongings and leave all of a sudden. That's a panic mode. I'd forget something, probably."

"Well, my wife and I took some preliminary steps to make it easier in case we had to leave. She left the canyon in late afternoon to escape the smoke. Alice has asthma, and she was already starting to notice the particulates in the air blowing in from Belle-vue Canyon. So, we loaded up the car and she drove out and returned to our house in Fort Connor. Meanwhile, I started putting stuff in the back of my truck in case I had to leave. By eleven thirty that night, police were ordering everyone to leave, and it was chaotic getting out of the canyon." He shook his head, obviously recalling the scene.

"I'll bet. One of Steve's friends lives near Poudre Park with his family, and he said it was all he could do to remember to grab some clothes and things for the kids. He and his wife both forgot to bring clothes for themselves."

Arthur nodded. "Firefighters and police went to all the houses in that area and ordered people to leave. And they didn't give them any more than a minute or two to grab stuff and leave. People were literally fleeing the canyon with only the shirts on their backs. And the smoke was thicker by then. Heavy. I was coughing, too. Of course, the drive went slower because of all the people on the road. Some people were actually hiking out of the canyon to get away. I saw a couple with their backpacks. I even gave a ride to one man who was walking alongside the road. He didn't even have a backpack or water bottle. He was coughing a lot when I noticed him."

"That was so kind of you, Arthur. Helping out someone when you're in the midst of handling a crisis yourself." She gave him a thumbs-up.

Arthur smiled. "Well, I wouldn't have done it if he'd looked scruffy, I admit. But this guy looked okay. He was really grateful when I pulled over. Said he and friends from Denver were camping in the Diamond Rock campground since Friday night, not far from Poudre Park. They were keeping track of the fire on their police radio. Once they saw the first flames cresting the canyon's ridge, they decided to get out of there. They loaded up and headed farther up the canyon toward Walden, away from the fire. They figured the firefighters and police would close the lower canyon road, and they didn't want to risk getting stuck in all that traffic. He said he lived in Fort Connor, so he told them he'd hike out of the canyon."

"Wow, that's a good hike from Diamond Rock campground out of the canyon. Did he have a car parked in Landport?"

"Nope. He said his friends picked him up Friday afternoon. So, he sure did need a little help. And, like I said, he looked like a nice guy. Told me he worked for one of the big insurance companies." Arthur chuckled. "I had to laugh when he said that. Told him I bet he didn't wear that KISS concert tee shirt to meet clients. Most insurance agents I know are kind of straightlaced sorts. We joked about that."

Arthur's comment caught Kelly's attention right away. *A KISS concert tee shirt?* Jim Carson was wearing a tee shirt like that Saturday in the canyon, when they rescued Jayleen's alpacas. Kelly's little buzzer went off.

"Yeah, I see what you mean. Tell me, Arthur, what did he look like? Greg said he had a friend camping in the canyon that weekend, and he hasn't heard word yet about how he got out."

Arthur mused for a moment. "Well, he was tall, not overweight, had dark hair. It was late night, so there was no light of day to see all sorts of details. But I did get a close-up look at him while he was in my car."

"Okay, I'll pass that along to Greg. How old, mid-thirties, mid-twenties, older?

"Early forties, I'd say. He was in decent shape, too, so maybe he worked out."

Kelly catalogued the description Arthur gave, and her little buzzer grew louder inside. Jim Carson looked to be that age, and from what Kelly could tell, Jim looked to be in decent shape. She thought she remembered Connie telling her that she and her husband belonged to a health club on the east side of town.

"Anything else you can recall? Something distinctive that Greg would recognize as his friend or not. Did he wear glasses or have a scar or an earring?"

Arthur chuckled. "Didn't see any scars or earrings. But I did notice that he had a tattoo on his left forearm. Looked like a dragon. I couldn't help but notice when he got into my car, and the light was on."

This time Kelly's buzzer became strident. She'd noticed a dragon tattoo on Jim's forearm when he was helping load Jayleen's alpacas into horse trailers the day of the wildfire.

But how could it be Jim? He told Burt he left the canyon while it was still light and arrived in Landport right before dark. Arthur left the canyon after eleven thirty, late that night. Why would Jim lie?

"Thanks, Arthur. That's an identifying trait for sure. Greg will know right away if that guy is his friend. Did you drop him off in Fort Conner?"

"No, he got out in Landport. Said he had friends there."

"By the way, do you know anyone who might have property near Andrea's? Her place is down from yours on the river side, yellow house and corrals with alpacas."

"Yes, I've seen it for years. Didn't know her personally, though. I've got some old friends who live near there. Great people. Raised their kids there. Of course, they have grandchildren now. Kids come and visit regularly." He peered at Kelly. "Why do you ask, Kelly? I sense there's another reason for your question."

Kelly grinned at him. "Now I know I've got to work on that transparency thing. I simply wanted to know if anyone had been hiking or camping or walking around the vicinity of Andrea's property. Apparently there was a loud and heated argument that occurred there that evening. And considering that the police are now looking harder at anyone who was at her place that Saturday, I was curious if anyone overheard or saw something.

"I thought so. You're sleuthing again, aren't you?" He grinned at her. "I knew you were up to something with those questions."

"I can't help myself, Arthur," she teased. "It's the curious and skeptical accountant instinct."

Arthur sobered quickly. "I certainly hope

my neighbor Dennis hasn't come under police suspicion. He's rough and tough, but a sweet-natured guy at heart. Andrea was his ex-wife, and he wanted to get back together with her. I remember him saying that. Poor guy."

Kelly weighed her words carefully. "Well, I can't speak to what police are thinking, but they've questioned one of the clerks at Lambspun twice and are calling her in again. And, I heard that Dennis's financial troubles caught the detective's attention as well. Apparently he used some of Andrea's money to pay the funeral home and hospital bills. And I'm sure I don't have to tell you to keep that information private."

Arthur stared back at her. "Of course, Kelly. And I'm really disturbed by that news. Dennis had financial troubles and hinted that he was having trouble paying his mortgage and some other bills. But I can certainly understand the reason he used his ex-wife's money. Unfortunately, we cannot excuse it." His brow furrowed, clearly concerned for his neighbor.

"I feel exactly the same way, Arthur. But the police have a much harder attitude when they look at someone. Because of that, Dennis has moved onto the police radar screen."

"Good Lord! Are police investigating her death as a murder? I cannot believe that!"

"All I know is that police are looking into everything and everyone that had a close relationship with Andrea. So, those of us at Lampspun are worried about our friend Connie, who angrily confronted Andrea earlier that Saturday. Connie's husband had left her for Andrea." Kelly gave him a condensed version of events.

Afterwards, Arthur sank back into his chair and stared wide-eyed at Kelly. "Good Lord in Heaven! I cannot believe my ears! This sounds like some . . . some soap opera on television. Unbelievable."

Kelly gave him a rueful smile. "I know what you mean, Arthur. It's a soap opera all right. Alas, the characters aren't actors, but real people we know and consider friends."

Arthur had no reply. He simply stared out the window of his office toward the foothills, smoking no longer.

EIGHTEEN

Kelly pushed open the heavy front door of Lambspun and stepped inside. The cool air-conditioning felt good. It was going to be close to one hundred degrees *again.* Yet another brutally hot day in northern Colorado. Thank goodness the nasty wind that whipped up the wildfire and spread it to several canyon locations had finally left this week. The firefighters that were working on the High Park fire had finally gotten it 75 percent contained, according to news reports this morning. The capricious wind had shifted to Colorado Springs to bedevil the firefighters' efforts on the Waldo Canyon fire there. Over six hundred of the eighteen hundred firefighters had gone to fight that horrible fire.

Rosa walked into the foyer, holding two new knitted garments to hang in the entryway, tempting knitters to try them. "Hey,

Kelly, you just missed Mimi. Detective Dan called Connie again and said they wanted her to come to the police department to answer more questions. So Mimi called Burt, and he said to take Connie to see a lawyer he knows who does pro bono work." Rosa's dark eyes showed her concern.

"Wow! So early in the morning?" Kelly said, glancing at her watch. "It's only ten after nine." She headed toward the main room and dropped her briefcase on the library table.

"I'd say it's about time Connie got legal help. We're all worried about her. Police keep asking her questions, so it's clear they're suspicious of her. Burt figured Connie had better have an attorney with her when she talks to the police again. And I'm relieved Burt suggested a good lawyer. Connie's definitely a suspect."

"It sure looks that way," Kelly said sadly. "*Damn!* If only she hadn't gone back into the canyon a third time. She was following us out of the canyon then turned off. Why would she confront Andrea again? I cannot figure some people out."

Rosa leaned against the table and folded her arms. Her dark hair was wrapped into an upswept style and held together with an old-fashioned hair comb. "Connie is compulsive, at least with anything to do with her husband. They've gone through break-ups before, but Connie begs and pleads with him to come back home." She shook her head. "It always sounded to me like Jim really wanted to leave her, but she'd make such a scene he'd give in. Of course, Connie would always be convinced that everything was just fine again, when it really wasn't. It was clear that Jim wanted to leave her. But Connie refused to see it. Meanwhile, she kept papering over their problems instead of solving them. Marriage counseling never seemed to work for long."

"That's so sad. The Saturday of the fire, it was clear even to strangers Connie was deluding herself about their relationship."

"Personally, I think Connie should have been in individual counseling. That would be the only way for her to learn the reasons for her actions. She's always been jealous of Jim. Really possessive."

"Mimi said Jim developed a wandering eye after a few years of their marriage. That's enough to set off alarms for a jealous woman."

Rosa nodded. "I'm sure that's it. I've heard her talk about how women at parties always come up to talk to Jim. If she'd had some counseling maybe she could have learned to deal with that without blowing up."

"Wise advice, Rosa. Lisa told me she also suggested counseling to Connie years ago. I wish Connie had listened to you both, then maybe all of this wouldn't be happening."

Rosa gave a dismissive wave. "Oh, Connie doesn't listen to anybody when it comes to personal things. She's stubborn as the day is long."

Kelly smiled. She hadn't heard that old saying since her aunt Helen was alive. "The days are summer-long now, that's for sure. The summer solstice has just passed."

The sound of the shop phone ringing from up front sounded then. "Talk to you later, Kelly. Gotta get that," Rosa said as she left the room.

Time for coffee, Kelly decided, and grabbed her mug, then headed for the café, where she settled at the table beside the windows. Kelly had wanted to talk to Mimi about her sweater project, but that would have to wait for Mimi to return. Meanwhile, accounts beckoned. Kelly popped open her laptop and prepared to disappear into the numbers as Julie refilled her coffee mug.

Immersed in her clients' accounting spreadsheets, Kelly almost jumped when her cell phone rang. She hoped it was Burt returning her call, but Jayleen's name and number flashed instead. "Hey, there, Jayleen. Have you heard yet when you and the other Belleveue canyon residents can return to your homes?"

"Yes, we have. At last! We've all been pestering the authorities every time we see them at those meetings, and they finally gave us the word. Bellevue Canyon Road will be opened at five p.m. tonight. Thank the Lord."

"Oh, Jayleen, I'm so happy for you! Please let us know tomorrow how it looks. You'll be too busy tonight."

"I sure will, Kelly. Right now, I'm itching to get up there."

"Keep picturing your ranch, Jayleen. See yourself driving up the gravel road with the ranch house up ahead. As a matter of fact, I've been doing it, too." Kelly took a deep sip of her hot coffee. Inside the air-conditioning, she could tolerate the heat.

"Lordy, Kelly-girl, you and Curt are a pair." She chuckled.

"What's Curt up to? Still helping build his neighbors' fences?"

"He's gone over to the Ranch shelter to see if they need supplies. I'm packing up some stuff in case we want to stay up in the canyon."

"You might not want to, right away. I've heard stories of food spoiling in freezers and dripping through onto the floors."

"I know. I'm planning on taking up more cleaning supplies. I'm gonna get started on it right away."

"Well, give us a call, and we'll bring a cleaning crew."

"You folks are unbelievable, you know that?"

"We're all trying to help out any way we can. Heck, I'm even knitting a sweater for Mimi's charity evacuee project."

Jayleen let out her rowdy guffaw. It was good to hear her laugh. Kelly hadn't had much to laugh about ever since the High Park wildfire started nearly two weeks ago.

"Good Lord, girl! I can't believe you're knitting wool in this heat."

"I almost said the same thing when Mimi suggested it. But she reminded me that when winter comes, the evacuees will need winter clothing of all kinds. So many of them lost their homes, especially in those Glacier View and Whale Rock subdivisions. Fire authorities said that most of the homes were burned to the ground. They're unin-habitable."

Jayleen's voice became somber. "Poor

folks. My heart goes out to them. I imagine lots of us will be contributing things they can wear. That reminds me. Tell Mimi I'll be glad to donate a big bag of wool fleece for sweaters if she finds the knitters."

"Oh, I think Mimi would love that. I'm in the café now working. I'll tell her as soon as I see her."

"Thanks. That would help me out. It seems I'm on the phone more these last two weeks than at any other time in my life. Have mercy."

Kelly had to smile. Listening to Jayleen's voice somehow helped her bring back memories of her aunt Helen. She was an earthy sort, too. "By the way, Mimi took Connie out to speak with a lawyer this morning. Burt told me Connie is on police radar big-time."

"Lord, Lord . . ." Jayleen released a sigh. "This morning is filled with bad news. I got a call from Dennis earlier, and he told me the police are considering charging him with misdemeanor theft. I tell you, Kelly, that has me seriously worried. We all know Dennis acted out of good intentions. He didn't have money for those bills, but he felt obligated to pay his ex-wife's hospital and funeral bills. But instead of coming to me or one of his other friends in the canyon, he made a stupid mistake and used Andrea's money. No one would have caught it if the police didn't happen to be investigating Andrea's death right then. Of course, his good intentions don't change the fact that he used money that wasn't his. That's still illegal."

"What's even more worrisome is the police may look at Dennis more closely as a suspect now. He acted out of desperation, that's for sure. The police may think that drove him to the desperate act of stealing from his ex-wife. And, perhaps . . . something worse."

"Oh, Lord . . . that could happen. Police might think Dennis was after Andrea's money as a way to rescue himself. I remember how crushed he looked when he learned that Andrea was serious about Jim Carson. I'm sure the police learned about that situation, too."

Kelly heard the beep on Jayleen's phone indicating another call was coming in. "I think you've got a call, Jayleen. We'll talk later, okay?"

"Thanks, Kelly. Keep me posted," Jayleen said, then clicked off.

Kelly drained her coffee mug and was debating getting a refill. She would definitely be working in the shop all day today to stay out of the heat. And that meant having one of Eduardo's wonderful lunches. She was toying between a chicken and walnut salad and a salmon salad when she saw Burt walk into the back door not far from where she sat.

"Hey, Burt. So glad you came in. I've wanted to talk with you about something I learned yesterday."

"Sorry I didn't get back to you, Kelly," Burt said as he walked over to her table. "I was submerged doing stuff and helping move some evacuees into a house they found to rent. Of course my phone ran out of juice last night, and I didn't even notice till morning. This afternoon I'll be over at the Landport evacuee shelter, helping over there. I just talked to Mimi as I drove over and she caught me up on the Connie project, as she calls it."

"Wow, Burt, you put all the rest of us to shame. You deserve a super volunteer medal or something."

"Simply trying to be useful. That's the thing about retirement. If you don't get involved in things that are important to you, you won't last long. You'll probably die of boredom." He gestured to her. "C'mon, let's grab some iced coffee. I figure you've learned something you want to share about

Andrea's investigation, so let's go outside where there's some privacy under the trees."

"Sounds good. As long as there's a shady table. That heat is brutal out there even though it's only late morning." Kelly rose and followed Burt to the grill counter.

Waitress Julie was lifting two sandwich orders to her tray. "Hey, you two. What can I get for you?"

"Two iced coffees, please, Julie," Burt said. "We'll be outside, in the shade hopefully."

"Sure, let me get those for you now." She quickly poured iced coffee into their empty mugs.

"Listen, if all those shady tables are taken, we may have to beat someone up and grab their table. Jungle law."

Julie laughed. "Hurry on out. I gave the check to a couple under the cottonwood tree a minute ago. They should be gone soon."

"Ooh, let's scurry, Burt," Kelly said, heading for the front door.

"You scurry, I'll walk," he called behind her.

Kelly rushed through the front door and skipped down the steps. The coveted shady table beneath the cottonwood tree was still empty. She tried to ignore the sun's heat and escaped into the shade. Unfortunately, even in the shade it was hot. You just couldn't escape heat this intense. Thank goodness there was really low humidity. Kelly didn't want to think of these temperatures *with* high humidity. It would be suffocating.

"First, catch me up on what happened at the lawyer's office. Did Mimi stay with Connie during the appointment? Or did Connie want to be alone?"

"Connie actually was glad Mimi had come along, I think. Mimi has a calming presence. Mimi said she kept patting Connie's hand throughout the interview."

"Mother Mimi's reassuring pats," Kelly said with a smile.

"You bet. They work, too."

"Did Connie feel better after talking with the lawyer?"

Burt nodded. "She thanked Mimi for taking her, too. At least Connie knows she won't be alone when she goes to talk with the police again, which might be this afternoon or tomorrow morning, from what Dan said."

"Jayleen called and said that Dennis is really worried the police may charge him with theft. Now Jayleen and I are worried. Did Dan let on what he was thinking?"

"I asked about Dennis, and he said they were considering charging Dennis with theft. Now, tell me what you learned yesterday when you spoke with Arthur Housemann. Your phone message said you'd learned something new about that Saturday."

Kelly could feel the sun's rays beating down even though there was a canopy of thick leaves overhead. The heat shimmered in the air like it had yesterday, so she sought to give Burt the quickest version she could manage so they could escape back into the air-conditioning.

"Okay, here goes. I'll talk fast because this heat is bad even under the trees."

"You young folk are sissies. You're spoiled by that air-conditioning. We didn't have it when I was growing up, and we played outside all the time in the summer." He gave her a wicked grin.

"Yeah, and you kids walked through three feet of snow barefoot to school every day, too," Kelly teased back.

"What did you learn from Housemann?"

"Okay, we were talking about that night the fire spread into Poudre Canyon. Arthur said he and the other neighbors were concerned earlier in the day because the smoke was building. His wife drove out that after-

319

noon because she has asthma and the air was getting bad. Arthur stayed and kept watch. When fire crossed the ridge near Poudre Park, volunteer firemen ordered everyone out of the lower canyon. Arthur drove off about eleven thirty that night, he said. Roads were jammed. Some people were hiking out. He saw a guy walking by the road, coughing from the smoke and with no water bottle. So he gave him a ride. The guy said his camping friends headed west out of the canyon toward Walden, so he started walking back to Landport. Arthur said he looked like a nice guy and was wearing a KISS concert tee shirt. Arthur dropped him off in Landport." Kelly looked Burt in the eyes. "Jim Carson was wearing a KISS concert shirt that Saturday, so naturally I got suspicious."

Burt's good-natured grin was gone, and he looked at Kelly. "The fact that it was the same shirt isn't enough to make me believe that guy was Jim Carson."

"I figured the same thing. So I asked Arthur for more description. Anything he could remember. And he remembered that the guy had dark hair, was slender, and had a tattoo on his left forearm. A dragon. Arthur said he noticed it when the guy got into the car and the light was on."

This time, Burt's eyes narrowed. He'd clearly met Jim Carson many times before while Connie was working for Mimi, so that bit of information was telling. "Well, in that case, you were right to be suspicious. In fact, I'm suspicious now."

"Didn't Jim tell you he left the canyon after the argument, while it was still daylight, and got into Landport about sunset?"

"Good memory, Sherlock. Yes, he did. So the question now is why would Jim Carson lie about the time he left the canyon?"

"Unless he was trying to hide something," Kelly conjectured. "Like, maybe he pushed Andrea in the heat of that argument, and she fell down the stairs. He'd be panic-stricken, of course. If she broke her neck right away, he wouldn't be able to feel a pulse. So he'd know she was dead. Then he'd be really scared. Maybe he simply re-acted out of basic survival instinct. Ran away as fast as he could."

Burt gave her a crooked smile. "Nice theorizing, Sherlock. If that scenario was true, then Jim might have decided to lie about the time he left, trying to protect himself. Then he got himself out of the canyon before Andrea's body was discovered. He sure wouldn't want to be discovered with her dead body lying there in a heap." Burt frowned.

"You're right. Jim would have wanted to flee the scene immediately."

"We're still not clear why Jim would lie about the time he left the canyon, but it certainly looks like he lied. Arthur's description is damning. And I'm really suspicious, too. In fact, I think Dan will have the same reaction, so I'm going to call him right now." Burt pulled out his cell phone. He looked back at Kelly and smiled. "Good job, Sherlock. Once again you've found information that police missed. You always find clues no one else turns up."

Kelly felt a warm flush of pleasure spread through her. It always made her feel so good whenever she was able to help detectives in their investigations. "Thanks, Burt. It's my naturally inquisitive nature at work again."

"Well, keep it up, Kelly. Lieutenant Morrison would never admit it, but Dan and the other detectives appreciate your help." He picked up his mug and drained it. "Brother, this heat is brutal."

"I really should get back to work. Better come inside as soon as you finish that call. Escape into the cooler air once more. You want me to tell Julie to bring you another iced coffee?"

Burt was already punching in Dan's number. "Thanks, Kelly. I'd appreciate that."

Kelly didn't waste another minute getting out of the heat. She practically leaped from the chair and hurried to the café's back steps.

"Hey, get me some popcorn, would you, please? Gotta take this call," Kelly said to Steve as she walked toward the Cineplex doors.

"Okay, we'll save you a seat. Look for us," Steve called after her.

Kelly paused at the door, watching her friends line up for tickets to the latest Hollywood action-adventure movie. "I won't be able to miss you. Not with Marty's jumbo-sized tub of popcorn."

"Hey, I didn't have much dinner," Marty joked to his friends lined up behind Steve.

Kelly laughed as she clicked on the call. Burt's name flashed. She'd already put her phone on mute for the theater. "Hey, Burt, I hope you heard from Dan. I admit I'm dying to know."

"We were right. Dan became suspicious as soon I told him Arthur's information. In fact, Dan was annoyed, I could tell. He said that Jim Carson was as unassuming and truthful-sounding as anyone he'd ever interviewed. Now Dan is kicking himself for buying Jim's story when he first heard it. He took Jim's story about arguing with Andrea then storming off for truth. Apparently Jim was really convincing, crying and blaming himself and all that."

"Is he going to question Jim again?" Kelly asked, walking away from a group of people approaching the Cineplex.

"He already did. In fact, he told me that Jim looked a little surprised when Dan showed up at his front door this evening. Dan proceeded to ask Jim what time he left the canyon exactly. And what did he remember about the driver who gave him a lift into Landport. He said Jim appeared more tense this time than previously. He repeated that he left when it was earlier and still daylight. And he didn't remember much except the guy was older than he was, but really nice. Then Dan asked him again if he was there when Connie returned to Andrea's ranch. Jim repeated that he wasn't. But we know that he must have been there. Maybe he was inside the house, not wanting to speak to her. Connie told Dan that she returned to Andrea's ranch when it was still daylight."

"Did Dan try to challenge him on his answers?"

"Nope. Dan doesn't work that way. He likes to circle around a suspect and get them to talk, and see if they will twist themselves up in their own lies. Sort of like a spider spinning a web. He just wanted to give Jim a chance to tell the truth, rather than spinning more lies."

"So what's Dan going to do next?"

"He'll probably start digging deeper into Jim Carson to see if anything shows up. He'll let Jim stew for a while, then come back and push harder. That's when he'll mention Arthur's description of his late-night rider."

"Okay, let's see what Spider Dan catches in his web," Kelly joked. She heard Burt's deep laughter over the phone.

NINETEEN

Friday, June 29

Kelly picked up her cell phone from her desk in the corner of the cottage. Jayleen's name and number flashed there. "Hey, Jayleen. I've been hoping you'd call. What did you see in Bellevue Canyon? Please tell me your ranch house is okay."

"Thank God, those firefighters were tellin' the truth. The ranch house is still there. In one piece."

Thank God. Kelly sent a brief prayer above, totally forgetting that she hadn't prayed in years. "Oh, Jayleen, I'm so happy for you and relieved." She felt herself relax inside. "I've been worried that those firefighters might have been mistaken."

"You and me both, Kelly-girl. We had to go in with police supervision, so it took longer to get up there. I swear, I felt muscles I didn't even know I had relax when we turned onto the driveway. I jumped out of

Curt's truck before it even rolled to a stop. I just had to get up close and take a look." She released a long sigh. "The entire ranch house is intact and so is the garage. The corrals and barn are okay, too. There's fire damage in the front pasture and below and along the sides. Some of the fences were burned, and that outbuilding in the pasture I used for corrals and storage was completely burned. Of course, there's that pinkish red fire retardant slurry over everything, but that's okay. Bless the retardant, I say. That helped keep blowing cinders from igniting. I'll live with a pink and red ranch. I'm grateful."

Kelly hadn't realized how worried she'd become until she'd felt herself relax. Even though it wasn't her property, Kelly felt like she was halfway invested in it. She was Jayleen's accountant, she'd overseen the financing, and she'd drawn up a new budget for her. Plus, and more important, she was Jayleen's friend and didn't want to see her lose everything she'd spent the last twenty years building for herself.

"I agree, Jayleen. And don't worry about that fire-fighting retardant. All of us will help you clean it off."

"Don't worry about it. It wears off. We'll have enough to do repairing fences and hauling away burned wood and brush. Most of the ridges on the north and west of the ranch are almost completely burned. So we'll have plenty to clear out on those hills as well. Then we'll have to do some restoration work there. Otherwise the monsoon rains will come in July and wash away both hillsides. Dirt, soot, charred soil. Everything in a black slush."

"Well, we'll be there. Steve's been champing at the bit, wanting to help. Marty and Megan and Greg and Lisa said the same thing. When do you think authorities would allow nonresidents to drive into the canyon?"

"I don't know, Kelly. We'll just have to wait and see on that. But I sure am grateful that you folks want to help out. That means the world to me. You know it does."

"I do, indeed, Jayleen. Watching you building your ranch and alpaca business step-by-step with hard work and smart decisions, well . . . that makes my little CPA heart sing. You're a role model, you know that?"

Jayleen gave a snort. "Well, I wouldn't go that far, Kelly. But it's nice to have your hard work recognized. Thank you for that."

"It's the truth." Kelly walked over to the cottage kitchen counter and poured the last of the coffee in her pot into a large tumbler glass.

"Tell me, what kind of song does a CPA's heart sing?" Jayleen teased.

Kelly chuckled. "I don't know, probably that television program theme song 'Money, money, money . . .' "

Jayleen cackled. "Kelly-girl, you are a hoot and a half. Listen, Curt's waving me over to the barn. He's figuring out how we can transport my herd back to the ranch without disturbing you folks like last time."

"Hey, we wouldn't mind. There's no smoke to choke us now." Kelly grabbed several ice cubes from her freezer bin and dropped them into the glass with her coffee. Iced coffee was becoming a necessity these days.

"And last time there was a murder, so Curt and I both figure it'll be better if we simply bring them over two at a time. Don't want to tempt Fate."

Kelly could tell Jayleen was kidding, trying to hide the fact that she didn't want to ask all her friends to give up another summer weekend for her. "Whatever you say, Jayleen. I'm gonna text the gang right now and let everyone know the good news."

"Oh, thank you, Kelly. That would really help me out. I've got enough folks to contact myself."

"No problem, Jayleen. Talk to you later."

Kelly clicked off and slowly walked to her patio screen door. A warm breeze was blowing through. Carl was snuffling in the flower beds in the backyard, finding faint odors of squirrel feet, no doubt. Elusive, enticing. Brazen Squirrel was nowhere in sight.

She sent a brief text message on her smartphone to her friends, including Mimi and Burt, spreading Jayleen's good news. Then she checked her phone directory and found Arthur Housemann's number. His secretary answered.

"Good morning, this is Kelly. I wonder if Arthur is in. I have some good news to tell him."

"He's meeting with an investor right now. I'll have him give you a call as soon as he finishes."

"That would be great. Thank you so much." Kelly clicked off, dropped her phone into her briefcase bag, already filled with her laptop and the day's account files, and checked Carl's jumbo water dish to make sure it was still full before heading to the knitting shop.

The moment Kelly stepped into the shop foyer, Mimi looked up from a nearby yarn display and beamed. "Kelly! I just got your text. That's wonderful news! Oh, I'm so thankful that Jayleen's ranch is okay. Burt and I were *so* worried."

"I know. We all were. She said she'd have us all up to the ranch as soon as she was allowed." Kelly walked into the main room and set her briefcase and iced coffee on the table.

Mimi followed after her. "That news has made my day. That, plus the fact that Connie found something that can help establish her whereabouts that Saturday evening."

Kelly blinked. "You're kidding! What was it?"

"Connie's lawyer told her to check carefully and see if she had any receipts from that Saturday evening that she could use to establish when she'd left the canyon. So Connie dug around in her purse and her car and found a crinkled receipt down between the front car seats. It showed that she'd stopped at that restaurant near the crossroads in Landport at eight forty-five p.m. And she remembers now that she talked to a waitress she knows." Mimi's face shone with excitement as she talked. "That proves Connie was in Fort Connor by that time. So she couldn't have been up Poudre Canyon." Mimi looked triumphant.

Kelly smiled at her dear friend. *Mother*

Mimi. Always looking out for and worrying about others. "That's definitely good news, Mimi. Let's hope it's enough to satisfy the detectives." She didn't say anything else. Kelly figured that Detective Dan was already on the trail of another suspect — Jim Carson.

Mimi let out a long sigh. "I declare, I feel like a load of bricks has been lifted off my shoulders, worrying about Connie and Jayleen at the same time."

Kelly reached over and gave Mimi a hug. "We're all relieved, Mimi. I felt the same way. Worry sure weighs a lot."

Mimi hugged her back. "It surely does, Kelly." Mimi's distinctive cell phone jingle sounded. She dug it out of her shirt pocket. "Oh, I've got to take this, Kelly. It's that vendor I've been calling since yesterday," she said as she walked toward the shop front.

Kelly was about to settle in for some accounting in the quiet morning when her cell phone rang again.

Arthur Housemann's name and number flashed on the screen. "Hey, Arthur, I heard some good news from my Bellevue Canyon friend Jayleen Swinson. She was able to go up to her property yesterday afternoon. So, that must mean all of you Poudre Canyon folks ought to be able to see your places this weekend, don't you think?"

"I sure hope so, Kelly. People have been calling me all morning with that good news. We've got a meeting tonight with the authorities, and I pray they'll give us the green light for tomorrow."

"I'll keep my fingers crossed, Arthur."

"I tell you, all of us are straining at the bit, dying to get up there. Please tell me that Jayleen's house was spared."

"Yes, the ranch house, barn, and corrals near the house were okay, but the property was burned all around the pasture edges. Fences were burned and an outbuilding was destroyed. Several trees were gone not far from the house, cut down by firefighters to help make a fire line around the house."

"I'd say she was damn lucky. Just about everyone up Whale Rock Road got burned out, from what I've heard."

"Be prepared for reddish pink fire retardant slurry. Jayleen said that slurry was all over the ranch house roof and the barn and on the ground around the house. So brace yourself just in case."

Arthur laughed. "I'll take it. Slurry wears off. It's still better than burned."

"Don't forget, Dennis told Jayleen that the wildfire didn't get all the way down to your house or his. So, you may luck out entirely, Arthur."

Arthur's voice sobered quickly. "Ah, poor Dennis. Have the police decided to charge him with anything yet?"

"Yes, Burt told me he'd heard they were going to charge Dennis with theft. I have no idea how much jail time is involved with that. Apparently he only withdrew the amount of Andrea's funeral bill and hospital charges."

"Well, I certainly hope the police go easy on the poor guy. He's a good man. Rough but good-hearted. He'd go out of his way to help you if he could. He helped me lug a huge old truck engine into my garage once. Even helped me cut down some sucker trees on the outer edge of my property, near his place. I asked him if I could borrow his chain saw, and he volunteered to cut the trees down. Of course, he might have been worried that I'd cut my hand off. Maybe that's why he offered." Arthur chuckled.

"That's probably what was going through his mind. I won't get near a chain saw. I'd cut down a beautiful plant by accident. I can reduce a forsythia bush to a hassock with long-handled garden clippers."

This time Arthur laughed out loud. It was good to hear him laugh. She hadn't heard

Jayleen or Arthur laugh loud and deep for the past two weeks.

"Kelly, that image will stay with me forever. I can picture you now trying to make that unruly bush behave. God help the forsythia."

"Sad, but true. Some of us should never be allowed to prune anything but numbers."

"I also can't get poor Dennis out of my mind," Arthur said. "I can understand the police charging him with the theft, but I certainly hope they're not serious about charging him with his ex-wife's death. What have you heard?"

"Well . . . to be honest, it sounds like Dennis is at the top of the suspect list, principally because of his taking Andrea's money. Detectives learned about his financial problems. He was behind in his mortgage payment —"

"Oh, no."

"Yes, and the police are thinking he may have had his eyes on Andrea's money as a way to solve his financial woes. The detective learned Dennis wanted to reconcile with his wife —"

"Oh, no . . ."

"*And* the detective also learned that Dennis was really disappointed that his wife was serious about this other guy. That guy was also there with her in the canyon, so Dennis could see them together. I mean, he'd told Jayleen many times and I'm sure she told the police when she and Curt were questioned."

"Yes, you're right. Dennis told me how he wanted to get back with his wife, and I'm only his neighbor."

"I was there in the canyon helping bring alpacas to Andrea's ranch. You could tell that those two guys, Dennis and Jim, were like two stags in mating season. They couldn't wait to tangle antlers. And they did. Jim pushed Dennis and Dennis grabbed Jim by the shirt and yanked him. He was ready to deck Jim, you could tell, until Steve and Greg stepped between them."

"Oh, brother. That's not good. No wonder the police have got him on their list."

"Yeah, and he's moved higher, now. Thank goodness our friend Connie who works at Lambspun remembers talking to a café waitress she knows that night and has a receipt that shows she was back in Landport the evening of Andrea's death. That will help her move from the top of the list."

"And poor Dennis moves up," Arthur said with a sigh. "I swear, if your friend was able to find a waitress that helped establish her whereabouts, then Dennis ought to be able to find people who can vouch for him. I saw him earlier that evening, at sunset. He told me he was going up to keep watch on the ridge in case the wildfire started moving our way. I know he wasn't up there alone, because I've talked with others since then who said they were up there, too. Maybe I should call one of those guys. Maybe some of them could vouch for Dennis with police. The wildfire crossed over that night, and firefighters and police were driving around evacuating everyone. I don't see how Dennis could be up on the ridge keeping fire watch and killing his wife at the same time."

Kelly pondered what Arthur said. "You know, Arthur, that makes sense. I guess I figured that Dennis would have already asked his friends or neighbors to vouch for him. But, then, he may have been embarrassed to admit that police suspected him of involvement in Andrea's death."

"I think that's exactly what went through his mind. Dennis strikes me as a stoic sort, who doesn't like to ask for help. He'll offer you help readily, but I wish he'd been more forthcoming with how bad his financial problems were. I've helped others in town in similar circumstances. Some people just go through a rough patch and need a little help."

"You're a sweetheart, Arthur."

"Don't let it get around. I've got to protect my hard-driving businessman image." Arthur chuckled.

"I promise, I'll never tell. Meanwhile, why don't you call some of those guys and see if they can vouch for Dennis's whereabouts that night."

"I think I will, Kelly. Of course, if they can, that may move your friend Connie back into first place on the police list."

"There's someone else who's shown up on their radar screen now, so I'm hoping he'll take the police spotlight off Dennis and Connie. And it's all because of what you told me about that late-night rider. You know, the guy you gave a ride to the night of the wildfire."

"Really? I'll be damned. Who is he?"

"Jim Carson. Andrea's boyfriend. He was the guy who was helping Andrea load Jayleen's alpacas that day. The one who Dennis squared off with at Andrea's ranch. He also happens to be our friend Connie's husband."

"Oh, brother. That is one messy situation. It really is a soap opera."

"When you said that guy wore a KISS tee shirt, that caught my attention fast. Jim Carson had on a shirt like that. I'd also noticed his dragon tattoo when I first saw him at Jayleen's ranch. That's why I was asking you more questions about his appearance. Once you said he had a tattoo of a dragon on his arm, my little buzzer went off loud and clear."

"My word, Kelly. You really are quite a sleuth. You shared all this with the police, I imagine."

"I told Burt. His old partner Dan was in charge of the case. Apparently Jim told Dan in his interview that he left the canyon while it was still light. So, Detective Dan was quite interested in your account of the late-night rider." She smiled.

"Well, that certainly does sound suspicious. Let me know what happens, please. I'm worried about Dennis. By the way, I remembered that you wanted to know if anyone was hiking or camping around Andrea's and heard anything that night."

Kelly brightened and sat up straighter in her chair. "Yes, was there anyone?"

"That friend of mine who lives in the canyon near there, well, his kids came up from Denver that weekend, and his son and girlfriend went camping right around Diamond Peak. They heard on their radio about the Bellevue Canyon wildfire and worried that it might come over into Poudre Canyon. They've seen how fast those canyon fires around Denver spread. So they decided to hike out in the early evening while it was still light and they could see. They packed up their gear and started hiking along the river, heading toward the mouth of the canyon and Landport. Anyway, they told my friend they passed by one house where a man and a woman were having a loud argument on the deck in the back. The man was yelling at the woman, and she was yelling back. They said they hurried past really fast to get away from it."

Kelly's little buzzer went off again. "Oh, really? That's interesting. And there was a deck in the back, huh? I think Detective Dan would find that interesting, too."

"And that campground is right above where you said Andrea's ranch was located. So, that could be important. Maybe a lover's quarrel in progress."

Kelly had to laugh. "Sounds like it to me, Arthur. Thanks so much for that information. I'm going to call Burt right now. I'll bet Detective Dan will want to interview you."

"Anything that can help out poor Dennis, I'm glad to do. You keep me posted, okay?"

"You bet, Arthur. Take care, now." She clicked off and scrolled through her directory to Burt's number and pressed it. Leaning back in the chair, Kelly listened to Burt's phone ring then revert to voice mail. As more customers came into the shop and started browsing through the yarn bins, Kelly started recording a message for Burt, detailing Arthur's intriguing information.

Suddenly Burt's voice cut in. "Hey, Kelly. It sounds like you learned something new from Arthur Housemann this morning. I'm tied up over here at the Ranch, helping out. Why don't you call Dan yourself and tell him what you learned."

"Me? But Dan is used to talking to you. I don't want to interrupt him."

"You won't interrupt him. Believe me, Dan will be happy to take your call. You've helped out a bunch of investigations. Besides, you know what a friendly guy Dan is."

Kelly remembered meeting Burt's former partner several times over these last few years she'd been sleuthing. Burt was right. Dan was a friendly, good-natured guy. "Okay, I'll give him a call. Main Police Department number, right?"

"You got it, Sherlock. I gotta go. Three people are helping me load these boxes." His phone clicked off.

Kelly scrolled down her directory to the

Fort Connor Police Department phone number. After telling a receptionist who she wanted to speak to, Kelly waited. Finally, a man's slightly scratchy voice came on.

"Well, hello there, Kelly Flynn. What can I do for you?"

Kelly heard the good humor in Dan's voice and relaxed. "Hey, there, Detective Dan. Burt told me I should call you because he's swamped over there at the Ranch. I found out something that you may find interesting."

"Oh, really. Well, let me get out my notepad. What'd you learn?"

"I called my client Arthur Housemann to let him know that residents were able to go up and check their homes in Bellevue Canyon last night. Arthur's been anxious to get into Poudre Canyon and see his house. Then he asked how the investigation was going into Andrea Holt's death. Dennis Holt is Arthur's neighbor."

"Oh, really?"

"Yes, and he's worried about Dennis. Then, Arthur mentioned that another neighbor's son was camping with a friend at Diamond Peak campground that Saturday. They heard the wildfire news and started hiking out of Poudre Canyon while it was still light. They followed the river, and it

sounds like they passed right behind Andrea's ranch house because the young guy
said he and his girlfriend saw a man and a
woman yelling at each other outside on a
deck in the back of a house. I'll bet that was
Jim and Andrea. The young guy said it
looked like a bad argument so they hurried
away."

"Well, now, I may have to give your client
Arthur Housemann a call and find out who
his neighbor is."

"I told Arthur that the police might want
to talk with him, and he said he'd be glad
to help."

Dan's soft chuckle sounded over the
phone. "Gotta hand it to you, Kelly. You
always manage to turn up information that
no one else has found. Thanks for passing
that along. I'll get right on it."

Kelly was almost surprised how good
Dan's comment made her feel. She was
used to being flattered by Burt. So she never
took him seriously when he said that Dan
and the other detectives really appreciated
her efforts.

"You're more than welcome, Detective. I
kind of figured you'd want to find out what
those campers saw. That's why I called right
away."

"You were right. Keep up the good work,

Kelly. I'll let Burt know what I find out."

Kelly heard his phone click off. She'd keep it up, all right. She didn't think she could stop sleuthing if she tried.

Kelly walked into the café and headed straight for the counter. Jennifer was there, checking her order pad.

"Don't tell me you're hungry again? After one of Pete's wicked burgers?"

"Naw, I'm still good," Kelly said with a grin. "I've come for more iced coffee. Do you guys have an extra-large mug sitting somewhere? You're going to close the café in a while and I'll be knee-deep in numbers without enough cold caffeine to sustain me."

"You poor thing," Jennifer commiserated. "I'll fix you a pot of iced coffee and leave it on your table, how's that?"

"Oh, that would be wonderful. Thank you, thank you, Kind One. Most merciful one to take pity on poor beleaguered accountants." Kelly bowed deeply, waving her hand before her in gesture.

"Yeah, yeah, yeah. You must really be lost. Numbers not adding up for you today?" Jennifer took Kelly's mug and walked to the fridge where she filled it from a pitcher.

"Nor subtracting, either. Not cooperating. I'm trying to decipher an income statement that Don Warner got from a colleague, and it's not balancing when I add up the figures. So something's off."

"Probably the other guy's numbers." Jennifer handed her the mug and pointed toward the other side of the café. "Your favorite spot is open, if you want it."

"I do, thanks. Talk to you later."

Kelly sped around the café corner and over to the small table by the window. The late afternoon sun was beating down outside, she could tell. The golf course greens had that super-hot shimmer to them. She settled in at the table and popped open her laptop once again to the spreadsheet she was working on. Glancing at the open file folder beside her, Kelly scowled at the disobedient numbers. Maybe Jennifer was right. Maybe these numbers were wrong. Time to change assumptions.

She was about to burrow into the income statement yet again, when Burt's voice sounded behind her. "Hey, Kelly, I thought you'd still be here working. Too hot back at the cottage."

"Right you are, Burt," Kelly said, eagerly shoving the laptop aside. "Unless you're a dog who loves to sleep in the shade and dream of squirrels. Animals seem to adjust more easily to these temperatures. As long as they have enough water and lots of shade to lie down in, they're okay with it."

Burt pulled out the chair across from her. "Not us, though. I tell you, if it weren't for air-conditioned cars, I'd stay inside, too. Do errands at night."

"Heard anything from Dan yet? He was really glad to have that information about those campers. Said he was going to call Arthur Housemann. I figured he would. Dan also said he'd let you know what he finds out."

Burt settled back in his chair and sipped from a water bottle. "He called a while ago. Got in touch with Arthur Housemann right away so he could corroborate your information. Next, Dan will contact that neighbor and find out how to follow up with those campers. Then, he'll probably call Jim Carson and tell him they've received new information and will want to question him again. At the department this time. If Jim's got something to hide, then he'll get nervous and start to worry. It'll soften him up for questioning. That's how we used to work. Don't let the suspect know everything you know. That way you can use the information one piece at a time." Burt smiled.

"Boy, I'll bet you two were a pair," Kelly said, grinning at him.

"We worked well together, we sure did." He took a big drink of water.

"Don't forget to refill that, Burt. Hydrate, hydrate, especially in this heat."

"You're preaching to the choir, Kelly," Burt said, upending the bottle.

Kelly heard Burt's cell phone ring. He dug it out of his pocket then glanced at her. "It's Dan. Let's see what's happening." He clicked on. "Hey, there. Did you talk to that neighbor of Housemann's?"

Kelly leaned forward over the table and sipped her iced coffee while she watched Burt nod and respond to what he heard on the phone.

"Okay, and the neighbor gave you their phone numbers, right? Really? Excellent." Burt smiled over at Kelly. "Kelly's sitting here with me at the café. She'll be glad to hear you're making progress. When are you going down to Denver? This afternoon? Good job, Dan. Keep me posted, okay?" Burt said, then clicked off.

Kelly leaned forward. "Sounds like Dan was able to confirm what Arthur told me. Has he spoken to one of the campers yet?"

Burt nodded. "Yep. He moved on it immediately. The neighbor was really helpful and gave Dan his son's office number, so Dan was able to get right through to him.

The young man said he'd be glad to meet this afternoon. So, we'll wait and see what that camper has to say. Meanwhile, we can't jump to conclusions. Maybe he didn't see anything except the arguing."

"Fair enough. No jumping to conclusions. But my gut is telling me the police have found their man."

"You may be right, Sherlock," Burt said with a smile. "We'll have to wait and see. Time will tell."

Kelly took another sip of the cold Fat Tire ale and savored it as she sat on Greg and Lisa's outdoor patio. The long hot day was over at last, and cooler air was finally mellowing the heat as she and her friends relaxed. She felt her phone vibrating inside her pants pocket and drew it out. Burt was calling.

"Save one slice of pesto pizza for me, okay? I gotta take this call. It's from Burt." Kelly pushed the wrought-iron chair back and headed toward the backyard.

"Don't tell me you're sleuthing in this weather," Megan called after her.

"That would be an affirmative," Steve answered.

"Sleuthing knows no season," Lisa joked. Dusk had darkened the edges of the neighboring houses and fences, softening them. Kelly paused in the middle of the yard and clicked on Burt's call.

"Hey, there. Have you heard anything from Dan?"

"Oh, yeah. The young guy in Denver had quite a tale to tell. It seems he didn't tell his father everything he and his girlfriend saw. He told Dan that they stopped to peer through the bushes at the yelling couple because they sounded so angry. And he saw the man on the deck push the woman so hard, she fell straight down to the ground."

"You're kidding!"

"No, Dan said the young guy was stunned and so was his girlfriend. Apparently they watched the guy scream her name, then run down the steps to check on her. That's when the campers took off. They didn't want the man to know they'd been watching. The guy said it really shook them up. They didn't know if they should report it or not. Dan said the guy actually looked relieved to talk to him. Oh, yeah. Dan asked the guy if he noticed what the man was wearing."

"Let me guess. A KISS concert tee shirt."

"You got it."

Kelly stared out into the encroaching night. "I think that should do it, Burt. Don't you?"

"I'd say so. Dan stayed in Denver to interview the girlfriend around eight o'clock tonight, and she confirmed everything her boyfriend said. So Dan and another detective will show up at Jim Carson's door tomorrow to take him in for questioning. Hopefully he'll cooperate. Two eyewitnesses to Jim pushing Andrea off the deck are pretty damning. Only Jim knows if he meant to kill her. Regardless, he definitely caused her death. People do all sorts of things when they're enraged."

Kelly had seen enough over the years to testify to the truth of what her friend and mentor said. "You're right about that. Thanks for updating me, Burt. Keep me posted."

"Don't worry, Kelly. I will. Right now, I'm going to bed."

"Sleep well, Burt. You've earned it. You and Detective Dan."

TWENTY

Sunday, July 1

Kelly stared at the blackened sections of pasture as Steve slowed his truck to turn into Jayleen's Bellevue Canyon ranch.

Charred logs were all that remained of the burned outbuilding at the edge of her property along the canyon road.

"Wow, that's totally gone," she said as the truck tires scrunched into the gravel. "Jayleen kept feed storage there, as I remember."

"Still, she's damn lucky not to lose anything more. Trees and pastures can be replanted and sodded. Those folks up Whale Rock Road lost everything," Steve said.

"Good Lord . . . look at all the fire retardant slurry." Kelly gaped at the reddish pink covering the ground surrounding the ranch house and the house itself.

"Yeah, they spray it from a big air tanker or a helicopter as it flies over. There's a nozzle thing hanging down. Covers a lot.

Looks weird, but it kept some houses from burning."

"Well, since everybody is driving up this afternoon, we might as well organize work parties once we get there," Kelly said.

"Good idea. We can start now. Everybody's got a different schedule, so we can alternate times to come back and help. Let's see what Jayleen needs first." He pulled the truck right next to an old gray pickup. Curt was standing in the ranch house driveway, directing the convoy of cars behind them into parking places.

Kelly jumped out of the truck cab and surveyed the pastureland, corrals, everything all around her, going in a 360-degree sweep. "Wow, Red Pink City."

Up on the ridges bordering Jayleen's ranch on the north and west, most of the pine trees were burned, exactly like Jayleen said. Both hillsides were charred. But there were still green pine trees mixed in with the blackened ones. It saddened her to see it, but trees could be replanted. Dead ones cut out, new trees planted to take their place. *New life.*

"Looks like we've got ourselves a convoy," Curt said as he approached Kelly and Steve. He squinted beneath his Stetson toward the line of cars turning into Jayleen's ranch driveway.

"Whoooooooeeeeeeeee!" Jayleen said as she strode over. "All you folks coming over at the same time. Now, that's something."

Steve shook hands with Curt then surveyed the surroundings. "It looks like you could use a good clean-up team, Jayleen."

"Amen to that," Curt added, waving Marty and Megan to park next to Steve's truck.

"All you folks didn't need to take your Sunday to come up here."

"Are you kidding? We've all been dying to see the canyon," Kelly said. "And judging from some of the damage I saw on the way up, I'd say most of you canyon folks were lucky. Spotty burned areas, blackened trees here and there, charred bushes. You can tell how that wildfire hopped and skipped around."

"Hey, there, Jayleen," Marty called out as he climbed from his car. "First brigade of volunteers reporting for duty."

"My heart was in my mouth all the way, Jayleen," Megan said as she walked up, staring at the pastures. "I'm so glad you didn't get burned out like those folks up Whale Rock Road."

"And Davis Ranch Road, too," Jayleen added, watching Curt direct Greg and Lisa

353

to park. "Don't forget those poor souls. I feel positively blessed to only have this kind of damage."

"Who's that behind Greg and Lisa?" Curt asked, continuing to wave at the last two cars coming up the driveway. "Burt and Mimi?"

"That's Jennifer and Pete and Cassie. They got Julie, Bridget, Eduardo, and a temp cook to handle the café lunch crowd. Burt and Mimi are bringing up the rear," Kelly said, checking out the reddish pink slurry closer up. "Are you sure this stuff wears off?"

"Yep." Jayleen nodded. "And I don't care how long it takes. That stuff helped this place survive."

"I see what you mean, Jayleen," Marty said, walking around the ranch house and surveying the stumps of cut trees along the side.

"You got a pot of chili on, Jayleen?" Greg called out as he climbed out of his car. "I work for food."

Jayleen cackled. "I sure do, Greg. A big one, too."

"All right! Now, we're talking."

"How can we best help you? We brought lots of work gloves. And tools," Lisa said.

"We've got trash bags. Lots of them." Curt

waved at Jennifer and Pete climbing out of their car.

"I figure we'll start by clearing out the burned brush and grasses the best we can." Jayleen pointed toward the large pasture in front of them. "With all these hands, we ought to make good progress."

The back door of Pete's car burst open, and Cassie emerged and raced over to all of them. "The ranch house is safe! And the barn! And the animals, too!" she cried, then threw her arms around Jayleen in a big hug.

Jayleen hugged Cassie back, her eyes closed. "They're all safe, thank the Lord. Other folks weren't so lucky, Cassie-girl."

"Yeah, we saw where some places had fire damage and others didn't. Weird." Cassie gazed all around. "Look at all that red stuff! Whoa! How're we gonna clean all that up?"

"Don't have to. It wears off," Curt said, tousling Cassie's hair.

Pete and Jennifer walked up. She was carrying a plastic container. "We brought some potato salad to go with Jayleen's chili," Jennifer said.

"I know you said you didn't need anything, but we had these great rolls left over so I figured we could use them with the chili, too." Pete grinned and handed over a package.

"You two are dolls," Jayleen said, taking the container and rolls. "Cassie, would you please run these into my kitchen and put it on the counter? Thanks so much, girl."

"Sure thing." Cassie grabbed them and was off like a shot.

"I can't tell you how relieved Mimi and I were once we saw your place," Burt said as he and Mimi approached the group.

"Oh, goodness me, yes!" Mimi exclaimed. "Some places had damage but, I declare, most of the houses weren't touched. I was so afraid they were all burned."

"Bellevue Canyon folks were damn lucky, that's the truth. Except for Whale Rock and David Ranch roads. They lost a lot, for sure," Jayleen said.

"Okay . . . where do you want us to start, Jayleen?" Marty asked. "Most of us brought shears and rakes."

"I picked up a couple bales of straw and some rope to make waddles," Steve said, then pointed toward the burned hillsides. "We can start over there. Those hills will need shoring up. Otherwise, the monsoon rains in July will wash all that soot and what's left of the soil down the hillsides onto your ranch. That area is ripe for runoff."

"Oh, yeah," Marty agreed, nodding. "I'll help you make those waddles, Steve. Yo,

Greg!" he beckoned. "Come on over and learn how to do something that's not plugged into a wall socket."

"Yeah, yeah, yeah," Greg said, sauntering over. "You just need more muscle. Those skinny arms of yours can't lift a tissue box."

Marty just laughed as they walked over to Steve's truck.

Lisa pulled on her garden gloves. "Okay, now that the entertainment has gotten busy, why don't I take some of those trash bags and head out toward the far pasture." She pointed to the burned edges of Jayleen's land.

"I'll join you," Megan said, grabbing two rakes. "You'll need one of these, too. Hey, Cassie, come with us and learn how we can make charred land look better," Megan beckoned.

"Sure!" Cassie said, starting in their direction.

"Wait, take a whole roll of black plastic trash bags," Jennifer said, handing over a roll. "You guys will need it for sure."

"Do you want us out there, Jayleen, or on the side of the house?" Pete asked, pointing toward the charred ground alongside the cut trees beside the house.

"Bless your hearts, Pete," Jayleen said. "We surely do need help along there. I try not to look at it."

Pete grinned. "Well, we'll try to make it look better for you."

"Well, I can start somewhere," Mimi said, glancing toward the ranch house. "Did you have any smoke damage or food spoilage in the kitchen, Jayleen?"

"Lord, yes. I had to clean that fridge out twice. But the smoke smell is still bad in those back rooms facing the west. And I'm all out of that pine cleaner."

Mimi beamed. "Well, we came in the knick of time." She pulled out a super-sized bottle of the pine cleaner. "Where do you want me to start?"

"Just follow your nose, Mimi," Curt advised with a wry grin. "It's pretty damn smoky in there." Mimi scurried off.

"Burt, I see some charred places out there, past the corrals. Why don't you and I start there?" Kelly pointed toward the pastures bordering the other side of the ranch driveway.

"Sounds good to me." Burt grabbed a rake and gloves.

Kelly took a handful of trash bags and some shears and was about to start for the pasture when she spotted an old pickup truck coming up the driveway. It looked familiar. Once the truck was closer, Kelly could see a bushy brown beard behind the windshield. Dennis Holt.

"Let's say hello to Dennis first," Kelly suggested to Burt.

Burt gave her a sly smile. "By all means. I was planning to update you once we had a moment."

Dennis parked and approached the group, carrying a toolbox in one hand and a chain saw in the other.

"Looks like you've come to do some work," Curt called as Dennis approached.

"Whooooeeee!" Jayleen said as she went to meet him. "Bless your heart, Dennis. We sure can use that."

"Well, I figured you folks would have some burned trees you wanted cut down," Dennis said with a smile. "I'm happy to help."

"Dennis, you're a jewel of a man, that's for sure," Jayleen said, putting her hands on her hips. "We'd really appreciate your help. But you're not gonna take one step toward those trees until I give you a check to pay for boarding my alpacas these last three weeks."

Dennis looked shocked. "Hell, no, Jayleen. I was glad to do it. You've helped me so much in the past, and I —"

"That's true, but the past is over and gone, Dennis. This is the present and future, here and now. And I pay my bills. Don't argue with me."

Dennis shook his head. "I can't take your money, Jayleen."

"Then you're gonna have to turn around and find someone else in Bellevue Canyon who needs trees cut down. You're not helping here until we go inside and you take the check I've written."

"Jayleen, I don't want —"

"I don't care what you want, Dennis. My mind's made up. Don't try to change it. I'm stubborn as a mule. You know that."

Jayleen gave a 'that's that' nod and lifted her chin in the way Kelly had seen her friend do in the past. Kelly suppressed her smile as she watched this exchange.

"I'd give in if I were you, Dennis," Curt advised sagely.

Dennis looked from Jayleen to Curt then back to Jayleen again. Then he gave a big sigh. "All right, Jayleen. I'll take the check." He set his toolbox and chain saw on the ground.

"There you go," Jayleen said. "C'mon to the kitchen with me, then we can all get back to work."

"Smart move," Curt opined as Dennis meekly followed Jayleen toward the ranch house.

Burt simply chuckled as he and Kelly started walking toward the pasture gate. "Jayleen is clearly not someone you'd want to argue with."

"You got that right," Kelly said, imitating Jayleen's favorite expression. She reached out and opened the latch on the gate which led into the open pasture and corral. "You said you had an update for me. Did Dan and the other detective question Jim Carson?"

"They sure did. Showed up at Jim's door yesterday morning. Dan said Jim looked surprised to see both of them. He followed them to the department and they let him sit in the interview room for a while, alone. Dan said Jim was pretty jumpy when they finally came in together. They read him his rights, then they told him there was conflicting information about when he actually left the canyon. A man claimed he gave a ride to someone who fit Jim's description, later at night when everyone was evacuating. Apparently Jim started stammering, saying that couldn't be right, he was already in Landport late at night. Then they told him the driver described his KISS concert tee shirt and his dragon tattoo. Jim stammered a little more. That's when Dan told him about the two campers who witnessed him pushing Andrea off the deck of her house. Jim went white as a sheet, Dan said, then he started stammering again, faster and faster. Saying he didn't mean to hurt Andrea, he was just so angry, seeing her kiss Dennis, he was angry she'd dump him, and on and on."

"Wow. Sounds like Jim had a meltdown. He'll be charged, right?"

"Yeah, second-degree murder. Not premeditated. Crime of passion. You know."

"Well, we brought some resolution to Andrea's death at last. And cleared Dennis and Connie from suspicion. That's what's most important to me."

Kelly surveyed the edges of this pasture which bordered the driveway and all the way down to the canyon road. No noticeable burned areas at all. She turned toward the northeast side of the pasture, which sloped downward. "Okay, let's check out this section while we talk. I want to be doing something if I hear bad news. Are the police still going to charge Dennis with misdemeanor theft?"

Burt matched her stride as they started through the tall heat-stressed grasses. Dry and brittle, even with a fine red mist. "Well, I can report some good news there. A bunch of Dennis's Poudre Canyon friends . . . some retired cops and firemen . . . and some other folks all showed up at the police department to vouch for Dennis. Not at the same time, mind you. But over these last two days. Dan told me they each said they thought Dennis should not be sentenced harshly. All of them swore Dennis was not a thief. He was 'honest as the day was long,' one of them said." Burt smiled. "Dan said he got a kick out of it."

Kelly stopped in the midst of the dry grass and grinned. "That's fantastic! Good for them! Dennis deserves that kind of support. Do you think that will really make a difference when he's sentenced?"

"Oh, indeed, it will," Burt said as they walked. "I'm betting that Dennis will probably be sentenced to a year or two at the most at the county detention facility. Maybe the last part could even be a work-release with one of those ankle bracelets. We'll see."

Kelly pondered that while they walked through the grass. "Well, I guess that's pretty mild, considering."

"If I'm not mistaken, your client Arthur Housemann might have had something to do with that. Didn't you say he mentioned alerting Dennis's friends in the canyon about his predicament?"

"Yes, he did. As Dennis's neighbor, he'd gotten to know him and like him. Arthur was really upset with what had happened to Dennis."

"Apparently, Housemann has also offered to pay Dennis's mortgage for him so he won't lose his home in the canyon while he's serving his sentence. And, Dan said Housemann also mentioned he's pretty sure he can find Dennis steady work doing repairs on some of his rental properties once he's released."

Kelly's smile spread inside this time. "Well, how about that? It's time Dennis had a break or two. Arthur mentioned he's helped out others in the past who've needed a helping hand. That old sweetie. I'm going to bake him some of Aunt Helen's ginger-snap cookies for a gift. He loves them."

Burt stopped in his tracks. "In *July*! Good Lord, Kelly! It's still in the upper nineties back in town. You'll swelter in that kitchen!"

"Hmm, good point," Kelly said, staring off toward the mountains in the distance. "Maybe I'll sit outside with Carl in the shade of the cottonwood trees while they're baking."

Burt and Kelly both laughed out loud as they continued to walk through the pasture of dry grass. No burned patches over here either. Small blessings were everywhere.

CANYON PULLOVER

Finished Measurements in Inches:
Bust (at underarm): 36 (S), 40 (M), 44 (L), 48 (XL)

Length*: 22 (S), 22 (M), 22 3/4 (L), 22 3/4 (XL)

*Length is easily adjusted between the bottom edge of the sweater and the armhole.

Materials:
Heavy worsted weight yarn or any combination of yarns to obtain gauge.

Yardage: 935 (S), 935 (M), 1000 (L), 1070 (XL)

Needles:
US Size 7 — double-pointed needles (for neck and sleeve ribbing)
US Size 7 — 32-inch circular needle (for ribbing)

US Size 8 — double-pointed needles (for sleeves)

US Size 8 — 16-inch circular needle (for sleeves)

US Size 8 — 32-inch circular needle (or size necessary to obtain gauge)

Additional Supplies:
Stitch holders
Tapestry needle

Gauge:
3.5 sts = 1 inch

Instructions:

Body:
With 32-inch US Size 7 needle, CO 126 (140, 154, 168) sts. Join in a circle being careful not to twist the sts. Work in k1, p1 ribbing for 2".

Change to larger needles and continue in st st until body measures 13" or desired length from the beginning to the armhole. Split the work by placing half the sts on a holder or piece of scrap yarn. Work back and forth in st st.

Back:

Continue working in st st until armhole measures 9 (9, 9 3/4, 9 3/4) inches. Work 23 (26, 29, 32) sts. BO the center 17 (18, 19, 20) sts, and work to the end of row. Place remaining shoulder sts on holders 23 (26, 29, 32). Leave a long enough length of yarn to knit the shoulders sts together.

Front:

Place front sts on a needle and work the front same as back until front measures 6 (6 1/2, 6 1/2, 7 1/2) inches.

Shape neck: Row one (RS): Work 28 (31, 34, 37) sts, BO next 7 (8, 9, 10) sts. The bind off area designates neck edge. Work to the end of row 28 (31, 34, 37) sts.

Row two (WS): Work to neck edge. Drop yarn and join a second ball of yarn after the BO sts. BO 2 sts at this side of neck edge; complete row.

Row three (RS): Work to neck edge. Drop yarn. BO 2 sts at opposite neck edge, using second strand of yarn. Work to end of row. 26 (29, 32, 35) sts remain on each shoulder.

Continue in this manner, binding off one stitch at each side of neck edge, 3 times; 23 (26, 29, 32) sts remain on each shoulder. Continue until the front measures the same as the back.

Join Shoulders:

Turn the garment wrong side out and join the shoulders with three needle bind-off as follows: Place the back shoulder sts on one end of the needle and the front sts on the other end. Hold the two ends of the needle together and with a spare US size 8 needle, knit one st from the front needle and one from the back needle together, k the second st from front and back. Pass first st over second. Continue until all sts are bound off from both ends of the circular needle.

Sleeves:

With the 16-inch US size 8 needle, pick-up 72 (72, 78, 78) sts evenly around armhole opening. Knit every round. Place a marker on either side of the center st at the underarm. Knit 5 rnds. Continue in pattern, decreasing 1 st each side of the markers every 4th row 20 (20, 21, 21) times. Switch to double-pointed needles when sleeve is too small for the circular needle. [32 (32, 36, 36) sts remain].

Neckline:

With the right side facing, use the 16-inch needle, begin at the right shoulder, pick-up sts evenly, skipping every 4th st, around the neckline. A larger or smaller neckline can be created by picking up more or fewer sts. Work in ribbing for 1 1/2". This neckline can easily be altered to make a turtle neck by working neckline in st st, or by extending the ribbing.

Wash in cool water with Lambspun Herbal Magic, dry flat, enjoy!

Pattern courtesy of Lambspun of Colorado, Fort Collins, Colorado. Designed for Lambspun by Laura Macagno-Shang.

CHOCOLATE FUDGE
BROWNIES

1/2 cup butter
2 squares (2 ounces) unsweetened chocolate
1 cup sugar
2 eggs
1 teaspoon vanilla
3/4 all-purpose flour
1/2 cup chopped nuts

In a medium saucepan, melt butter and chocolate over low heat. Remove from heat. Stir in sugar, eggs, and vanilla, then beat with fork until combined. Stir in flour and nuts. Spread batter into a greased 8″ × 8″ square baking pan. Bake in a 350 degree F oven for 30 minutes, then cool on wire rack.